Mosquito 8

Mosquito 8

Cover Art and Design by John Hackett

Interior by Melissa Williams Design

Published in the United States by Tyler H. Jolley

ISBN: 978-1-958734-27-8 (paperback)
ISBN: 978-1-958734-28-5 (hardcover)
ISBN: 978-1-958734-29-2 (eBook)

Mosquito 8

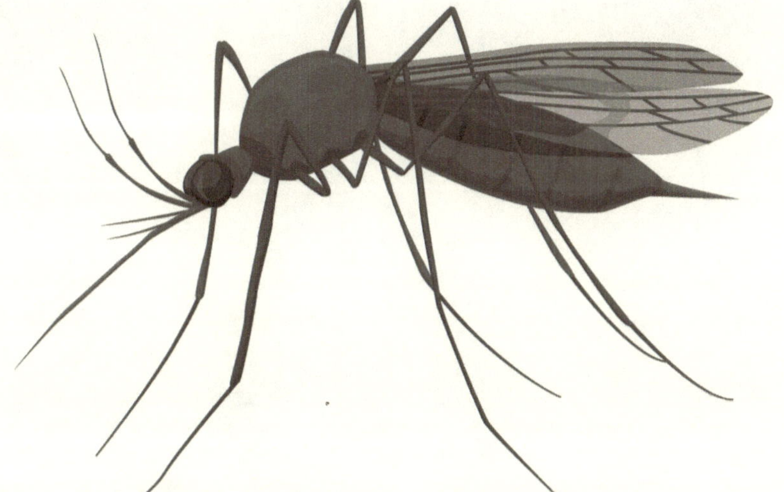

TYLER H. JOLLEY

JARED PETERSON

JOLLEY CHRONICLES

To my mom, who let me have imaginary friends and
who put fingernail Xs on my mosquito bites.

Part 1

IDENTIFYING MARKERS

"A proboscis (biting organ) protrudes from the head several millimeters longer, followed by one pair of wings. Present in the wings' veins are scales, which also fringe the hind edge (though these cannot be seen without the help of magnification)."

—*Dr. Zane McCallister, PhD*

1

The microscope's top light went out the moment Travis Grant bent toward the eyepiece. Not the ordinary soft *click* he'd heard in the past, but a violent *pop* that made him question if the light exploded. He jumped back in surprise and inspected the light. Luckily it was still intact, just burned out.

The bulbs had only been used for seventy hours, max—enough to start weakening the light, but they should have had a hundred and thirty hours more in them. Now, though? He looked again. Complete darkness.

"Geesh," he said.

Being so close to the eyepiece had made his glasses fog up. He took them off and wiped them with his shirt, leaning back in his chair with a frustrated sigh.

"What is it?" a phlegmy voice said from Travis's right.

Dr. Zane McCallister was back from his smoke break, a steamy cup of strong coffee in his hand that Travis *knew* was more Jack than coffee. The bitter, bitey smell of alcohol and caffeine blotted out everything else. Not even the whir of a centrifuge or fetid smell of acids in the cabinet above distracted him.

"One of the lights just went out," Travis said.

Yellow tobacco stains highlighted the tips of Dr. McCallister's mustache and scraggly soul patch. He narrowed his eyes. "Should have some in the supply closet. You want me to—"

Travis shook his head. "I got it."

The last thing he needed was for his mentor to be getting him light bulbs. Travis could barely handle the embarrassment of the thought. He glanced at the specimen on the dimly lit stage plate, entirely anatomically correct, but *off* in a way he couldn't articulate yet. It seemed to stare at him, its silhouette cold and spindly.

While McCallister settled onto a stainless-steel stool next to the stereo microscope, he pinched the stem of the pipe and tucked it into his stained brown lab-coat pocket. Meanwhile, Travis headed toward the supply closet. He straightened his back and held his head high.

He wanted a lab coat like that one day—though he'd keep his clean and white, not permanently stained like Doc's. Not the techie one he had on now, but a *real* lab coat, with his name and degree meticulously monogrammed over the pocket. For just a moment, his mind ran back to the possibilities of what they'd caught and what lay on that stage plate behind him. What if it was some great discovery? Something that would end up in journals and land him a guaranteed position into any entomology doctorate he wanted.

Calm down, Travis, he told himself. *It's not that earth-shattering.* Not yet, anyway. And he'd only just graduated from Deep Rock High School—a far cry from tenure and the effervescent prestige of the scientific community.

The sign on the supply closet read "GMMC"—Grand Marsh Mosquito Control. The best place Travis could have chosen to work in Botella, Florida. The connections here had gotten him into college. He was sure he would have eventually found a program to attend, but with McCallister's recommendations, he'd received several emphatic yeses. The decision was an easy one. The University of Florida was the best school in the country for entomology, and they had also said yes.

So Travis figured a light bulb was the least he could do for the old geezer.

He entered the storage room and fumbled around in the dark until he found the right switch. The sterile white hurt his eyes, but he soon found the small rectangular box he needed tucked away on a high shelf next to other less-needed lab necessities—spare fluorescents, hydrochloric acid, yellowing Petri dishes that needed to be thrown out.

Travis was so focused on his thoughts that he didn't notice Camila sauntering into the lab. He stopped himself only just in time to not run into her, his heart jumping into his throat.

"Watch it, buddy," she said with a laugh, not missing a beat.

"Right," he managed to say.

Camila took out both earphones and faced him, smiling. Perfectly aligned, smooth white teeth filled her smile from corner to corner. Travis always liked when she smiled at him—it made his gut tingle in the best way possible. But that was it. The tingle stopped there. Always stopped because he had too much to do in the lab. He couldn't let it rise up to his mouth, where he might do something insane and ask her out. And anyway, with her tomboyish persona and Nirvana tee, Camila was . . . there was no other word for it . . . *cool*. Travis's shaggy brown hair and glasses could never compare.

So it stopped at a tingle.

She pulled her thick dark dreadlocks behind her head, wrapping them in a tie. "What'd I miss?"

Travis held up the new bulb, like a fragile bird's nest still in its box. "Not much—we haven't been able to make out much of anything yet."

"Glad I got here when I did."

The two walked through the halls back to the main lab.

"To the naked eye, that thing looks weird. Like a mutant mosquito or something," Travis said.

"What does that even mean?" Camila asked.

"That's all you got from that?"

"No," she said. "I got that naked eyes see weird things, mutant things."

Travis smiled. "Close enough. Anyway, something is weird with the specimen."

They were interrupted with a sputum-filled cough, then, "You two darlings done yet?"

Travis and Camila looked at each other. It had been this way during the entire summer internship, Dr. McCallister teasing them on account of being the same age.

They both entered the lab proper, wrinkling their noses at the blue haze of pipe smoke. If it weren't in an absent-minded professor way, it might have been disconcerting that Dr. McCallister smoked indoors when stress levels reached capacity.

More than anything, it let them know something was wrong.

Fans turned on overhead, metal squealing as it forced AC in and out of the space. The large lab was occupied with stainless-steel counters and glass-front cabinets lining almost every inch of wall space. Multiple collections of file boxes were stacked on the back counter, filled with mosquito specimens impaled onto cardstock through the thorax and labeled with typewritten Latin names in Times New Roman font. To anyone else, they might sound slightly ominous, but they were as comforting as a bedtime story to Travis.

He tried to keep his hands from shaking as he replaced the small top light bulb. It was difficult, sitting so snugly behind the stereo head—and he kept flicking his gaze down to the specimen on the stage plate, so spindly, so unnaturally rigid.

A dead mosquito wouldn't be so stiff. It would be bent and flaccid, the organic matter in it no longer supported by life. Maybe it was still alive, only paralyzed?

Once he'd screwed in the bulb, he made sure it was connected to the overhead, and Camila turned out the lab lights. There was only a dim red glow, from the emergency button under the counter and the exit signs, augmented by the white of the projector.

Travis took a breath.

He flicked the switch. The microscope hummed to life, and the top light lit up.

"Dial in closer if you can," Dr. McCallister said.

"That doesn't look like a mosquito I've ever seen," Travis said.

"I think we've discovered a new genus of mosquito!" Dr. McCallister said.

2

Travis wiped the fog from his glasses, then adjusted the diopter beneath the eyepiece and fiddled with the focus knob.

The image of the mosquito, dormant on its perfect circle of pale-yellow light, zoomed, blurred, then focused again. Camila and Dr. McCallister could view what Travis was seeing projected onto an LED flat-screen mounted on the wall above them. This time, the picture became clear, crisp, almost unreal in its detail.

"All right, kids," Dr. McCallister said quietly. "Where's Waldo?"

Camila stood next to Travis, staring up at the screen. He stuffed his hands into his pockets, jumbled with his phone, spare pens, gum wrappers.

Camila crossed her arms. "My naked eye sees a weird mutant mosquito something."

Dr. McCallister raised an eyebrow. "I don't get your generation."

She shrugged and winked at Travis.

The identifying features of a mosquito were easy to point out: the head with antennae and eyes, the wings in the thorax, the abdomen.

"There are only three sections," Travis said, moving

forward and prodding its abdomen gently with the scalpel. "There should be ten."

He looked to Camila and Dr. McCallister for approval; they both nodded in agreement.

"Is that . . ." Camila walked forward until she was flush with the table, as close to the projector screen as she could get. The artificial light shone harshly on her dark skin. "Is that a screw?"

Travis peered through the eyepiece, slowly moving the scalpel to one of the mosquito's six legs. There, at the joint. "What the . . ." he breathed.

"Travis, son," Dr. McCallister said, "I think it's time you opened that thing up, hmm?"

"Should I use the same instruments we use on commonly known mosquitoes?"

"I don't see why not. It's the same size, plus we don't have any instruments smaller than those." Dr. McCallister took a long drink of his boozy coffee.

Travis selected a micro scalpel and tweezers. After taking a deep breath to steady himself, he cut into the abdomen. A high-pitched screech shot out at them, so distinct it could only have been metal on metal. Careful not to go too deep, Travis continued the incision, until the entire abdomen lay exposed.

Unlike flesh, the edges of the incision curled in jagged lines. Inside, complex connections of red-and-blue wires ran through intricate circuitry and minute cogs. Enough to make a small machine fly.

"Okay," Camila said. "Now I'm confused."

"It's a drone," Dr. McCallister said, as though it were the most obvious answer in the room.

Both Travis and Camila looked to him. He finished a sip of coffee-and-Jack before biting down on the end of his pipe.

A high-pitched humming rang in Travis's ears. He flipped around, staring at the "mosquito drone" on the plate. It didn't move, but he thought he saw blue sparks running along its insides.

Both of the microscope's lights popped and went out. The projector screen went black.

Now, they saw only by the red emergency lights.

Dr. McCallister shuffled to the wall to turn on the series of lights.

"It's totally a conspiracy being proven true," Camila said as the fluorescents flooded the lab again, some of them flickering, still warming up.

"A conspiracy of what?" Travis couldn't keep his eyes off the small mechanical mosquito he'd dissected.

"Government spying on us?" Camila said, maybe with too much enthusiasm.

"Are you crazy?" he asked. "That's just a conspiracy."

"That's why I said proven to be true."

"How? We haven't even seen if there's a camera on it."

Camila pointed to the screen. "How? We just proved it to be true. Look at those inner workings and I'm positive you'll find one. That's anatomy made out of metal and gears."

"So you're saying the government made a mosquito drone to spy on us?"

"Yes!" She nodded vigorously. "And we have the proof!"

"Whatever it's for," Dr. McCallister said, "I'm sure you have caught more of them in the traps. I need you two to go see what we've got on our hands. Can you do that? Hmm?"

"Sure," Camila said.

She caught Travis's eye. *Conspiracy theory*, her expression said. *I'm telling you.*

As they headed out, Travis took a left turn where he should have taken a right.

"What's up?" Camila whispered, her voice still too loud in the undecorated industrial hall.

Travis smiled. "Just come with me for a sec. There's something I want to show you."

* * *

The beetle would only have stood three inches high if it were alive—but that was the point, Travis thought. It would have *stood* up, thick red pincers in the air like a male elk fighting for a cow. As it was, it lay flat in the frame, its shell a shimmering scarlet-black. The pincers looked sharp enough, and bony enough, to pierce skin.

"Holy Moses," Camila whispered. "How did *you* get your hands on a stag beetle?"

"One of the professors at the University of Florida is good friends with Dr. McCallister," Travis said. "I asked him if I could give it to the doc as a thank-you gift."

"For what—a summer wading through swamps?"

Travis gave her a look, eyes widened, hoping she got his meaning. That signature punky smile crept over her face.

"You got in," she said. "Holy—*Travis*, you got in?"

"I did."

Camila gave the most un-tomboyish squeal ever.

"Shhh," he said, laughing. "I want to keep it a surprise. He's done a lot. He deserves it."

"Sure. The old geezer does. Course."

For a moment, Travis's gaze settled on her mouth and he let his mind wander, something he was usually so careful not to do. He pictured himself stepping close enough that he could feel her breath on his lips.

And for just a moment, he thought he could do it. Thought he could finally lean in and—

But the moment was gone. *Geesh, you're a coward, Travis.*

How many times would he run away from this feeling before he finally stopped feeling it altogether?

This wasn't like him. Normally he was so engrossed in bugs and insects and Latin names like lullabies that he didn't have another thought left for anyone else, let alone girls.

But Camila was different. Camila *was* into bugs and insects and Latin names that sounded like lullabies when she said them. That was much more attractive than he'd ever thought possible.

Travis ignored the *Rhopalocera* fluttering around his stomach with their linen-paper wings. It would never work between them; he forced himself to mentally run the other direction.

He tucked the stag beetle, safe in its frame, under his arm. He'd give it to Dr. McCallister when they returned from checking the traps. That was as good a time as any, right?

"You know," Camila said, "if that were alive, you could be a millionaire already."

"Yeah, well, if that was all I cared about, I wouldn't do bugs for a living, would I?"

"*Do* bugs?"

"You know what I mean."

"Yeah . . . do me a favor and don't ever say that again?"

"You two done with—" Dr. McCallister began to call from the hall over.

"We're going! We'll see you in an hour, Doc!" Travis yelled back, but he couldn't shake the unsettling feeling he got from the tone of Dr. McCallister's voice.

3

If the lab smelled mostly of rubbing alcohol, Clorox, and nauseating whiffs of coffee and pipe smoke, the GMMC's vehicle bay reeked only of pesticides, sulfur, wet concrete, and clumps of mud—an imbalance of pH that made Travis's head spin. Suits and backpacks hung on racks on both walls.

Travis walked them past the rows of identical white F-150s and Ford Rangers parked diagonally down one side of the bay. Slanted sunlight peeked in from the open doors and shone on high transoms, making them seem newer than they were.

They walked until they reached the end of the line and stopped at the old, banged-up Ford Ranger that Travis had grown a certain pride for.

"Wow," he said, nodding while he unlocked the doors. "Carol needs a bit of a wash."

"Would you stop calling her that?"

"What did you want her to be called?"

Camila rolled her eyes.

"Just get in," he said.

Camila chuckled, clambering into the passenger seat. "Don't listen to her, Carol. I think you're great the way you are."

Travis started the truck, and it rattled to life, echoing inside the cavernous bay.

"How 'bout Sir Vincent Wigglesworth," he said.

"Come again?"

"*That*'s a good name to replace Carol. Sir Vincent Wigglesworth."

"Let me get this straight," Camila said as they waited for the enormous garage door to open. "You want to replace Carol with *Wigglesworth*?"

Travis shrugged. "He was the first scientist to really look into the organ systems of insects. Without his *Insect Physiology*, we wouldn't—"

"Yeah, I know who he is."

"Wigglesworth it is, then," Travis said again, almost defensively.

But then he caught Camila's pretend annoyance out of the corner of his eye, and he couldn't help smiling as they pulled out into the hot sunlight and sped off down the vast driveway.

Travis let her choose the music—surprise, alternative grunge, Nirvana—while he drove them down narrower and narrower pavement, until it wasn't pavement anymore but dirt roads, then mud roads, then barely road at all.

"I mean, Kurt Cobain"—Camila pointed to the radio as if pointing to Nirvana's lead singer directly—"was found dead in his home of all places, and he'd shot himself in the head with a shotgun. But he used his toe to pull the trigger? I mean. I *mean*. You can't tell me that isn't suspicious."

"Crazy," Travis said. "Just crazy. Is that one of your conspiracies?"

"No," she answered. "Well, I mean kinda. I don't know. Toe pulling the trigger? Or was it someone else whose name rhymes with Ourtney and starts with C?"

"I don't know either."

The road ended abruptly, a line of mud, after which only swampland reigned.

The truck bounced wildly, and Travis slowed down to a crawl. "Do you *really* think the government made that mosquito?"

"I do." Camila looked at him. Her piercing green eyes showed how serious she was.

A chill cascaded down Travis's spine. He shook it off.

"What if we find more?" he asked. "What are we going to do? How do we prove it? Who's going to believe us?"

"Settle down, whistleblower," Camila said.

"Well . . ."

"I don't know what to do or who to tell. Let's just see if we did catch more."

She sounded so serious that, for a moment, Travis looked at her, speechless. He turned off the truck and waited, thinking they might be having a real serious conversation. But then she winked. "Put your waders on, whistleblower."

"Okay, conspiracy theorist."

Travis shook his head, then got out with her, pulling his waders out from the back seat. He slung one enormous rubber shaft over his left leg, the other over his right, securing them both to the belt loops of his jeans on their respective sides.

Bugs hummed, chirped, and buzzed, an assault of Latin lullabies that begged for Travis's attention, for him to name them, understand them like very few humans ever bothered to do. But he put all those thoughts out of his mind and set about doing his job instead.

And that was collecting a particular insect from a very specific trap.

Camila moved into the swamp with him, rubber waders sloshing up against floating clouds of algae. Pickleweed succulents sprung from the sandiest bits of mud like small trees. Red-and-black mangroves seemed to grow *downward* instead of right way up, their roots a massive scaffolding for clumps of teardrop leaves. In breaks between smooth sheets of cordgrass, purslane overran the ground with its red stems and sprinklings of purple and pink sea-star blossoms. Here was the best place for catching mosquitoes: stagnant water, a mesh of ecosystems full of flesh, sitting, ready to exsanguinate.

The traps waited for them more than a dozen steps in, and it was slow going. Every move required a double check to see if a log was beginning to transform, if that slither by his thigh was a rope of algae or something longer, thicker, ready to kill.

Even the thought, the need to double check, made Travis want to run away. Bugs he could do. Gators and anacondas could go f—

"Are you excited for school?" Camila interrupted his thought, which he was thankful for. Best not to think about what lay beneath.

"Yeah," he said, clearing his throat. "I'm leaving right after the summer. Which means you'll be . . . doing what, exactly?"

"Taking your job," she said. "Duh."

"We have the same job."

"Yeah, I know. But you and I both know the doc likes you better."

"No, he doesn't."

"That's such a *lie*," she said playfully. "I think you remind him of himself or something."

"What—a chain-smoking alcoholic?"

"You know what I mean."

Slosh, slither—*check*. "Geesh . . ." Travis breathed.

"Just a little fish," Camila said, "don't be scared."

They continued on. They could see the traps now, just a few steps away.

"Honestly?" she said. "I think he likes you better because you're going to college."

"Why don't you do that, then?"

"Not really for me."

"Come on." Travis smirked. "*You*? You'd be perfect for college. They'd have to be crazy not to accept you."

Camila shrugged. "There's more than one way of doing it, though. I'm not saying I'll never go, but . . . life just started for us, Travis. Like, it *just* started. We have so much to do, so much we *could* be doing. I don't wanna miss all of it. Sometimes slow is okay, you know? Right now, I want to work for the doc. Then I'll see what I want to do next."

Travis didn't have an answer to that, so he nodded and gave her a smile that he hoped showed he approved.

He reached down, twisting the track of the metal stake the trap was mounted on. It was the size of a large lantern, with the top cap open to allow mosquitoes in. Once in, however, they shouldn't be able to escape.

"Ever since my parents moved to the US to raise me," Camila said, as Travis unscrewed the trap, "they've been working. Days. Nights. Weekends. Holidays . . . just trying to get ahead. For me. We never go back to Brazil, not for anything. That's how badly they wanted to give me something else."

Camila had stopped speaking, and Travis met her eyes, listening intensely now.

Her face shone. "I'm not gonna waste that, Travis. Not this one life that I have. I'm gonna face it with everything I've got."

"I think that's really brave," he said, voice nearly drowned by the buzzing symphony of the swamp.

"Thanks," she said, sounding like she really meant it. "What's in the birthday box?"

Travis looked down into the trap, the blue light inside illuminating the otherwise black interior.

Multiple little bodies lay on the bottom, each of them full of blood—and flaccid, lying in clumps.

Not drones.

A different thought hit Travis, sending his nerves spiraling into his gut.

The doc sending them out now the way he had was clearly some sort of distraction. But he had never had reason to lie to them before—not so far as Travis could tell, anyway—so why had he dismissed them like this?

"What is it?" Camila asked.

"Dr. McCallister sent us out here looking for more drones," he said.

"Yeah . . ."

"But the trap uses CO_2."

They shared a look.

"The traps wouldn't catch a drone," Camila said. "CO_2 is an organic signature bio mosquitoes follow. The drones wouldn't have the same programming."

Travis nodded, then frowned. "You know that one back at the lab?

"Yeah."

"Remember Doc said he caught it in a trap? But Dr. McCallister had it on the scope ready for you and me to study. Ready for *us* to study."

"Then why send us out here to look for more?"

"So many questions with not enough answers," Travis responded.

4

Now, of course, Dr. Zane McCallister could say that he should have seen it coming, but he knew he couldn't actually have had any idea what was about to happen next.

What he'd seen on that dissection microscope—that was drone technology the likes of which he hadn't seen in years. A technology he thought had been stopped, defunded, "moved on from," as the memo had read.

And the way the drone had sucked the energy from the microscope, shattering the bulbs . . . that meant it wasn't broken. Perhaps it was the nicotine paranoia shaking his fingertips, but he was pretty sure—*certain*, actually—that someone was spying on him, had been spying on him since they found the drone.

Dr. McCallister resorted to staring at the dissected drone for several seconds at a time, absorbed in the jagged metal aperture Travis had cut through its abdomen, at the lack of scales along its hindside, the thinness of the wings. All these observations—each of them trivial, and yet each of them *paramount* in what they might mean later—he scribbled into a notepad. Half of it became his shorthand, the other a jumbled string of run-on sentences, a stream of consciousness that only he would be able to make out later.

Later.

Because he was in a fog, because he could not peer into even the next few moments, Dr. McCallister took for granted that there would *be* a later.

He did not notice the half-dozen metallic insects that buzzed into the lab. They silently dropped down the HVAC shaft near the glowing red emergency exit, hovering for a moment as though awaiting instructions. Maybe spying . . .

By the time Dr. McCallister recognized the intrusion by the high-pitched buzzing of their mystery wings— they'd flown past, *to get a visual*, Dr. McCallister thought, *to make sure it's me they get*—it was too late to keep them from seeing, spying, taking.

Then instinct rose up.

Not to go quietly.

Fight, Zane . . . You got it in ya. One last go, hmm?

Dr. McCallister let out a growl, a guttural pirate cry, and whacked at the scourge.

Scourge, he thought. Only now did the collective name for mosquitoes seem relevant.

He missed.

He swiped again, felt a metallic ping as his hands came in contact with one of the drones, denser than swatting a real mosquito, but almost just as effective.

As Dr. McCallister watched the single drone zigzag away from its group, two others flew straight at him— small enough that he didn't know where they had gone . . . only that he could feel them like gnats prickling at different parts of his skin, tickling, almost stinging.

He swatted at them—at all parts of his body—but only succeeded in backhanding himself.

Then the drone Travis had cut into, still sitting on the

observation plate of the dissection microscope, buzzed to life and rose into the air to join the fight.

It dove toward him faster than should have been possible—for insect or machine—landing on his neck, biting tube first. The puncture burned with an itchiness that was more stinging nettle than mosquito, cold and much, much sharper.

Dr. McCallister backed into the bench behind him, became vaguely aware of the stools clattering and falling as he hit them one by one in his attempt to secure an escape.

"H-help . . ." he managed to say, though not loudly enough.

And he was the only one left in the lab.

The only one—he'd made sure of that, hadn't he? Sent the kids off to collect useless traps when . . . when . . .

More sharp stings. He slapped at them, but it was no use. No use at all. Never had he felt so useless in his own lab.

His lab. In an attempt to feel some modicum of control, Dr. McCallister's analytic brain turned on, lighting up for him like the amygdala might in others. Even while being stung—even flinging himself around, knocking beakers and stools and equipment like a madman—his thoughts cleared the way enough to wonder.

These were not automatons, he concluded. Their flight pattern wasn't random enough, and the dissected one's dormancy far too deliberate. He was right. *Someone is controlling them.* Someone here to spy on him, or . . .

A final sting, however, from one of the drone's proboscises, sharper and deeper than any he had yet experienced, made him reevaluate the drones' goal. If they'd only wanted to spy . . .

Hindsight, he remembered. Hindsight was twenty-twenty. But Dr. McCallister's eyesight wasn't, not anymore.

At first, it was just a blur around the edges, a vignette like the slow focusing of a microscope lens, creating a circular pad of soft light where he could *see*.

Words croaked out of his throat, unintelligible now, even to his own ears. Words for help, words in protestation.

Half-blind, the buzzing of the drones rattling through his jaw, turning the roots of his teeth to sore, rotting liquid, Dr. McCallister lifted his hands in front of him. He didn't bother to swipe away at the drones this time, only needed to find a handhold, a way out of the captivity of the lab.

Past the front slab of stainless steel now, to the front. A microscope fell over next to him; the bulbs and lenses cracked.

He tripped over his own big feet, fell hard onto the floor, nose spattering against the industrial tile. He cried out, but he knew now that whoever was there watching was only going to do that—watch.

Run, he thought, *run, you miserable old ogre.*

Up now, up, up—his hands found the projector screen, which came crashing from its wall mount. That sent erasers and sticks of chalk showering from the blackboard behind it, and Dr. McCallister coughed on the dust. He might inhale smoke every day, but mineral particles were where his lungs drew the line.

The circular light in his vision was dimming, though the edges remained blurred and dewy like a dream.

Standing, Dr. McCallister took a deep breath, facing his reflection in one of the glass cabinets lining the wall opposite.

Every cell in him iced over. His hands began to shake. And deep in his belly, coffee and whiskey boiled up.

Larvae crawled out of his skin, wrinkled themselves from behind his eyes, poked out of his pupils, poured from his nostrils and ears. As he watched them curl from around his lips, he *felt* them in his airway and began to gag.

Help me, he thought. *Help me, somebody—please!*

5

The screams were useless.

Dr. McCallister knew this.

He screamed anyway.

Screeching echoed through the empty halls of the Grand Marsh Mosquito Control as he scratched at his skin, at the larvae flooding from his orifices in a bloody, pus-filled deluge that would never end.

His beard began falling out.

It must have been all the pus and blood, he thought, barely capable of coherence now. *Must have gotten into the follicles, acid, messed with it somehow, must've . . .*

Clawing at his face, bits of pus-filled larvae and clumps of gray whisker in his hands, Dr. McCallister watched his own image in the reflection of the glass cabinet.

Watched himself and screamed and choked on the screams with the larvae in his airway.

But they were *in* him, crawling *from* him, and was he going to just stand here? Stand here while he died of a nightmare?

No, he concluded. Not going to go quietly.

Rage.

The line, that line, from that favorite college poem of his. It rang through him like a mission bell.

Rage.

Whatever it took.

Rage.

Rage, rage against the dying of the light.

"Dying," he whispered.

He was spurred toward the wash station. He turned the faucet on, splashed the thick streams of water into his nose, mouth, and eyes. His eyes. They were taking his eyes, they were—

Dr. McCallister held them open as wide as he could, near being sick with the feeling of them crawling from inside of him.

The more he tried to get them out, however, the more he felt them. There were so many of them now. A full scourge, working their way up from his belly. This, he realized, this was the boiling, sick feeling—not coffee and Jack, but the pregnancy of these larvae.

He gagged. The gag turned into another scream.

Out, he thought. *Out, out, out!*

Shaking, he reached up to his eyes. He plucked at them with his fingers, feeling them squirm tightly from between the sclera and the socket. He pulled—satisfying, the little thing finally out. But then another one. And still another one.

Out. Ouuuut!

Harder he pushed, faster he pulled. Not enough.

His nails scratched his eyes, but he didn't care. Those wounds could be dealt with later.

Later. What a silly assumption; how stupid he'd been.

Clawing now, pulling, raking.

Nothing stopped them, and still they came. And still Dr. McCallister continued to scream to no one but himself.

It wasn't going to work.

There were too many of them.

Crazed with his new idea, smiling through the larvae and clumps of beard and epidermis continuing to fall from his chin, Dr. McCallister made his way just outside the lab, to the door with the sign Grand Marsh Mosquito Control.

It would be inside; that would get rid of them.

He reached up onto the top shelf. Next to yellowing Petri dishes and spare light bulbs, he found the bottle that would finally do the trick.

He unscrewed it, already feeling the gluttonous triumph.

Then he poured it over his eyes, sighing as the hydrochloric acid began to devour the soft tissues. All of it. The larvae, the remaining eyelids, the deeper muscle. His tongue. The cartilage of his nose.

Smoke whitened.

Flesh bubbled.

Unable to feel the larvae now, unable to feel much at all.

It was working.

But not—it was starting again. That nagging feeling in his gut. The rest of them about to come up.

Not enough; not yet anyway.

In his blindness, Dr. McCallister stumbled his way toward the storage again, rummaging through bottles, trying desperately to remember which acids were on which shelf.

There. A full jug of it.

He had no smell, no ability to discern what it was. All he knew was that it burned going down his throat, and it felt good, so, so *good*—enough that he knew it was working.

Those little worms, those larvae, were dead where they squirmed. It was only a matter of time.

Relief.

Dr. McCallister sunk to the floor, the jug in his hand, and drank, glugging the acid like a pirate drinking rum from a dark brown bottle.

"Rage . . ." he mumbled. "Rage . . . rage . . . *dying* . . . rage . . ."

Something melted onto his burning skin, sizzling in his cauliflower ears. *My clothes*, he thought vaguely. His lab coat, so beautifully monogrammed, melting into him. Becoming one with him.

For a moment, there was peace.

And then the drones returned. He registered them as swirling differences in the air, neither visual nor quite auditory, but he knew they were there—spying, killing.

It needs to end. Make it end, you miserable old man! Get up!

With inhuman sounds, sounds that only his bones heard, Dr. McCallister crawled from the storage room. The tile was slippery under him and smelled of chemicals and blood. So much that the scourge could devour.

No, whoever it was, Dr. McCallister wouldn't let them win.

Scooting, dragging . . . *into the lab now*, he thought, *have to be*. Amidst the shock of the larvae, the acid, his mind became clear, the fog of the future lifting.

Because now there only remained hindsight. These were the thoughts of a man about to die.

Dr. McCallister found the table near the front of the room, could picture in his mind the dim red glow it cast whenever they turned the lights off in the lab, the one echoed by the emergency exit signs.

It was the ultimate emergency button, one that existed

in very few places, very few labs. In the mosquito control center, they dealt always with the possibility of a contagion, of a nuclear scenario in which every square inch of air needed to be purged. When it came to disease, rats were one thing, mosquitoes another, and public safety required contingencies.

He burned from the inside out, coughing up pieces of his own organs. No separation now, he knew vividly, between his esophagus and his larynx—all was an interconnected soup. The liquid slowly filled his lungs.

It was almost to his heart.

Can't let them get out.

Couldn't let these ... *things* spread to the outside world, do whatever they'd done to him.

His last thought was of the kids, Travis and Camila. He hoped they weren't back yet, that they were clear.

As his heart finally skipped a terrible, bloody beat, Dr. McCallister slapped the backlit red mushroom-shaped button ... and let out a rasping sigh.

6

Travis pulled into the bay. Camila started to get out immediately, but when he hesitated, she said, "What's up?"

"It's still bothering me," he said.

"That he didn't tell us why he sent us out?"

Travis nodded.

"Then why don't you ask him?"

He set his lips in a line. "You're right. I'm sure there was a reason."

But as he got out and joined Camila in the adjacent washroom to rinse off their waders and the used traps, he couldn't help thinking that it went deeper than that.

He was about to gift his mentor one of the rarest beetle specimens in the *world*, as a thank-you for everything he'd done. And here the doc was, acting suspicious in a way he never had.

All the way here, Travis had tried to rationalize it. The doc just wanted them to check the traps; it didn't go any deeper. *But he* knew *the traps wouldn't attract the drones.*

"Travis," Camila said, forcing him to look up at her. "Drop it. Okay? We don't know anything yet."

We don't know anything.

That was the problem, wasn't it?

A mosquito drone? What use was that? What purpose?

Water ran clear and cool in every direction. The grated floor drank up every ounce of it from the wands as they cleaned the boots and washed their faces and hands in the deep stainless-steel sinks.

Travis was still deep in his head as they put their equipment in the dryer. He watched it cycle. He felt Camila watching him as he watched droplets of water evaporating. Wary, he shuffled his bare feet across the cold metal grating then slipped his shoes back on.

A sound like breaking glass bounced toward them.

"You wanna go check it out?" Travis said after a moment. "I can make sure this stuff gets put away."

Camila shrugged. "McCallister probably just broke a beaker or something. No biggie. Right?"

"Sure."

"I'm gonna run to the bathroom, though. Be right back."

She strutted away, some of the bounce seeping out of her step. Travis thought he knew why.

A quiet drip of water from one of the wands hanging next to a sink and the tumble-thrum of the dryer were all he heard now.

That and . . .

Travis perked his head up, would know that sound anywhere. He pulled his glasses off, wiped the smudges of water away with the corner of his shirt, then put them on and squinted at the air in front of him.

Just outside the washroom door, he made out the sound of small bodies passing, wings vibrating at a rate that *should* be impossible . . . it was a miracle that real mosquitoes could fly and even more amazing that mosquito drones flew the same way, and Travis wasn't certain which was which anymore.

He followed them out, watching them carefully. He counted a total of seven and knew with a sinking feeling that they weren't organic—one of them had the unzipped metal abdomen he'd left on a microscope slate over an hour ago.

He thought about calling for Camila, but if they *were* all drones, that meant someone could be listening, and he didn't want to scare them off.

Instead, he followed, stealthily. He wasn't very good at it, he knew. He'd never been able to sneak out of the house as a kid—never needed to, because he was too busy following curfew.

Now he wished he had some of those skills.

They're going into the lecture hall, he thought.

They curved around the southern half of the building, in and out of squares of light from the windows opposite, before finally making it inside the back doors to the auditorium. Here, it was mostly dark.

Travis tiptoed in, looking around for anything he could use to capture them. There—a snack cart, with stale crackers from the last event, and small plastic cups for lemon water.

The drones continued to press forward.

But then one of them paused and stayed behind from the rest of the group. Travis held his breath, the plastic cup already growing sweaty and slick in his palm.

Only a few feet away, he watched as it began to turn, slowly, hovering in place like no *normal* mosquito should have ever been able to do.

Like someone was controlling it.

Like someone was watching.

Panicked, he did the first thing that came to mind, dropping to the ground so he was behind a row of seats.

Overreacting. Stupid. This is ridiculous.

But was it?

His glasses fell off as he hit the ground, and he fumbled for them, clutching them with the hand not holding the cup.

Waited for a breath, then two.

Get off the ground, you paranoid weirdo, he thought. *Geesh.*

Slowly, Travis shoved his glasses back on and lifted himself up, peering from behind the row of chairs. The entire dimly lit auditorium was blurry, but he saw seven shapes heading away, toward the windows by the lecture area.

One of them was propped open.

Travis rushed forward, unbending the plastic cup as he went.

What was going on? First, the mosquito they found was a drone, and now, he was certain he was being watched and acting like a crazy person.

It was clear: He just needed to get a couple of these trapped, then confer with Camila.

Not caring who saw him now—likely, he reminded himself, they already had—he sprinted down the steep incline on the left-hand side of the small auditorium. With the dexterity of someone who had been practicing insect catching with everything from Mason jars to butterfly nets since he could walk, Travis slammed two of the buzzing insects inside the cup and placed his hand over the top to keep them from escaping.

Heart buzzing along with their wings, and wanting to avoid getting bitten, he ran back up to the snack cart and found a small lid. It wasn't a perfect hold for these two, but even the opening for the straw wouldn't be enough for them to escape. He could replace it later with an official vial.

"Gotcha," he said, looking back around the auditorium.

The other mosquitoes had already left through the open window.

Dr. McCallister had asked them for more drones. Now they had them. With this and the stag beetle, it was about to be the doc's lucky day.

* * *

Travis was jumbling around through one of the storage closets near the washroom, where they kept all their glassware, when he heard the garbled scream.

He looked up, knew it was coming from the lab.

What the . . .

Quickly, he dumped the furious mosquitoes into a vial, sealed it, then set it on the shelf.

"Travis!"

It was Camila, clearly, distinctly. She'd never sounded like that.

"*Travis!*"

Leaving the vial on the shelf, he ran toward the lab.

7

"Camila!"

Travis ran toward the lab. Several steps before he reached it, the fetid air hit him. There was something so acidic about it that even the *scent* seemed to want to burn his sinuses and boil the water around his mind.

He coughed, covered his mouth, and wiped the moisture away from his red eyes.

The lab lay in several epicenters of chaos, like a dust devil had run through only certain sections. Microscopes were toppled, chalk dusted a patina on the floor, stools lay askew, the normally pristine counter was a disaster, the projector screen was pulled down, and beakers were spilled and shattered.

The washing center must have been on, and for a long time, too—the swirl of water still slurred toward the drain, where it made a gurgling sound on the floor, next to a body.

"Camila?" Travis said again.

She stood over what had to be Dr. McCallister, though so much of him had become unrecognizable. The acidic undertone made sense—burning flesh and bubbling skin. Melted pools of goop sizzled where his eyes should've been, most of his nose was gone, and his lips had peeled off.

She turned and threw her face into Travis's chest. He grabbed her and hugged her, staring in horror. Dr. McCallister's body seemed to be smoldering—no, *steaming*. He covered his mouth with the back of his other hand.

His eyes took in the scene and his brain tried to make sense of what he was seeing.

On the back of one hand, in the only spot unburned by whatever had done this, two large, purple bite marks stood out like blinking lights.

"I think I'm going to be sick," Camila said, still with her hand over her mouth and nose.

Even though he felt the same, neither of them looked away. They couldn't.

"He's dead," Travis said, "isn't he."

Camila didn't respond. Probably, he thought, because she knew just as well as he did.

"How could he do this to himself?" she said.

"Who says he's the one who did it?" Travis pointed out.

"There's no one else here—"

"Shh," he said.

"Don't—"

"Do you hear that?"

"Hear—"

But Travis put his hand up. Both of them listened, and when Camila asked, "What's beeping?" he knew he wasn't making things up because of his raised cortisol levels.

Trying his best not to panic—and largely failing—Travis navigated the maze of glass, water, and acid to the table closest to the projector. That's where the noise seemed to be coming from.

Camila followed his movements. "I thought he told us that was only for emergencies."

Travis looked around them. "Well, I guess this was an emergency."

"What does it do?"

He bent down, staring at the little red button that had seemed so innocuous all summer, but which seemed sinister now that it was beeping incessantly.

He knelt on the tile, putting his head under the table so he could see it properly, and nearly had to swallow his throat.

"It's a countdown," he said, coming back out.

"To what?" Camila asked, her eyes going wide.

"Decontamination? Keep the spread of infection down." Travis looked wildly from side to side, trying to take everything in.

"That can't be good for us, right?" Camila pressed her palms into her eyes.

"Don't think so."

"We need to get out of here!"

Travis was about to agree, when a sound issued from Dr. McCallister—a wet grunt, like seaweed had slithered down his throat.

His gut twisting, Travis thought about what to do next. The logistics they could figure out later . . . and right now, he said what they were both thinking. "What about him?"

"I'll call nine-one-one," Camila said, pulling out her phone.

"Right."

Already she was holding the phone up to her ear. "How long did the timer say?"

"It was at eight minutes maybe twenty seconds ago."

She nodded, then spouted off in great detail, and with forced calm, the situation to the 911 operator.

"Thank you," she said finally, "how long?"

But someone was already here.

Travis and Camila caught each other's narrowed eyes, both of them asking what was going on—even though he was certain she didn't have a better idea than he did.

There was a pounding of footsteps down the hall, then three people entered the lab. Their polos were navy blue, with the EMT crest over the breast. Two men, one with biceps as large as his head, another with a wristwatch he kept glancing at, and a woman with fire-engine-red hair. All three wore blue masks and nitrile gloves.

"Yes," Camila said distractedly into the phone. "Thanks."

"I'm assuming Dr. McCallister called you?" Travis asked.

"This the guy?" Biceps said, leaning down over Dr. McCallister, who was now coughing. "Oh geez."

"I don't know what happened," Travis said, aware now that his nerves were doing the talking, not him. "I don't—he sent us out to check the traps. Camila—that's Camila over there—she's the one who found him like this. There are weird purple marks on his hand there, but I don't know where they came from. I don't . . . I mean, I guess maybe it has something to do with the drones we found? Those stupid little . . ."

He felt a hand on his shoulder from behind and stopped talking long enough to feel Camila squeezing him, keeping her teary eyes forward, where Biceps was slowly picking at the doc's body.

His beard was burned right off his face with the acid, Travis noticed. Weird, seeing the old man without a beard.

"Is he still alive?" Camila asked.

"Barely," the redhead said. "You said this might have something to do with . . . drones?"

Wristwatch was looking at Travis carefully, in a way that made him shuffle his feet and glance at the glass-dusted floor.

Camila stepped in. "We found something this morning—drone seemed like the only explanation."

Biceps, Redhead, and Wristwatch looked at her blankly.

"Isn't this a mosquito control center?" Biceps asked.

"That's what it looked like," Camila said.

"Can we see one of these drones?" Wristwatch asked.

Travis looked down to Dr. McCallister, his breath suddenly catching in his throat. Shouldn't they be doing something about *him*? Something wasn't right.

"I captured a couple," he said, shrugging—trying, maybe too hard, to make light of it.

But Biceps was now giving him a look that seemed to say, *Well, where is it, chump?*

"I'll just . . . go grab them for you," Travis said.

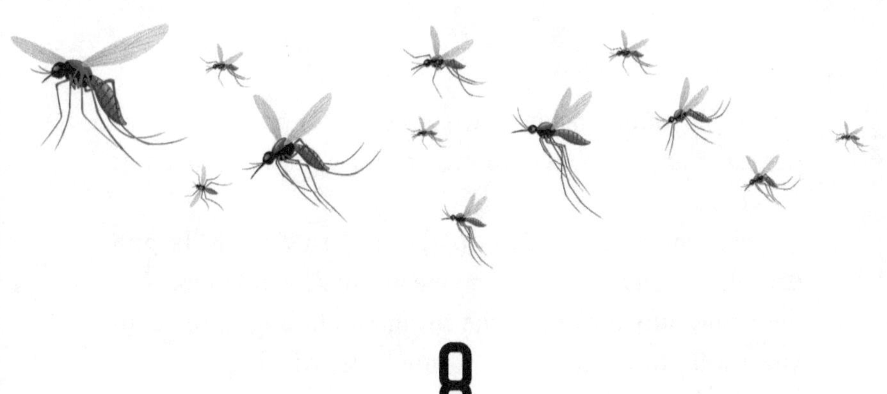

8

Travis walked all the way to the far room for the vial with the specimens for the EMTs—the EMTs who he wasn't sure were EMTs at all. He tried to get control over his breathing.

The industrial waxed tile flashed with blood and shattered glass—images of what he saw and what he'd *seen* superimposed over each other. Melting marshmallows in bone-porcelain sockets, a skull jutting out of cartilage, and dissolved muscle made him swallow back bile.

Dr. McCallister . . . Dr. McCallister is . . .

No, not dead.

He thought of the stag beetle, waiting for him in the truck, just feet away. He should have given it to him an hour ago—but how could he have known there wouldn't be time?

He wouldn't be able to give it to him now. He would wait to give it to him at his hospital bedside. He sprinted to his truck and snatched the prized beetle and shoved it in his pocket.

Dripping water echoed from the wash bay to his left in time with his soft footfalls.

Feeling queasy, grateful for the quiet and being alone, Travis carefully picked up the vial with the drone insects buzzing around inside and stared at them anew, wondering if anyone was looking at him while he looked at *them . . .*

He was headed back to the lab, to the EMTs and Camila, when he heard someone whispering into a phone. He could only make out the rising and falling of the conversation, the tones, not a single word. *That doesn't sound like an emergency call.*

When he finally got the courage to walk back to the lab, Wristwatch saw him first. He was the one talking on the phone, but he quickly hung up and gave Travis a smile that made his stomach curdle.

"Find those drones?" Wristwatch asked.

For reasons Travis couldn't comprehend, he left the vial of mosquitoes in his pocket and lied. "Er, no. They must've got out or something."

Camila shot him a questioning sideways glance.

Wristwatch took a step closer to them. "They got out, huh?" The questioning tone was dripping with sarcasm. "Like unscrewed the lid of this *vial* you put them in?"

Biceps held his hand to his ear and spoke into his wrist. "Still on him, you say? Copy." He looked at them and joined Wristwatch, closing the gap between the two young scientists.

The hair on the back of Travis's neck stood, then he grabbed Camila's arm and pulled her toward him, and they started to run. He slammed the door behind them, and they rushed into the bay of trucks.

They dodged and ducked behind a truck as the EMTs entered.

"This will be so much easier if you just give us the drones," Wristwatch said. "We can tell they're on you. Maybe in a pocket or something."

"How does he know that?" Travis whispered to Camila.

"Duh," she answered. "Drones probably have some visual lenses, like I said! Or maybe just a locator. It doesn't matter. They know you still have it."

"What do I do?"

Bang!

Bang!

Travis looked under the trucks. The EMTs were searching for them, and a tip of a shovel hung low. One of them was hitting the trucks as they searched.

They must've gotten it from the tool cabinet. Travis got after himself for not thinking of grabbing something like that so they could have a weapon to defend themselves.

"We need to get out of here!" Camila hissed.

He looked to the man-door next to the large garage door. He grabbed a fistful of Camila's shirt. "Let's go!"

Both ducked and weaved between the trucks. It was a tall order to think they could make it out of the bay without being seen, but they tried anyway.

Hearts thumped in rib cages just as they pushed the door open. EMTs sprinted out onto the back lot as well. Gravel crunched under their feet as they scrambled to find safety. Travis could hear the EMTs gaining ground, but he could also hear a siren in the distance. He and Camila veered left and raced toward the sirens. Could they trust it? Their pursuers were obviously fake emergency medical technicians, but could the sirens be a ruse also? Left with no other options, they ran as fast as they could toward the red and blue lights cresting the hill. To their surprise, the EMTs faltered and beelined it to their vehicle. Travis and Camila circled back around.

"We can't let Dr. McCallister just die back there," Travis said.

Camila agreed and the two dashed across the back parking area and back into the building.

"Travis . . ." McCallister forced out between melted jaws.

"Travis!" Camila shouted.

"What?!"

He spun around, eyes wide, the stench of the acid and flesh burning. His nostrils flared.

Camila pointed at the dying doctor. "He's trying to say something."

Dr. McCallister stirred, spreading glass across the tile underneath him. Whatever was left of his lips began to move, and when he finally was able to get words out, they sounded burned, crackling and charred.

"G-get out," he said.

"Doc," Travis said, "it's us. What do you need?"

More sirens blared distantly outside.

He and Camila shared a glance.

"Get . . . o-out . . ." Dr. McCallister said again. "Explo—"

But he never got to finish.

A coughing fit overtook him. Blood and bile boiled out of his mouth, coloring his teeth pink, dribbling down his chest, like an unset raspberry jam.

Camila swore and covered her mouth again, turning away.

"The timer," Travis whispered. "He needs help . . . *He needs help!*"

And without waiting for Camila to follow after him, he sped out of the lab, down the hall, and slammed through the doors. He heard her following behind, coughing through her tears.

"How long do you think we have left?" she yelled.

Travis couldn't respond, didn't want to think of how many seconds were left on that dim red, ominous glow.

By the time the swampy sunset air splashed onto his face, sharp in its contrast to the putrid smell festering inside, the ambulance was pulling out of the lot, speeding away, no sirens blaring, and lights turned off.

Fake EMTs.

Then he saw more lights down the street, appearing through the waving trees and greenery. He stopped and put his hands on his knees. The 911 dispatch.

"Then who were they?" Camila asked, watching the two ambulances pass each other.

Travis could barely hear the siren, or the rush of the damp wind, over his own thudding heartbeat.

The image of Dr. McCallister's face dribbling blood, like chopped-up raspberries, made his stomach lurch.

"What'd he say?" Travis asked. "The doc?"

He wondered if she didn't want to say it out loud. But then she took in a breath. Exhaled. "Explosion."

From behind, there was a resounding thud, followed by an echoing whoosh.

"Run," Travis breathed, an instinct. He grabbed Camila's hand from behind.

They rushed down the steps.

The air grew hot, every movement seemed to slow, and the palm trees on either side faded in his vision, Camila's hand clutched in his own. Heat licked at their backs while they frantically sprinted.

Without remembering how, Travis found himself on the other side of the front asphalt parking lot, Camila breathing hard next to his ear.

He turned around.

All of it happened at once.

The thud from the inside finally reached a crescendo, and the heat blossomed, higher and higher. Travis put his hands up to cover his face from the blast, twisting his body away.

Chunks of concrete, slivers of glass, steel bars, and asphalt flew in all directions.

The razor-sharp shrapnel clawed at his forearms and the back of his hands.

He was aware of his body being picked up and thrown several feet against its will, where he slammed against the parking lot, scraping his chest and his kneecaps.

Travis stayed where he was, curled now in the fetal position, shaking, struggling to breathe the hot tar-like air.

After ten breaths, he peeked out from the shell he'd made of himself. His ears were ringing, disorienting him further, but he still scanned the area and found Camila a few feet from him, already sitting up and staring where the lab had been.

"He blew it up," she was saying, "I can't believe . . . he actually blew it up."

9

What just happened?

A series of snapshots flashed in Travis's mind, each loosely connected like newspaper clippings and strung together by yarn on an investigation cork board.

One:

Foil around his shoulders, Camila talking to a young woman with long dark hair, wearing gloves. An EMT emblem watched Travis from her chest, mocking him, making him wonder . . . Pounding noises, screeching tires, crackling. Smoke in his eyes—smoke everywhere—burning underneath the parking lot lights as they flickered on, off, on, off, on—

What just happened?

Two:

"They just left," Travis was saying to the long-haired woman. But *was* he saying it? That didn't sound like his voice. The woman asked him to open his eyes so she could shine a piercing, painful light into them. It felt like a needle into his skull. A memory flashed—Doc's skull, showing through skin, flaps of cheek missing, eyes like . . . "They just left him. Didn't try to do anything, you know? Like, I thought they might have taken him outside, tried to save him. But they just *left*."

"Who left?" the woman asked. She smelled clean, like rubbing alcohol. The sting of it made Travis breathe easier. "Swallow for me."

He swallowed, then said, "There was another ambulance here. They said he was alive."

"Who?" she asked. "Was there someone in there?"

Travis nodded, could tell he was nodding by the way the interior of the ambulance cab bobbed up and down, but he didn't feel it. He couldn't feel much of anything.

"Was there someone else in there?" the EMT—a real one this time, he thought—asked again.

"McCallister," Travis croaked.

She turned away, said something frantically in Spanish to someone he couldn't see, then turned back to him and told him he must've hit his head pretty bad. They didn't see another ambulance.

Three:

There were three cop cars. Two fire engines—their bright red trucks and blaring sirens were overwhelming. A drop of sense began to rise slowly to the surface of Travis's thoughts, the shock beginning to wear off, and the full reality of his bruises and cuts screamed at him.

Three times, Travis blinked three times, stretched out his jaw—which cracked—and shrugged off the tinfoil blanket around his shoulders.

Camila sat only a couple feet in front of him, clutching her tinfoil around her and swinging her legs over the back bumper of the ambulance. With a grunt, he got off the gurney they'd laid him on and joined her.

She glanced at him before returning her gaze to the destruction, the buzzing mess of newscasters and helicopters and general pandemonium.

What just happened?

"They went to call in to dispatch," she said.

Travis nodded. Instead of disassociating from the shock, the motion now made a flush of vertigo jump down into his solar plexus.

"Those guys who were in the lab with us weren't EMTs," he said.

"Totally," Camila agreed. "Give me the vial."

They seemed dead, the specimens, or at least dormant. *Dormant*, Travis thought as he fished the vial out of his pocket. He shook it, trying to wake up the mosquitoes. "I'm fairly certain they're out of batteries at a minimum," Travis said. "I don't think they can spy on us if they're dead."

"Conspiracy's not far off," Camila said with no hint of spunk or sass. She was dead serious, maybe even a little bitter.

Travis took the vial from her, staring at the metallic glints, lit by the hazy parking lot lights and the flashing blue-white-red on all sides. The lights brought out that stark, biting silhouette from the mosquitoes again, the one that had first clued Travis into the truth of their makeup.

"Something really messed up is going on," Camila whispered.

"Thanks for that," he said.

The lightness in his tone made her let out a laugh, and for a second they could breathe. For just a moment, they weren't staring at a heap of steel, glass, and concrete that once had been the Grand Marsh Mosquito Control center. The thing that was leading to Travis's schooling, and Camila's foreseeable path. All of it had literally exploded in front of their eyes.

She let out a tight breath, shot between her lips. "He's really gone," she said. "Isn't he?"

Tears sprang up in the corners of his smoke-burned

eyes, clouding his vision. He looked down at the vial and didn't reply because of the lump swelling in his throat.

Something terrible had happened to Dr. McCallister. What had done it to him? Had he done it to *himself*? That idea was almost too much. He was a kook, absentminded in the most cliché way, but he wouldn't have gone to such lengths . . . would he? Unless something made him do it?

Holding the drones, with only a layer of glass between them and him, put his nerves on edge again.

A TV news helicopter landed in one of the cleared spaces a few hundred yards away. The chopper blades stirred up concrete dust and smoke. He and Camila both looked away, trying to breathe the clean air between the ambulance and a firetruck.

After coughing, she said, "The government made them."

"Come on," Travis said, even though he felt his face blanch. He knew somehow that they were probably the only entity with enough resources to create something like this—something that could drive a man to insanity.

"I'm serious, Travis."

"What would they make them for?"

"Are you really going to debate this?"

Travis looked in her eyes, saw how serious she was, how *right* she was. Shattered glass glistened in some of her dreads, and he thought how badly he wanted to get it out of her hair.

He relented. "No."

They looked away from each other. "What now?" Travis said.

"What are those?"

He looked up, following her finger to the west, where a line of black SUVs were cresting the hill.

Travis coughed, trying to keep his voice steady. Conversational. Yeah—conversational. "FBI?"

A man with a paunch and a bald head approached them. He was wearing a dark suit, and the way he looked them up and down, the way he stood, told Travis he was probably a detective.

"You have a way off the premises?" he asked them.

"I have my car," Camila said, pointing to the far end of the lot, where she'd parked the small tan Toyota Corolla in employee parking. It was banged up but, remarkably, *there*.

The detective nodded. "We just need to ask you both a couple questions before we let you go. That all right? Just for processing, you know, protocol. Might be another hour or so, until we get the scene wrapped up like Christmas. Just wait around here until we call for you."

Travis nodded, dizzy again. "Of course."

The detective got called over by a ridiculously tall man with a camera, leaving them both at the ambulance.

The black SUVs were getting closer. No descriptor—FBI, CIA, who knew? Government issued? Mafia?

Camila looked at the vial Travis was holding, just to make sure the drones weren't starting to twitch. She looked back at the SUVs, back at the vial. At Travis.

"Conspiracy, man," she said. "We gotta get out of here."

Before he could even form a reply, she had checked that the detective wasn't looking, then yanked Travis's hand and pulled him headlong toward her car at the other end of the lot.

They left their foil blankets behind, the only sign that they'd been there at all.

Part 2

ANATOMY OF THE HEAD

> "Insect anatomy dictates the existence of three sections: head, thorax, abdomen. All sensory data centers in the head, from which protrude its proboscis, antennae, and compound eyes."

—Dr. Zane McCallister, PhD

10

The smell of vanilla enveloped Travis as he flung his aching body into the passenger seat of Camila's Toyota Corolla. The yellow tree-shaped air freshener swung back and forth on the rearview mirror, like a pendulum.

A lurching sound erupted from the car.

"What's wrong?" Travis said. He wiped his glasses, then wiped his hands on his sooty pants.

"C'mon, baby," Camila muttered. She turned the key over and over. "Not now, we had an agreement. I need you."

She revved the engine again.

The detective grew in the passenger-side mirror, an elongated insect with black suit-clad limbs, reaching.

"Camila . . ." Travis whispered.

She looked up. Saw the detective—six feet away, now four.

"I'll get you fresh oil next week . . . just—" With a final mechanical jolt, the Corolla's engine clattered to life.

Camila spun the wheel, turning the small car out of the parking lot. The place that Travis had grown to love, now McCallister's tomb, was still smoldering, ashy, red with the sunset as a backdrop.

All he could focus on was the slender black stretch of

the detective growing smaller and smaller in the mirror as Camila sped them away.

Not far behind the detective, the black SUVs screeched to a halt. Someone got out and started speaking to the slender shape in the black suit, who didn't take his eyes off them.

But Camila turned a bend.

In the fuzz of rushing blood and shallow breaths, the red mangroves looked like hundreds of bloody legs running to catch them. Travis ground his teeth. "Go faster," he said, which was a mistake, because Camila only glared and set her knuckles on the wheel so hard, he thought it might break.

A low-hanging majesty palm slapped against the windshield.

Travis gasped.

"Breathe, man," Camila whispered. "I got it."

She fumbled with the stereo dial. It turned on, blaring rock at full blast.

After the shock wore off, Travis leaned his neck against the headrest. He took off his glasses and wiped them once. Wiped them again. Pinched the bridge of his nose. Looked at the world around them, which was somehow more comforting in its blurriness.

Nothing could harm him if he couldn't *see* it, right?

Nonsensical. It calmed him anyway, so he let it continue.

Camila found the alternative station she was looking for, the sort of music that didn't calm the nerves.

The AC blasted vanilla-scented aroma into Travis's nose.

He knew she must be thinking the same thing he was, though he didn't have enough energy to say it, much less *discuss* it.

What were they going to do now?

* * *

"Turn down here," Travis said when the intersection, so familiar its normalcy sent an ache through him, sped toward them.

Camila glanced at him, but stopped at the red light and hung a sharp right, leaving the Starbucks and Burger King to light up the road behind them.

"You have an idea?" She sounded as exhausted as Travis felt.

"Maybe." He shook his head. "Don't know yet."

They reached a section of town divided by blocks of apartment buildings. The wind was picking up around them—it threw up small whitecaps in the green-glowing swimming pool behind wrought-iron bars to their left. They sped past it.

"You can park in there," Travis said.

"In *there*," Camila said, deadpan.

"You don't think they're looking for us?"

She bit her lip. "You know they are. They're putting a BOLO out on us right now. We need to ditch this car."

"You're right. That's true," Travis said. "I know just the place."

* * *

"That place gave me the creeps," Camila said in a near whisper. "Where we headed, then?"

"My friend Alec's apartment," Travis said. "He's a scientist at another lab. Thought we could get his advice."

"Shh! What if they aren't dead? What if they can hear us?"

"They haven't moved since the explosion. They're dead."

"If you say so. Lead the way."

Travis led her out of the alley where they'd parked and across the street, toward one of the bigger blocks of apartment buildings, twenty stories high, shimmering with the light of evening traffic and coming rain.

The closer they got, the more *normal* the world seemed to become . . . Instead of the fire and acid that still hung in Travis's nose, the wind brought him whiffs of clean laundry from blowing dryer vents, the sound of kids arguing over the pieces of a puzzle on the patio of the second floor—and someone, somewhere, was making a gorgeous pot of sizzling curry. His stomach grumbled.

* * *

As they entered the building, neither of them noticed the body—falling, from the top of the twentieth floor, her slender limbs cascading one over the other, then she landed, twisted and broken, on the concrete.

Crack.

Crunch.

Silence.

* * *

Travis took them to the fourth floor, found 457, and knocked. The television was blaring from inside. It turned down, and then footsteps came toward the door. Travis noticed the Ring camera watching him and Camila, recording their every move.

The door swung inward. A man in his twenties stood there, tall enough that it was almost awkward, but only if he didn't spend every day in the gym. He'd pulled most of his blond hair into a hasty bun, but a few strands still hung round his face. The whole apartment smelled of incense.

Alec took them both in. His jaw dropped, and then he swore, his face paling fast.

"Sorry I didn't call," Travis said.

"Yeah, a little heads-up would've been nice. I just saw."

Travis's eyes narrowed. "Saw . . . ?"

"I'm Alec, by the way," he said, holding his hand out to Camila, who shook it with a polite enough smile.

"Nice to—" Camila started.

But Alec was already waving them inside, shutting the door behind them. Ambient lighting accented the walls of the apartment and lit the bookshelves—full of thick entomology textbooks and dozens of science-fiction paperbacks. Leftovers from his tofu pesto dinner sat on the stovetop.

The TV was still going in the background.

"I was honestly just about to call *you*." Alec glanced between them, reaching for a cupboard. "Do you want pesto?"

"Sure," Travis said, feeling bad that he was imposing, but also unable to ignore the ache of hunger for much longer.

"I thought you'd be . . . older, *scientist*." Camila interrupted, eyeing Alec suspiciously.

"Skipped a few grades." He winked.

"How old *are* you?" she pressed.

"Old enough to drink, not old enough to drive a minivan."

"Camila, he's cool, trust me. I've known him since I was a freshman."

"Anyway, as I was saying, I didn't know if you were inside when it happened, or what," Alec said, dishing them up lovely yarns of pasta, basil, olive oil, and tofu. "But I was pretty sure you were. Scared the living crap out of me, dude. That explosion. I mean, that's one of our worst fears, you know?"

That's when Travis noticed exactly *what* was on the seventy-inch flat-screen, the one he had always thought was disproportionate to how small the living room was. Now, he watched in 4K-clarity as the news channel shifted to an aerial shot of the explosion site—the rubble of the Grand Marsh Mosquito Control center.

The anchor's voice came over the footage, stiff and as cold as silly putty. "There are two eyewitness survivors who fled from the scene and are wanted for questioning. Authorities say any news on their whereabouts should be reported to . . ." She spouted off a number that Travis had a hard time paying attention to, because his and Camila's driver license photos flashed onto the screen.

Wanted for questioning.

Fled the scene.

"Travis," Alec said, setting the two bowls of pesto on the bar. "You gonna tell me what's going on, man?"

11

Alec spotted the vial Travis was holding. He tightened his grip on the glass, which became increasingly difficult as sweat began to break out on his palm.

"It's not what it sounds like," he said.

"You two in some kind of trouble?" Alec asked.

Travis eyed the pesto. Geesh, he wanted a bite of it. But he had a feeling that neither of them would be eating soon.

"Shut up, both of you," Camila said. "Who is *that*?"

They moved their attention back to the too-large screen, where someone they'd never seen before came on. From the way they presented him, Travis would have thought he was an authority on the institution that had just gone up in flames.

And he *looked* like he would know what he was talking about. He wore a navy-blue suit with white pinstripes, sparkling diamond cuff links, and a tie done up in a perfectly dimpled Windsor. His short black hair had been meticulously faded to his black skin. He appeared to be emotional.

"Dr. McCallister and I were great friends," he was saying. "Have been for years. I'm absolutely devastated by what has happened here, and I'm willing to help out however I can, to make sure the one responsible for it is caught."

"Dr. Cowan," Camila read from the screen caption. "We don't know him, do we?"

But Travis didn't have time to respond.

"Any thoughts on the two eyewitnesses who took off shortly after the explosion?"

Dr. Cowan shook his head. "From what Dr. McCallister had told me, they were just field techs he'd hired for the summer. A couple of lazy kids, didn't care about the field. Entitled—you know the type."

"Sure," the offscreen reporter said.

"He was planning on firing them," Dr. Cowan said. "Today, actually. Bit ironic, if you think about it."

"That would give them motive," the reporter said.

Dr. Cowan shrugged, a glint in his eye. "I wouldn't say that, of course. But I do find it to be an interesting correlation."

"Interesting correlation," Travis said, practically chewing the words, wishing he could spit them out, that's how bitter they tasted. "He basically just told the entire world that *we* did it!"

"Did you?"

Travis turned to Alec, who was staring at him and Camila with a hard scowl. He was leaning with his back toward the sink, his bare arms crossed.

"Are you kidding?" Travis said, the unjust anger of it all coming out with more vehemence than he'd intended.

"That guy has a good point."

"We've never seen *that guy*," Camila said. "He definitely doesn't work for GMMC, and I'm pretty sure he didn't even know the doc."

"You don't know that," Alec said. "I've known—

knew—McCallister for years. Doesn't mean I know everyone he's friends with."

"Alec, why would we blow it up?" Travis said.

"Why did you leave the scene like that?" he countered.

Good point.

Travis glanced at Camila, tried to have yet another conversation with just their eyes.

"It's a little hard to explain," she said.

"Look," Alec said, "all I'm saying is if there's nothing wrong—if you *did* nothing wrong—there's no reason to leave. Just tell the coppers what they want to know, move on with your lives."

"We can't," Travis said.

Alec looked between them. Travis's gut rumbled.

"Look," he said. "We think this is bigger than even the news channels want to admit, okay? I think if they let it out . . . people might panic. Right? I mean, the doc was dead before the building exploded. *He's* the one who did it."

"It's a conspiracy," Camila said.

Geesh, Travis thought. He threw his head back and turned around, trying to hide the exasperation on his face.

When he turned back, Alec was grinning. "A conspiracy?"

"I think it's time we tell him," Camila said to Travis.

"Tell me what?" Alec asked.

"I trust you, Alec," Travis said, "or I wouldn't have come here. All right?"

"You two are in deep," he said. "Aren't you?"

Travis set the vial on the quartz countertop. The glass pinged . . . like when the Ring camera dinged, announcing their arrival. He thought of a recording, of who was seeing what.

"We found one of these this morning," he said. "We were dissecting it with Dr. McCallister . . ."

And he told the story. What he found when he sliced the abdomen open, how Doc had sent them away. How they'd come back to more drones in the building and the lab a wreck. Camila had to pick up for Travis when his throat choked talking about Dr. McCallister. Alec looked like he was going to be sick when she told him what had happened to him.

Then the fake EMTs and the final explosion. The black SUVs.

"Conspiracy," Camila concluded.

"Conspiracy," Alec breathed.

All three of them were silent for a moment. Hearing it all out loud, it seemed to Travis as though it had never happened—the plot of some summer blockbuster he'd been to instead of the last twelve hours of his life.

He was getting to the point where exhaustion was beginning to override his hunger . . . and after the story, the tofu clumps in the pesto looked less appetizing than fifteen minutes ago.

"And that Dr. Cowan?" Alec asked.

"He's lying," Travis said.

"And we've never seen him in our lives," Camila added.

"Drones, huh . . ." Alec came in closer, looking at the vial, the cold metallic specimens sitting at the bottom.

A dark sinking feeling came over Travis, and he had the urge to tell Alec to move away, not to get too close . . . he thought he even saw the light above the stove quiver.

"They're real," Travis said. "And . . . dangerous."

"You think they did something to McCallister," Alec said.

"That's the idea," Camila said.

"They're the only factor that changed," Travis added. "It's like those drones showed up and we think the doc went insane."

"It's Illuminati-level crap," Camila said, also leaning down to inspect the drones on the opposite side of Alec. Travis wanted to tell both of them to knock it off. "Or maybe the CDC. Some kind of disease control, or . . . disease *spread*? But why?"

"How do we know they're still not tracking you? Watching," Alec asked.

Travis grabbed the vial. "I don't. But I think it's dead. If it wasn't, they—whoever they are—would have caught up to us already."

Camila and Alec looked to him.

"The truth is," he said, holding the vial up to the light, "we don't have any idea who made them."

"Where do we start?" Alec asked.

12

Dr. Victoria Swain looked out the open french doors to the terrace, to the empty sky behind it, full and bulging with the storm it was about to give birth to. Sometimes, even though she loved it and had worked hard for it, being this high up could be downright dizzying. But she'd insisted, hadn't she?

Victoria pressed her phone to her shoulder so she could use her hand to pick up the stem of her wineglass. The merlot, rich and bitter, swam along her tongue and down her throat. She caught sight of herself in those french doors, flung across her chaise lounge like a classic peacoat: classy, useful, utilitarian, and maybe a little out of style.

Even though she was approaching her late fifties—or perhaps because of it—her high cheekbones shaped her face into a sculpture of beauty. Her hair was buzzed short—her ancestors on the Continent had been confident in this style, and now so was she, after decades of soul-searching and fighting the internalized hatred of her coarse, unyielding curls. Her black skin practically shimmered with gold tones, always well oiled. Even with merlot every night, she'd maintained a whiteness in her teeth that made other women glance at her every so often in envy. Her teeth, her body, her apparent youth, her confidence.

Her penthouse.

It's all very enviable, isn't it? she thought, pulling herself briefly from the telephone conversation to congratulate herself. She had become everything every woman wanted to be. This, after all, was what success looked like.

"Where do you think they ran to?" the voice on the other end of the telephone asked.

"Sorry—who?"

"The witnesses."

"Does it really matter?" Yet another sip. "Zane's gone. Finding out who did it isn't going to change that."

"Did the old guy have any family?"

"Just the one daughter," Victoria said, waving the idea away with her free hand. "They've been estranged for years, though. Last I heard, she was in Colorado."

"Maybe you should call her, you knew him best."

Victoria smiled. She had, hadn't she? Known Zane very well. But *no one* knew Zane that well. There had always been a piece of himself that he kept subterranean.

A buzzing from the deck interrupted her focus. A subtle, low-pitched hum, like an insect, flitting.

She glanced briefly at the wide-open french doors, her warbled image cast back at her, the scarlet stain of the merlot's reflection in her hand.

"Victoria?" the voice on the phone said. "You still there?"

"Sorry, Georgia . . ."

"Did you hear what I said?"

Bzzz.

"No."

"You don't think it's related to Titus, do you?"

Titus. It had been a long time since Victoria had heard any mention of her old employer. It'd gone up in flames what felt like a lifetime ago—metaphorical flames, of course, but just as destructive as whatever had happened at the GMMC.

"They're not interested in that sort of thing," Victoria said. "Not anymore. Titus Pharma has moved on."

"But—"

It was a mosquito.

The rest of her friend's gabby falsetto faded as she realized that a mosquito had made its way into the room, despite the blue-burning trap outside the doors.

She reminded herself to find the flyswatter if this conversation ever came to an end.

". . . all I'm saying," Georgia continued, "is that they didn't really have a good taste in their mouth for Zane when everyone left. You told me that, remember? What a fiasco it was?"

"It wasn't all bad," Victoria said. "There were good times, too. In the beginning."

But that was so long ago. Odd how an ultimate experience with something could leave such a memory that nothing good ever seemed to have existed.

"Sure there were," Georgia said. "*We* had a good time before I left. And I'm glad I did, you know? Zane would've . . ."

Pinch. The mosquito had landed on her upper arm. The wine sloshed in its high-stem glass as she set it down. Little bugger. She flicked it away.

"Look," Victoria said, "I'm going to have to call you later."

"All right, all right, no worries . . ."

Platitudes, condolences—and then Victoria hung up. She breathed a sigh of relief at the quiet solemnity of the penthouse now. That breeze really did feel good. Now to get rid of the pest.

She scratched at her arm. She'd had enough wine that her cheeks flushed, the blood pumping through her, sponging to the surface of her skin—burgeoning into the location of the bite, itching beyond toleration and already visibly inflamed.

And she must have been more intoxicated than she'd realized. The moment she stood up, her head spun, and her vision began to blur at the edges, like she was on the verge of tears.

She blinked. It cleared, but only for a moment.

No—she shook her head. That little bugger needed to *go*. The audacity of interrupting this perfect life, when she'd done everything to keep things like it *out*. The itching in her arm, the wine-induced dizziness, the grief over Zane that somehow had been more shocking than she'd ever thought it would be, all bottlenecked into one goal only.

Get the swatter. Kill the mosquito. That parasitic, worthless little insect. That redundant waste of life and good cells, sycophantic and *lazy*.

Victoria entered the kitchen, almost knocking over the merlot bottle on the counter in her dizziness. She found the swatter in the pantry by the fire extinguisher.

She returned to the living room, swatter held high, her eyes searching—her mind warning her of what was to come before she saw the evidence of it.

The buzzing had increased, and the hum became overwhelming.

And in her living room, nesting in the buttoned upholstery of the chaise, undulating on the floor in impossible waves, were hundreds—no, thousands of *thousands*—of mosquitoes.

13

The swatter fell from her hand, landing on the carpet of wriggling, bulging mosquitoes, being *swallowed* by it, disappearing as wholly as though it had been digested.

The swarm moved as though it were one thing, not many. *Scourge*—she remembered the word now. Hadn't Zane taught her that term? She didn't feel a single prick, a single sting—but rather a burning flush on every inch of skin.

Any scream she might have uttered was blotted out by a chaotic scourge. They landed and crawled around her lips. She clasped a hand over her mouth to keep them from entering. *They won't go down my throat, will they? Down into my esophagus . . . into the bloody soft tissue inside?*

Several of the insects popped and splattered, their guts red and congealed like pus. They painted her mouth with their insides.

Warm.

Bzzz.

Why am I just standing here? Why am I just standing here, doing nothing?

She needed escape, craved it like someone wandering

a desert for generations, a thirst so clear and striking, it seemed to intertwine with her DNA.

In a panic, Victoria turned slowly about the room, keeping as tight a grasp as she could over her mouth to keep her sanity. Still, the insects crawled on her eyes, bit her lids—and *still* the blur grew.

But now the scourge had overtaken the kitchen, too.

"Help!" she screamed into her hand.

Her penthouse was no longer a home. It was a series of dunes in a sandstorm, every surface a windswept stretch of Sahara that moaned and called with a sound like flapping wings.

The sand grew thickest near the front door, spilled from it in waves.

When did I open it?

Don't just stand there.

You didn't get where you are by standing there, Victoria.

Remember who you are, she thought. *Remember where you come from.* This she would not stand.

So she turned from the obvious exit, saw that the french doors, now only a sandcastle impression of the graceful, paned portals they had been, still yawned open for her.

And beyond?

Clear air. Pregnant storm clouds, near bursting.

Her sigh of relief caught in her throat, tugging against the vacuum of air cupped in her palm.

She would get out. She, Victoria Swain, would *live*.

As she approached, however, the color of the mosquitoes around her darkened, slowly turning inky, navy black. A current swept her hand away from her mouth, and cold ocean water smacked against the warmth of her lips.

Now, she really could not open her mouth.

Terror shot through her in ribbons like slimy, chilly kelp.

The doorway was no longer a doorway, but jaws, impossibly large, Megalodon teeth like razors, filled with old carrion, and swimming toward her with the strength and speed of a warhead.

Victoria's entire body was frozen. She summoned her will. Kick forward, duck down!

Screaming.

The shark missed her by inches, its belly grazing her bare head and drawing blood as though she'd shaved with coarse sandpaper.

All at once, the water rushed down around her in currents and ribbons, as though, maddeningly, someone had pulled a plug in the ocean floor.

She gasped, precious oxygen inflating her lungs.

How long had she been holding her breath?

She looked around . . . *I'm on the terrace*, she thought, before the reality of what that meant overtook her. She was on the terrace, yes, but the terrace was no better than the penthouse anymore.

The mosquitoes had overtaken the furniture—the umbrella, the coffee table, the wicker loungers, all now an amalgamation of swirling sand.

And below her feet, the world began to shift and tumble. Not just sand, not anymore.

Quicksand began to swallow her feet; it had taken her ankles already, devouring her.

Victoria scrambled, falling forward and grasping the terrace's rails. Mosquitoes buzzed and popped under her palms, sticky with blood—but she clung tight, pulling herself out of the quicksand and carefully onto the wrought-iron railing.

Her teeth clacked together. She looked down. Twenty stories, wasn't it? That was what she'd asked for. This was what success looked like: twenty stories cutting a straight line to pavement she could barely make out. A young man and a young woman walked through the front doors down there. Victoria was too distracted by her own indecision to notice the way their heads turned from side to side, making sure no one noticed, making sure they weren't being followed.

Victoria closed her eyes.

She would stand here all night, she decided. Would cling to this railing in the hopes that someone would see her up here, maybe think it was a suicide about to happen and call 911.

Go back?

No—she turned her head, enough to see that there would be no going into her apartment.

Those two, going inside—she should have called down to them, called for help.

A rigidity stole through her hands; rain splattered on them, chilling them. She blinked away the raindrops from her eyes like tears. Her calves burned from keeping the full weight of her body balanced on the thin wrought iron, but even one step back and . . .

The railing shuddered. Wobbled, like it was in an earthquake.

As Victoria opened her panicked eyes, she saw the dark metal dissolving underneath her grip, a deep black sand falling twenty stories, spilling onto the quicksand of the deck—shimmering like ground obsidian, like mica.

"Help!" she screamed. "Help! Someone!"

Victoria heard her own voice, but she couldn't scream, not anymore. She barely had the wherewithal to keep herself on the edge of the terrace.

For a moment, she thought she'd jumped. Wind whipped at her, and in the split seconds before, she saw the truth.

Nothing was sand. Everything was just as it had been.

She, Dr. Victoria Swain, stood *on top of* the wrought-iron railing, barely balanced at all. Behind her, the terrace winked at her, her apartment affectionate and inviting.

Just behind her head, a handful of mosquitoes hovered.

Watched.

She only had time to narrow her eyes before her left foot slipped. Vertigo shot her stomach up into her throat.

And Victoria Swain fell to her death.

14

Where do we start?

Geesh. That was as good a question as any, and one Travis had been mulling over for a long while. He wiped his glasses and blinked around at the other two, his vision clearing. His stomach made empty gurgling noises.

"You wanna eat something there, buddy?" Alec asked, clearly having heard.

Indignant, Travis picked up his bowl of now-cold tofu pesto and took a bite. It tasted all right; the texture of the tofu in his mouth made him a little squeamish, though. He'd always thought the stuff tasted a bit like Play-Doh.

Camila picked at her bowl but only took a couple bites.

The food did its job, though. While Alec cleaned off their dishes, Travis's mind began to fire in the right direction again. "We need to take a closer look at those drones," he said.

The three of them glanced at the vial.

Travis had noticed they'd all done their best to pretend that they didn't exist for the last few minutes—but they'd all taken their turns eyeing them.

"Alec," he said, "we need to use your lab."

"Alec," his friend said mockingly. "I have a huge

favor to ask. Would it be at all possible to use the lab? Even though it will probably cost you your job and we're on the run from the friggin' FBI?"

Camila looked down, hiding her smile.

"What?" Travis said.

"You wanna just march into Aust Biotech," Alec said, "use my ID, and look at these little government-level buggers?"

"Yes," he said, as though it were the most obvious thing in the world. "Nive University has some of the best equipment in the state—you wouldn't work there if that weren't true! And we need to figure out what these are."

"And why's that?" Alec said, shrugging. All sarcasm had left him. "You could just turn them in, Travis. You told me yourself, you two didn't do anything *wrong*, which means you're not going to prison. You didn't blow up the GMMC, you didn't kill McCallister."

"That's just it." Travis met Camila's eye. "We didn't kill the doc. But *someone* did. I don't know if it was someone who showed up and did it to him, or I don't know, maybe the drones made him do it to himself—but that means someone is controlling the drones. It might be the FBI, might be the cops, someone else—right? We *don't know*.

"But whoever that Dr. Cowan is, he's lying. To the press, to the cops, to whoever was in those black SUVs. And come on, they're not going to believe a couple intern kids over him. You know it, and I know it."

"I know how crazy it sounds, but . . . I have a feeling even if we turn them in, it won't be the end of it, and we need to clear our names," Camila said.

Travis felt it then, the urge in the bottom of his gut that told him he was wrong, about everything he'd said. That the best thing would be to turn in the drones and forget any of it ever happened. Go to college and . . . just deal with the fact that the man who got him in had died, and that he, Travis, hadn't done anything to fix it.

He wanted to run.

But could he live with that? How much of himself would he have to compromise in order for that to happen, to keep going through all his programs, an entire career, when the man he owed all that to was dead?

He thought of the stag beetle, the one he'd meant to give the doc before they'd found him in the lab. He thought of McCallister's eyes, those melted pools of bloody marshmallow cream.

Travis knew he would have to sacrifice part of himself if he said no to figuring this out, and to stopping this from happening to anyone else—maybe even to himself and Camila, and now Alec. Was that a part of himself he was willing to risk?

Who would he be then? A coward? A murderer by omission?

Certainly not himself, not a person he would *like*.

Alec sighed, looking between them. "You really wanna bring drones into Aust Biotech Lab?"

This is it, Travis thought. *No going back after this.* Whatever they found out now, it would push them further and deeper. He would have to see this through to the end, or not at all. It was the only way to clear their names and set everything right. Was he ready?

Travis and Camila answered at the same time. "Yes."

Their pronouncement together made his heart leap. He was scared, of course, but also excited. Exhilarated that at least they would be doing this together. He resisted the urge to take Camila's hand.

"Okay . . ." Alec shook his head, smiling despite himself. "Okay. We'll take them in, take a look. All right?"

"When can we—" Camila started.

But a siren blast interrupted her, followed by a roll of thunder. Blue-and-red lights flashed through the windows.

Travis's heart jumped into his throat.

"How did they find us?" he said, though his eyes automatically searched out the vial, the drones.

Alec held up a hand. "Just . . . hold on, okay?" He tiptoed to the tall window next to the too-big TV and peeked through the blinds. The flashing lights created a banded mask on his eyes.

"Don't think it's for you," he said. "There's an ambulance." Then he swore. "*Oh.*"

"What?" Camila asked.

"Someone must've fallen off their balcony."

Alec turned to them. His face paled; he looked like he was about to be sick. "It's pretty bad."

"How bad?" Travis said.

"You really wanna know? Let's just say her brain's not exactly where it should be."

Travis closed his eyes, fighting the image.

"We gotta get you two out of here," Alec said. "A fall like this . . . reporters can't be far behind. And they can't see you two. There's already, like, three cops outside."

"Any black Suburbans?" Camila asked.

Alec glanced through the blinds again. The lights shimmered off his irises. "Two of them just pulled up."

Travis narrowed his eyes. "It can't be connected . . . can it?"

"I'll get you guys something to wear," Alec said, marching away from the window. "Something they won't recognize."

15

Camila got the *Rick and Morty*. Travis grumblingly accepted the Queens of the Stone Age pullover with 1990s pink fantasy lettering, then pulled the hood over his eyes.

Alec grabbed his ID and keys. Every siren beat, every squeal of tires and brakes, shot panic through Travis in miniature waves.

"You okay?" Camila whispered.

He gave a weak smile, though that was the last thing he wanted to do.

"Really," she asked, "you good?"

"Are you?"

"No."

"Good."

"Good?"

"Me either," Travis said.

"Ready?" Alec looked between them, chuckling at the length of the hoodies, the way they almost reached their knees.

What was more suspicious? Travis thought. The clothes they were last seen in, or stoner pullovers that clearly didn't belong to them?

"Let's get out of here," Camila said.

* * *

Oversized or not, Travis was grateful for the warmth—the instinctual security—of being wrapped almost head to toe in cotton comfort.

Rain splattered on their hoods. In the distance, thunder tripped and tumbled through the sky.

"Just keep moving," Alec said from behind. "Just get to the car."

Rainwater splashed up around Travis's shoes; he felt it squishing into his socks. And though he tried not to, he couldn't help turning his head once they passed the scene.

Rivulets of blood and . . . other parts . . . snaked their way along the cracks in the pavement, chased down the gutter, hemorrhaged onto the asphalt.

The body, what was left of it, lay under a bloodied white sheet.

A chill racked him.

He spotted the SUVs, and kept his grip on the vial in the front pocket of the Queens of the Stone Age hoodie.

Men in black suits exited the black vehicles. Each face could have been *the* detective—and Travis wished he remembered exactly what he'd looked like, so he could pinpoint him and know when to run.

They walked around the yellow caution tape, keeping along the warm brick side of the building. Alec couldn't stop looking behind them, either. The longer Travis looked, the sicker he became—and the more he wanted to *know*.

"Hold up," he said. He and Alec stopped.

Without knowing it, they'd gotten ahead of Camila. She stood a few feet behind them, staring at the brick, both hands gripping her hood to keep her face concealed entirely. The bulk of her dreads made the hood bulge up like thick arteries under skin made of cotton.

Travis wiped the rain and mist from his glasses, then put them back on. Alec gave him a look—a "what's up with her?" sort of glance—then they reluctantly approached her.

"Hey," Travis said. He reached out a hand and slid his fingers into hers.

"Hey," she said.

Alec and Travis shared a look.

Camila took in a deep breath; the exhale took four seconds.

"Hey," Travis said again. "Let's get moving. You all right? We can talk about it, just not here. Let's go."

He glanced back at the body as they wheeled it into the ambulance. A limp hand stuck out of the sheet. He noted the swollen purple welted bite marks.

"Not again," she said.

A man was approaching them from the other side of the caution tape, his paunch almost bursting the buttons of his police uniform.

"C'mon," Alec said.

"Right," Camila said. She wiped at her face. "Right."

They began walking away again, all three of them, when a sound caught in Travis's ear, like a fly strung in the sticky fibers of a web. It was like the sound of a quiet, low electric razor.

He'd heard it before, but now, his nerves on edge, he recognized just how different it sounded from a mosquito. He wondered how he'd ever thought they were similar.

Travis turned his head, seeing them in his periphery just before they were too far away: A small scourge of them, sticking together like no *real* scourge of mosquitoes would do, floating in and around the crime scene.

Remember that sound, he thought to himself as they picked up the pace, rain pelting him now, soaking through the hoodie and making it almost twice as heavy. *Remember it . . .* that whirring ping. A machine. Not an insect. Machine.

He was so stuck in his thoughts that he didn't notice Camila had been holding out her hand to him for several seconds already. Travis grabbed on to it, both their fingers cold, becoming warmer as they held each other.

"Do you think they saw us?" he asked.

"Whoever *they* are, no, I don't," Camila said. "They were focused on whoever was under that sheet."

It could've been me.

It could have been any of them.

And it still might be.

16

"Turn off your phone," Camila said. She pulled hers out in the back of Alec's station wagon. "And probably take out the SIM card for good measure."

When Travis didn't act right away, she said, "The last thing we need right now is for those SUVs or the police or whoever is after us to ping our location." She raised her eyebrows at him. "Right?"

Travis swallowed. Of course. He took out his phone, glancing nervously at every flash of windowpane-melted light that came through the rain-splattered glass.

He turned it off, then took out the SIM card.

A bump in the road caused him to suck in a sharp gasp of air.

"I thought you said you weren't old enough to drive a minivan," Camila said, breaking the tension.

"I did," Alec said. "Mom's old station wagon isn't a minivan."

"It's minivan adjacent," she retorted, then laughed.

Aust Biotech was only a couple miles from the apartment complex, a jutting steel-and-glass needle in the center of downtown. It was a part of Nive University's campus, and they had chosen hexagons as a motif. Even from the outside, Travis made out hexagonal sculptures, strung in gravity-defying patterns over the main lobby, dotted here and there with bare decorative bulbs that glowed yellow like bees among glinting honeycombs.

But then the view of the magnificent lobby disappeared, replaced with a cavern of dripping concrete and sheets of unlit parking garage.

Alec let them in through the employee door using his ID card, to which Travis whispered, "Thank you," and received a soft nod in return. A security guard wearing what could have only been a toupee waved as Alec passed, giving Travis and Camila an interested glance.

"Evening, A," the guard said.

"Bert," Alec said.

The interaction didn't go any further than that, but calm didn't find Travis until they'd entered the lab and closed and locked the doors behind them. Most of the other labs and office spaces were pitch black, illuminated here and there with the soft glow of an emergency hall light or an exit sign.

Just the sight of that blackness, of that eerie red, made Travis think of the doc. Of catching these drones only hours ago. How had that only been hours ago?

"All right," Alec said, "we won't have much time."

Travis took out the vial and set it on the counter. He glanced at the glass doors they'd entered through, then at the black hallway beyond it, where anything could be lurking.

The lab had a metallic tinge to the way it smelled. Lights still clicked on one by one above them, the fluorescents taking time to warm up. Somewhere, a machine whirred. Another one beeped. Most of them kept a steady green light, a sleep mode that Travis and the others were about to interrupt.

"First things first," Travis said. "We need to confirm

that these guys are dead or out of batteries, then we will consider them decommissioned. Use them to find out everything we can about what happened at the GMMC."

He watched with growing nerves as Alec booted up a computer the likes of which the GMMC, with its public funding, never would have seen. Travis was familiar with dissecting microscopes, but this high-tech piece of machinery was a sight to behold. Next to it, completing the array of technologically advanced scopes, was a sophisticated scanning electron microscope, SEM. Tonight, though, their scope of choice was the dissecting microscope. A square pad of light surrounded on five angles by microscopic lenses. The pad pulsed with its soft light, once, twice, three times.

"Put 'em on," Travis said.

Alec pulled a long set of tweezers from an antiseptic jar near the device and pulled one of the captured drones from the vial, setting it on the pad.

Another soft blink emanated from the computer terminal.

"Initial data scan complete," a charming female voice said.

An enormous screen, maybe a hundred inches in diagonal, came to life in front of them. It showed a three-dimensional rendering of the drone in real time, and in immaculate detail. Next to it, a drop-down tab hung the data for them in a nice line.

"Twelve point three milligrams," Camila said. "Over twice the weight of a normal mosquito . . ." Her eyes scanned the list. "Mass, five milligrams. Molecular density of *eight point nine*?"

"Mostly copper, looks like," Travis said. "Makes sense given the wiring. The outer shell needed to be light, too. Cheap, if you're going to make hundreds of them."

He looked to Alec. But the expression on his friend's face said it all—slightly slack jaw with wide eyes, studying the image intently, trying to make sense of it. The drones were so tiny, and if they were really so cheap to make? No . . . Travis shook his head at the thought of *hundreds* of these. Anywhere and everywhere.

"So are they spying on us?" Alec asked.

"I have no idea," Travis said.

Camila rubbed her chin. "Of course they are! There's no other reason for it. I just don't know why."

Alec pressed some keys on the computer, and like a flipped switch, the model became transparent, all of its wired-and-screwed insides lighting up.

"Can you move in on the abdomen for a sec?" Travis said.

The three-dimensional model whirred as Alec got closer to the abdomen. It grew to a grotesque size, but ultimately showed what Travis thought he'd seen.

Blood filled some sort of sack inside the abdomen, and in a second sack sloshed an oozy yellow substance that he couldn't make out off the top of his head.

"Is there a way to get that out?" Camila asked.

"Too tiny," Alec said. "I don't have a syringe small enough to get to it."

Alec zoomed in on the eyes. And at this magnification, in three dimensions, Travis saw that the mosquito's dozens of eyes, much like a fly's, were actually an illusion: transparent glass beads created a dome around the actual eye, a camera. He could even make out every blade of the aperture. Unmoving, staring—at least for now.

He wiped his glasses. "Back at the GMMC, it sucked power from the microscope. Ended up shattering two of the light bulbs because of it."

Alec was picking at the drone with the tweezers.

"This one's as dead as it's going to get." He glanced at his computer screen, narrowing his eyes. "I can't find an electrical pulse in it anywhere."

"So we're in the clear?" Camila asked.

Alec shrugged. "For now, at least."

"How do we know if it's *dead* dead," Travis asked, "or just . . . I don't know—*dormant*, or something?"

"We can't," Alec said. "But unless they've got some next-level tech, or there are actually little teeny-tiny people on the other side of that aperture, no one's watching."

That made Travis let out a breath. He helped Alec replace that drone with the second, and they ran the same diagnostics. Same non-electrical pulse. Even this one, with its split abdomen, had the same sacks, with the same liquids.

"Those weren't there before," Travis said, shaking his head. "I would've remembered seeing them."

"I say we figure out how to get it out," Camila said. "Yeah?" She looked between them.

"Nothing but time," Alec said, sighing.

She smiled. "I'll get us coffee."

17

They drew the drone, each of them doing sketches and labeling its drone-specific anatomy. Travis admitted Camila's was the best sketch of the three of them. So he focused on his more.

The coffee *did* help. What had once felt like a rainwater-slogged chore became a bit more fun and games. Even Alec, who'd appeared tired under all his curiosity, seemed to be only curious now. He leaned over the dissecting microscope where they'd placed the first specimen, blond hair falling out of his man bun and almost into his eyes. He swatted it away.

Travis glanced at Camila's drawing again. His and Alec's mock-ups of the drones might have been passable. They were utilitarian, geometrically accurate, to scale, labeled properly with ruler-straight lines. But Camila's . . . seemed almost to *hum.*

"Yours really is the best one," Travis said to her. He finished off his creamy coffee with a swig.

"Kids," Alec said, "Daddy's a genius."

Travis nearly snorted coffee through his nose, and the gulp to get it down properly made his Adam's apple hurt.

"What?" Alec said, looking up from the eyepiece innocently.

"It's fine," Camila said.

"What'd you figure out, Father Dearest?" Travis asked.

Alec rolled his eyes. "Right, right—look, I don't have a syringe small enough, but . . ." He shuffled over to the computer and the three-dimensional scanner, tucking hair back behind his ears. "Then I thought, what if we could use *it* to hack *into* it?"

As though he'd copy-and-pasted it, a duplicate of the drone's proboscis popped off the head and floated into the air. A moment later, a syringe appeared, attaching itself to one end so that the proboscis became the needle.

"That could work," Travis said. He wiped his glasses and pushed his own scraggly brown hair out of his eyes.

"Only question is," Camila said, "where to insert it? I mean, the last thing we need is to damage the thing. What's the use of it damaged?"

Travis and Alec both agreed.

Alec took the exact width of the drone's proboscis, and after waiting ten minutes for the render to complete, he ran a simulation in which they inserted it for extraction.

There wasn't so much concern for the drone's outer shell. The proboscis was small enough that the hole would be negligible—or easily repaired with a quick soldering. And anyway, they all agreed they should do the extraction on the partially dissected drone first—better to see in.

The first two simulations failed, the program turning the entire drone a washed-out red color as though it'd been soaked in dye. There were nano-wide parts that, even in a three-dimensional model the size of a small dog, all three of them had missed.

"Simulation failed," the AI voice chimed again, so

much like an airline stewardess and yet somehow sinister in this context, Travis thought.

"What about inserting it here?" He pointed at yet another point that seemed to be clear.

Alec nodded, too in the flow of the task to be talkative, and began running the simulation.

This time, instead of the drone simply turning red, it turned red, *flashed*, and then the computer began to beep, as though sounding an alarm.

"Whoa, whoa, whoa," Alec said, "down girl . . . c'mon . . ."

The sound ceased, but the drone continued to blink.

Camila stepped closer to the screen. "What'd we hit?"

In response, Alec spun the digital model around to an angle they'd never seen it from before. A small cube, with wires coming from either end, lay between the insert point and the sack with the unidentified yellow liquid.

Travis looked to Alec and saw him squinting at the screen. Then he closed his eyes. "Well, that certainly complicates it."

"What is it?" Camila asked.

"An explosive," Alec said.

After a clack of keys, the simulation stopped, leaving the model just as "normal" looking as ever.

"No matter where we extract it from," Alec said, "I think it's safe to assume we'll have to bypass the explosive. There might even be a mechanical fail-safe the extraction could trigger. The whole thing could self-destruct, electrical current or no. We just can't be sure."

"But not . . ." Travis said, having a difficult time phrasing the question.

"No," Alec said, "nothing like what blew up GMMC. There'd be a lot of smoke. It might take out some of the devices in here. But no, it would only be big enough really to destroy the drone and give us a little shake. Maybe like lighting a match."

"Right," Camila said.

If her tone meant anything, then Travis considered that she was just as convinced as he was—i.e., she wasn't.

"So wait," he said, "you're saying there's a real possibility that if we extract anything—the blood, or whatever the other stuff is—it might hit the suicide button?"

Alec nodded.

"Is that something we want to risk, then?" Travis looked from Alec to Camila. Whatever new resolve had pumped through them a couple hours ago with the coffee seemed to be crashing. And crashing fast.

Camila sighed, defeated.

"No," Alec said. "Not until we're sure. These two are dead—like I said, the kill switch is more than likely mechanical. But getting your hands on other specimens? Good luck, right?"

"I agree with Alec," Camila said. "Not worth it. Not until we know for sure we're not going to lose them."

"And if we never know for sure?" Alec asked.

Neither of them seemed to want to answer that.

"Okay," Travis said. "Well that's that, then."

Exhaustion and defeat had replaced whatever anxiety had been in him when they'd entered Aust Biotech. All he wanted now was a hot protein-heavy breakfast to fill his empty stomach and to lie down for a few hours.

"Come back later?" he said. "I'm sure the apartment's mostly clear by now."

He realized he'd basically invited himself and Camila back to Alec's place, and he was about to apologize about the assumption when Alec said, "You guys can crash at my place tonight. I got a spare bedroom and a pretty comfy couch. Not a big deal."

"Thanks, man," Travis said. "I don't know how I'm ever going to pay you back for this."

Alec winked. "I'll be phoning it in soon, don't worry."

18

Travis walked out of the guest bathroom early the next morning, wondering whether or not to bury himself in the blankets of the gray incense-scented sectional for a couple more hours, when he saw Camila and Alec sitting at the bar waiting for the coffee maker to finish. That made up his mind for him.

"How'd you sleep?" Camila asked.

Travis noticed that both of them were still wearing their hoodies from the night before. They'd been too exhausted to worry about changing, and anyway, they'd been comfy enough.

"Like uranium," he said.

Alec spluttered something like "ridiculous," but Camila only narrowed her eyes. "I don't get it."

"Give it a second," Alec said, getting up and grabbing bowls from the cupboard.

Travis watched, bleary-eyed, as she thought, understood, and let her shoulders drop. "That is the lamest crap—dude, we need to work on your sense of humor."

Travis turned to her and whispered, "We should do something to say thank you."

Alec returned from the kitchen counter, where he'd

been prepping coffee for them. "Sorry, coffee maker shorted out."

"We've got this, coffee's on us." Camila smiled. "And if you're lucky, we'll buy scones, too."

"Hey, can we borrow your car for a while?" Travis asked, changing the subject.

Alec shrugged. "Sure. The keys are in the dish by the front door."

"We'll be back in a bit. Let us go get coffee for all of us." He grabbed Alec's car keys by the dish before leaving the apartment.

* * *

Travis wondered if they would ever get to the point where he could wear anything other than a Queens of the Stone Age hoodie. But it was what it was—wasn't it? He put his hood up as Camila pulled them toward the closest coffee shop and he held the shop's door open for her. A waft of *coffea arabica*, ground fresh, made his eyes go wide, as though he'd taken a shot of caffeine just by smelling.

It's like everything's normal again. Travis could imagine this was just another morning, that none of yesterday had ever happened. There was no TV, which meant no news; instead, the smooth jazz made a warmth trickle through him from the inside.

He smiled.

The woman at the counter, her eyeliner thick, eyes smoky, asked what they wanted. "Three coffees," Camila said—the more the better, at this point. Travis added two lemon pound cakes and three cheese Danishes. Comfort food.

As the barista gave them the total, he took out his card

and was about to hand it to her when Camila slapped it out of his hand.

It fell to the tile with enough of a clatter to draw several eyes to them. The smoky-eyed barista looked between them; though her expression didn't change, she was clearly waiting for the explanation to make itself known.

Travis's ears burned. The bell chimed behind them as someone opened the door.

"Everything okay?" the barista asked.

"Fine," Camila muttered. "I'm sorry, can you get one more thing? A decaf would be nice."

"We haven't started any—"

"That's okay," Camila said, flashing a smile that Travis knew was fake but passed with the barista. "We can wait."

The barista smirked and headed to the back, nearly running into the tatted guy in a beanie doing double-time at the espresso machine for the morning rush out the drive-through.

"What's up?" Travis hissed.

"Really?" she whispered back. She had a vinyl glove that she put on her right hand, then reached into her wallet and began counting out money from a huge wad of cash and dropped it on the counter. "Cash, dummy. It's untraceable. And I'm not leaving fingerprints, either."

The barista looked between them again, then counted the money out, added the decaf, and reached out to give the change back to Camila.

"Keep it," Camila said.

The barista rolled her eyes and turned away from them. "It'll be just a few minutes."

"Thank you," Travis said, his voice cracking. He cleared his throat.

"Take care," she said dully.

They picked up the drinks in their cardboard holder and collected the Danishes and lemon loaves. They waited with the rest of the phone-glued patrons at the other end of the coffee bar for the decaf.

Travis could've sworn he saw people looking at him, glancing at him, trying to see under his hood. Paranoia? Truth? Did it matter? Every cell in his body told him he needed to be out of there, out of public *anything*.

With another smirk, Camila took the decaf from the barista, and then they left.

Travis walked the block back to Alec's car, Camila behind. "Sorry about that—fingerprints," she said. "No credit cards. We can't be tracked."

He swallowed. His ears were still burning. Of course—how could he have been so stupid? "Where'd you get all that cash?"

"Pfft. You really think I trust banks?"

"Guess we're going underground."

Any appetite he'd had left him.

"Guess so," Camila replied. "And Alec said we could use his car, so that's a start."

19

Travis leaned his head back into the cloth driver's seat headrest. The newscaster continued to spew teleprompter text in his bland Midwestern accent, too bright, too cheery, too . . .

"If there's something on there about us—about the doc, or GMMC? We gotta know. I know you said last night that we're going to do this. So, *Travis* . . . are we gonna do this?" Camila asked.

Travis sighed and drove in the direction of Alec's apartment, worried coffee and Danishes wouldn't be a big enough thank-you for letting them borrow his car and taking them to his lab.

"We're not going to win, you know," Camila said.

He looked at her, shocked.

"What I mean," she said, "is me and my family . . . we know something about survival. I'm not sure if you do." She glanced at him. "*Do* you?"

Travis opened his mouth and thought he had a reply, but realized he didn't. Was she right?

"We're going to have to do stuff we've never done," she said. "We're going to have to figure out solutions to problems we've never even thought of before."

"Okay. I can do that."

His pulse raced—but not because she was wrong.

"You okay with that?" she said.

"Yes."

Travis leaned his head back again. Both of them were breathing irregularly. She glanced out the window with glazed eyes.

She turned up the volume, and Travis swerved to miss the basketball rolling into the road from a kid walking to school on the sidewalk.

A reporter replaced the anchor. And *of course* they were reporting on the explosion. What was it, ten hours ago?

"In a bizarre turn of events," the reporter said, "a second former Titus Pharma scientist has died the same day as the first, Dr. Zane McCallister. Now, a Dr. Victoria Swain.

"Witnesses say Travis Grant and Camila Scott were at the scene. They are still at large and wanted for questioning. They are persons of interest. If you see them, do not approach, and call nine-one-one."

The hoodie became scalding, suffocating, stifling around Travis's head, squeezing him down to his wrists. He pulled at the neck, making sure the ties were as loose as they could be.

"Nothing we didn't already know," Camila said.

They pulled into the lot for Alec's building around back since there were too many cameras and ribbons of crime scene tape still near the front entrance.

"With us this morning is Dr. Cowan," the reporter said. Wind picked up from on location, and static flew through the speakers. "Dr. Cowan, you worked with Victoria at Titus Pharma some years ago, is that right?"

"She was a colleague of mine, yes." It was the same voice of the man they'd seen the night before.

"Dr. Cowan, what is your opinion on these deaths? Are they coincidental?"

"All leads point to these deaths being deliberate," he said. "Victoria was on the precipice of something big. She is—was—one of the most successful people I had the pleasure of knowing. She'd never kill herself."

"What *do* you think happened, then?"

Travis and Camila both held their breath.

"In my opinion, I think that couple pushed her off that roof. Pushed her, then ran away just like last time."

"You're referring to the eyewitnesses who ran from the scene of the explosion last night?"

"Yes."

"Do you have anything else you'd like to add, Dr. Cowan?"

"Only that I hope these two come forward soon— that they fess up to what they've done. These are peoples' *lives*, good people. Zane and Victoria were my friends. I'd like to know why they had to die. And maybe grue- somely, I can't help but wonder if . . . if I'm next . . . you know? Can't help it."

The news switched to the next topic—something about a famous concert pianist coming into town—and Travis parked them in a stall that was as far away as the one he had before. He balanced the coffee and food as they entered the apartment building.

"So last night," Camila said, "on the sidewalk. That must have been Dr. Victoria Swain."

"What have we got ourselves mixed up in, Camila, what?"

* * *

With some effort, and a heaping amount of "this is totally

normal and nothing at all is wrong," they carried the coffees, Danishes, and lemon cakes up to the fourth story and rang the doorbell to Alec's apartment.

Nothing.

Camila narrowed her eyes and pushed the bell again. Again, no answer.

"You don't think he went to work already, do you?"

"No," Travis said. "He doesn't go in until eleven. It's only nine . . . and anyway, he knew we were coming back." He knocked on the door, hard. "Alec! It's us!"

He thought he heard the camera doorbell whirring, maybe watching, but nothing else.

"Do you have his phone number?" Camila whispered.

"You sure that's a good idea?"

"Just one phone call," she said. "You can turn it back off after that. Here"—she reached for the drink holder with the coffees that were getting colder by the minute—"I'll take 'em."

Travis handed them over, got out his phone, and powered it back up with the SIM card. Text messages and voicemails dinged and flooded his home screen. He ignored them and dialed. One ring, two, three.

"Hello?"

"Alec?" Travis said.

"Travis Grant," the voice said. "I'm glad you've called."

With shaking hands, Travis put him on speaker so Camila could listen in. "Who is this?" he said.

"Drone Handler J," the voice said. "I believe you have something that belongs to us."

20

"Drone Handler J," Travis said. "That doesn't mean much to me."

"It doesn't matter," J said. "We're coming for you like we did Alec. You're lucky you left, but we'll easily track you down. You and your girl really only have two choices—you can stop running, or we can keep killing your friends."

"My friends?" Travis asked.

"It's your lives or theirs," J said. "But I'm afraid it's too late for Alec."

"What did you do?!" Camila shouted.

"*There* she is!" J said.

"What'd you do to Alec?!" Travis asked.

"The same thing I'm going to do to you if you don't give up this ridiculous goose chase. This is the deep end of the pool, kids. And there aren't any lifeguards for interns."

"Hang up," Camila said, grabbing the phone out of his hands even though hers were full. She terminated the call.

Or we can keep killing your friends.
It's too late for Alec.
No.

Travis pounded violently on the door, then jiggled the handle. Only resistance greeted him.

"Alec!" he shouted. "Alec! It's us!"

He imagined Alec's eyes melting out of his skull, dripping down his face, and matting itself in the strands of hair that had escaped his man bun.

Here Travis was wearing Alec's ridiculous Queens of the Stone Age hoodie. And why? Because he had helped them when he shouldn't have. They knew this was a dangerous situation. *Travis* knew.

I knew and I put him in danger.

"Alec!"

Pound, pound, *pound*.

"We need to get in there," Camila said. "The drones are in there."

Travis nearly scoffed. The *drones*. The stupid *drones* were in there—so they needed to get in, didn't they? For the drones.

But we're not getting through a locked door, he thought. Until Camila jiggled the keys in front of his face. "I could see what you were thinking, Travis."

He fumbled with the keys, trying to find the correct one until he was successful, unlocking the door and twisting the knob.

He listened for a moment but didn't hear anything else.

"Wait, Travis!" Camila said. "Listen for buzzing."

"No time to be paranoid," he said. "I'll tell you when it's safe to come in."

She paused, then said, "All right—just, be careful."

"Thanks for that."

For a moment, panic stole through him—*what am I doing?*—but it subsided after he decided to *move*. After that, simple action took over.

The next moment, he was standing inside the dark apartment, curtains fully drawn. With effort, he tried to catch his breath and hoped against hope that he was wrong about what he would find or hear. Silence. He'd half expected to have a swarm of drones attack him.

"Travis!" Camila said, voice muffled from the outside.

He shuffled his way toward the door, putting his hand along the wall so he could feel for the shelves, the light switches—there, the handle, which he turned.

Light hit him like an interrogation lamp. Concentrated and all at once. He put his forearm over his eyes.

He turned to where Camila was coming into the apartment and watched, as though from the other end of a tunnel, as her mouth dropped open. The coffee holder flipped from her hand. The pastries fell from her fingers. Coffee splattered, lids flew, and flakes of pastry tumbled through the entryway and stuck to the carpet.

Travis turned slowly, heart in his throat.

No. Please no.

With the light on, he could see the sofa where he had slept the night before. The spare blankets and pillows still lay messy over the cushions.

And atop it all—red. Crimson lakes pooling in the cushions and pillows and blankets. Rivers of it dripping onto the carpet, drawing from the multiple wounds in Alec's dead body.

His open eyes stared up into nothing, still wet and glistening in the jaundiced light.

Camila stepped next to Travis and put a hand over her mouth.

"Alec . . ." he whispered. His own eyes burned. He said it again, louder this time—as though the louder he said it, the better chance he would have of the word reviving him, bringing him back. "*Alec.*"

Camila closed the door, the sound making him turn. The entire gruesome scene came into focus at once.

Furniture, lamps, and books were strewn over every surface of floor, broken, ripped, and toppled at extreme angles. A few smears of blood covered the TV, which barely clung to its mount.

"What do we do?" Camila said.

Her sharp breaths, so focused, brought life back into Travis's senses. *She's right*, he thought. This was now another crime scene, and both of them in the middle of it again.

A radical idea came to him, one that assuaged his conscience even though he wasn't sure how valid it would be.

"We could turn ourselves in," he said.

Camila shook her head and put her hands on her hips. She walked toward the kitchen, picking her way around debris. Travis knew what she was looking for.

"Won't work," she said. "We'll be found guilty for sure."

"You don't know that."

"Travis, we ran away from the explosion at the GMMC, right after we watched the doc die. There are three very *not* EMTs who're probably working for some secret division of the police or some crap. And a BOLO is out on us for sure now.

"Then we stayed overnight in the same building as the second victim, Swain." She was counting on her fingers now. "And that *same morning*, the guy we're staying with just happens to be brutally murdered in his own home, and we don't have so much as a receipt to prove we were actually out."

Travis wiped his glasses with the borrowed sweat-shirt. Alec's. "Okay."

He walked toward Camila in the kitchen, where she was pulling the spice rack open. She went to the bottle of basil—the one Alec must have used in the tofu pesto the night before.

The thought brought tears bursting through his eyes, and he kept his back turned away from the living room. Guilt weighed on him for how carefully he wanted to avoid the grief.

Later, he told himself. *You can think about it later.*

"Alec's a smart guy," Camila said, pouring the basil into her hands over the counter, until two small metallic insects dropped into her palms. "Knew he wouldn't just leave them lying around anywhere."

"So we still have the upper hand," Travis said.

"Sure." Camila put them back in the now-empty basil jar and screwed on the lid. "But against what? *Who?*"

Travis took the jar from her and pocketed it in the hoodie. "First things first," he said. "I think we need to be completely off the grid."

"I agree."

Then, standing in Alec's broken apartment, his body staring at them from behind, Camila looked Travis square in the eye and said, "This was Cowan. That's it. He's been there for every death. It's gotta be him. That's the connection. We find him."

21

This feels wrong.

"Just do it, Travis," Camila whispered, looking around even though it was still just them in the apartment.

Yeah, just us . . . just us going through Alec's stuff like it's no big deal.

"Look, we need a way to access computers," she said, "or we're never going to figure this out. And clear our name."

Travis looked at the card, feeling numb. "I just . . . Camila, it's my fault he's dead."

"No! You didn't murder him. *Cowan* did. He's responsible."

Travis sat, still staring at the card. "Camila, how do I move on from this? He was my friend."

Impatient now, she snatched it up from the drawer and stuffed it in her pocket. "You move on by not getting yourself killed. It's a library card. It's not like we're stealing his identity. Would you get a grip?"

"Sorry," he muttered.

But then she also grabbed Alec's Nive University ID card. Travis opened his mouth to protest—because hadn't she just said that's what they *weren't* doing? Her expression, though, all raised eyebrows and high cheekbones, said, *Don't you even dare.*

* * *

Back in the kitchen, they listed off the plan, repeating it back to each other so there were no misunderstandings.

If ever there were a time to be on the same page, Travis figured that was today.

"Burner phones or land lines," Camila said.

"Burner phones," Travis repeated. "Ambulance."

"Right—so they can pick up Alec."

"Then we head to the library."

"Maybe not." Travis opened Alec's laptop and punched in a few passwords. "Crap, I think I bricked it. Library it is. What else do we need?"

"Wigs first so we won't be recognized. Well, for you anyway. I don't think I'm getting any of this into a bald cap."

"Wig," Travis said, "then we look up everything we can about Titus Pharma."

"And be sure to get change so we can print out as much as we can. We won't have internet after we leave."

After we leave.

And where were they going to go after that? Travis wanted to ask. But he knew she'd have just as many answers as he did, so he kept his mouth shut.

They truly had nowhere to go now.

* * *

They got almost everything in one trip—the burner phones, the change, snacks for the road. The wig was the only thing that took a while, because Camila insisted it couldn't be some Halloween crap.

"That's more suspicious than not wearing anything, to be real with you. I mean, it's a sauna outside. You'd have to be crazy to walk around with plastic suffocating you like that."

So after shelling out a larger chunk of cash than Travis would have liked, he ended up with a cap and a blond wig that, he had to admit, did most of the legwork when it came to disguising him.

Looking in the mirror, the lace-front taped down to his skullcap, the front glued to his skull, he had to double take just to recognize himself. The blond hair coifed back like a supermodel's and gave him a broader forehead than he knew he had. The only thing that might give him away were the glasses.

"Wow," Camila said, looking him up and down from her place in the driver's side. "Like a whole different person. You look kinda cute with blond hair, you know."

Travis flipped the passenger mirror back up. "Let's just hope it's enough . . . Call the ambulance now?"

Her smile disappeared. She got out the TracFone and called 911, stating that she was visiting her aunt for the weekend and ended up finding one of the windows to one of the apartment's doors wide open. "There's a dead body in there, and . . . and . . ." Travis didn't think the tears she summoned then were fake—though he had to admit that the ease with which she lied surprised him.

Camila gave the address and put on her seat belt. "Thank you. Yes—yes, I'll be sure to stay on the scene until . . . of course . . ." Then she hung up.

She picked up the cheetah-print sunglasses she'd gotten at the store, ripped off the tag, and put them on. Then she dabbed on a scarlet lipstick.

Travis's stomach fluttered.

"What?" she whispered, seeming half-scared, half-amused.

"Just never seen you with any makeup is all."

"And?"

"You look good."

"Oh, so the implication being that I don't look good *without* makeup, then."

"No, that's not what I—"

"I'm messing with you, Travis."

"You just . . . you look good."

"Thanks. You, too. Even if you do look like Ross Lynch."

* * *

They got into the library no problem.

It probably helped, Travis thought, that he was a blond now. Depending on how often Alec frequented the Botella public library, he probably could have passed for him.

And maybe it *was* a little odd that Camila didn't take off those outrageous sunglasses even in the middle of a moderately lit computer lab, but no one paid any attention. Or rather, maybe the sour pucker she made with those scarlet lips kept everyone at bay.

The computers hummed and buzzed.

Too much like the drones. Travis expected one of them to come around the corner at any minute.

Still, he typed and clicked, opened tabs and dug down rabbit holes. Camila watched over his shoulder—the card only got them one computer privilege—sometimes giving him input, saying, "There!" or, "No, that's not it."

"Do you wanna do the clicking?" he whispered.

"Don't lose your crap, Travis. It's not—there it is!"

He looked where she pointed, surprised she'd even been able to see a hyperlink that small with those glasses on. But there it was, cited in a journal on philanthropic work in Africa from nearly ten years ago.

"Titus Pharma," Camila said.

"Gotcha," Travis said, and clicked it open.

22

The time on the computer was almost up, and still Travis was scrolling, waiting to find the end. Some niche science blogger and fringe conspiracy theorist had written an article about them. About Titus Pharma and everyone involved.

"Wait, hold on," Camila said. "We don't have time to read the whole thing. Can you print it?"

"Yeah." Travis clicked Control + P and followed the pop-up menu to give the right commands.

While Camila went off to fill the printer with enough dimes for the job, he scanned through what he could.

It surprised him just how small the company had been. Just eight scientists and a president. They'd been well-funded, and their size was more due to the elite nature of the team than anything else.

The president had dismantled the company years ago after a shift in focus brought ruin on the financial aspects. Travis tried to read between the lines to figure out what they'd been doing before and after, but couldn't find the information fast enough—because the author of the article had been less interested in *what* they did and more in *who* was doing it.

Eight scientists.

Several feet to his left, coins clinked as Camila inserted them. The printer whirred to life.

Travis pulled one of the notepads by the computer toward him and took the half-sized pencil in his hands. It was dull, but it'd have to do. Man, did he want to itch his wig. But he didn't want to draw any more attention to himself.

Scrolling more, his eyes flashed across text in lit-up phosphorescent. The president had gotten into what should have been a fatal car crash just before the company shifted focus. But due to the miracle of technology, his own nanobot invention saved his life. His lengthy absence and strange non-contact with the ongoings of the company were the final linchpins—like the downfall of an emperor in Rome, or the board kicking Steve Jobs out of his own company. After that, the company switched gears, and it was downhill from there. A little exaggerated in the comparisons, Travis thought, but at least he got the picture.

Eight scientists . . . All of them lined up in a black-and-white photograph that looked to be a scan of a newspaper clipping.

Dr. McCallister, Dr. Swain, and an angry-looking man who could have been an MMA fighter, named Dr. Briggs. He scanned the rest of the names below each scientist, Dr. Cornelius, Dr. Norcroff, Dr. Armstrong, and Dr. Ulrich. But the nicest-looking one, at least according to the photo, was Dr. Samantha Tabby.

There was only one minute left on the computer timer, and Camila was coming back with the printed article.

Travis opened a new tab and typed in "Dr. Samantha Tabby."

She was close—as in, just a couple towns over close. He scribbled down the name of the university where she taught, as well as what subjects she taught and her office hours.

"Who's she?"

With ten seconds left on the clock, Travis closed all the tabs. The computer logged him out automatically.

"I'll tell you in the car," he muttered.

Camila nodded, clutching the sheath of papers and folding them in half while they walked out.

Travis kept expecting it to happen—for the librarian with the chain glasses and the mole on her cheek to tell them to come with her, that she *knew* they weren't their dead friend and how terrible of them for killing all those people, then using *his* card to get into the library.

But she didn't even look up at them as they passed.

He let out a breath.

"You, too?" Camila asked.

"Yeah."

Outside, looking both ways, looking up at the sky, Travis's whole body buzzed like he'd overdosed on caffeine.

Inside the car, he told Camila about the original eight scientists who worked for Titus Pharma.

"It's like they're being targeted," he said. "First the doc, then Dr. Swain. Whoever Cowan is, he's onto something. Whoever's next is in this photograph . . ."

"Which means they're all in danger."

"There are gonna be more Docs, more Swains. And besides us, I don't think anyone's bothering to warn them they're all about to die, horribly."

"One thing at a time, though," Camila said, getting Travis out of his thoughts. "We need to find out everything we can about Titus Pharma. I feel really good about that lead. Do you?"

He nodded. "I do. We have nothing else to go on."

He shuffled through the article, looking at the various photographs—but especially at the one of the eight scientists together, along with the president.

"No, it's more than that," Camila said. "Do you feel like we're being framed?"

Was that . . .

"Travis?" Camila asked. "Did you hear me?"

"Look . . ." He gave her the sheet with the black-and-white scan of newspaper clipping. "The president—"

"That's Dr. Cowan," Camila said.

"If anyone's behind this," Travis said, "if we are being framed? I bet my friggin' blond hair that it's him."

"So let's get this douchebag. Dr. Tabby's our best bet into Titus Pharma. Where'd you say she teaches?"

For Alec. For the doc. And to save the rest of the scientists.

A sad anger began to trickle through Travis's body, starting in his chest and making his legs restless. He couldn't tell if he needed to cry or break another window.

"University of Florida," he said with an ironic grin, letting the grief fuel him into their next action. "Guess I'm checking in to fall semester early this year. The dean'll be pleased."

23

"What do you mean she's on sabbatical?" Travis said.

The receptionist at the Biology & Nanotech department for the University of Florida gave him a patient smile that didn't come close to her eyes.

"Dr. Tabby took a two-year sabbatical for individual research purposes," she said. "It's not uncommon, especially for a tenured professor of her caliber. She's emeritus, you know."

"Do you know where we can find her?" Camila asked. Travis had grown too anxious to be able to get any words out. Anger and fear were making him shake and turning his vision hot.

"Is your friend okay?" the receptionist asked instead of answering Camila's question.

Camila didn't even look at Travis, only said, "He's fine."

"Where can we find her?" he said.

"I'm afraid I can't tell you. We're not really in the business of giving out our faculty's private information to . . . I don't know, whatever you two are trying to be . . ."

Camila cleared her throat and adjusted her sunglasses. "Thank you for your time."

"Hope to see you around," she said in a monotone that would have made Alan Rickman green with envy.

Camila grabbed Travis by the arm and steered him away, walking them out of the just-cleaned glass doors of the Biology & Nanotech department.

"It's fine," she said, leading him down the hallway with the professors' offices.

Enormous windows on either end of the hall let in swaths of light, and the air felt cool and well-conditioned.

"Good thing you've got that on," Camila said, eyeing the wig. "I don't think they'd be too happy with their premiere entomology student breaking into one of the professor's offices."

"What?"

"Shh," Camila hissed, "would you be quiet? Do you want to figure out where she is or don't you?"

Travis took a deep breath.

When he thought of it that way, not even his schooling seemed to be much of a priority.

"Let's just not get me kicked out before I even start."

"Right-o," Camila whispered, stopping in front of the large oak door and taking off her glasses long enough to peer through the rectangular window next to it.

Semi-darkness met them.

"Give me a card," she said, holding out her hand.

Travis sighed and took out his wallet, handing over his credit card. At least it was finally useful for something.

Camila slid it between the jam and the lock, jiggling it until the handle began to loosen.

Travis looked around nervously, even putting his hands behind his back to try to feign innocence. A mechanical *click* echoed down the hallway.

But not any louder than a proper key unlocking a proper door. Nothing out of the ordinary.

"Get in here, Ross Lynch," Camila said.

She was already inside, gesturing for him to come in. He did, then shut the door behind them.

No sooner had he closed it and twisted the blinds shut than he heard footsteps outside. Maybe it was Travis's imagination, but he thought he heard them pause outside the door . . . pause . . . listen . . . then move on down the hall.

"Right . . ." Camila breathed.

"I'm so getting expelled," Travis said.

"Just try to find her address. I don't know—a piece of mail, a contract, paystub. Whatever."

Travis shuffled through several of the pieces of mail in the inbox on her desk, though there wasn't much. It seemed that most of it had been forwarded to her. Anything that couldn't be sent had simply been left here for her to find when she returned, which meant the address was for the university, not Dr. Tabby.

The file cabinet squealed too loudly when Camila opened it, and Travis grimaced before looking to the door, listening for any incoming footsteps. Nothing . . . in the clear, for now.

This is so illegal. This is so friggin' illegal.

So was killing Alec. If he didn't do something, Dr. Tabby could be next.

Travis took a deep breath. "Anything?" he whispered.

Camila was shuffling through several papers in meticulously labeled folders. "There we go," she said, smiling. "A parking ticket. That should do it."

"We're not going to take that, are—"

"No, Travis."

She took out the burner phone and snapped several pictures of the address before putting it back in the file cabinet.

Silence.

"Okay . . ." Travis said. "Everything just as we left it?"

Camila put the phone back in her pocket and put on the cheetah-print sunglasses. She smacked her scarlet lips. "Far as I know."

"Let's get outta here, then."

Travis peeked through the blinds of the thin side window. The coast looked clear enough.

"On the count of three," he said.

"Just open the door."

Fine.

Travis turned the handle and swung it open. They shuffled out, and he thought they were going to make it, that no one had seen them come out of Dr. Tabby's office.

But just as they were turning to leave, a door at the end of the hall opened, and the receptionist was saying, "Thank you, Dr. Anderson. I'll be sure to—oh for the love. What're you two doing?"

She saw which door Travis had just closed.

"Time to go," Camila whispered, taking his hand.

"Hey!" the receptionist said, running after them. "What do you think you two are doing? That's not—I'm reporting you!"

Travis and Camila ran from her, into the stairwell, taking them two and three at a time and speeding past every landing until they got to the ground floor and rushed into the humid air outside. Four o'clock, and students were honking and playing loud music, trying to get home in time to enjoy their weekend.

Travis laughed, remembering the receptionist's face. Camila cracked up, too, and he took her hand as they sprinted down the sidewalk, into the parking lot. He ripped the parking ticket off the windshield and got into the driver's side while she pulled an old map out of the glove compartment.

"You're so getting expelled," she said, trying to stifle her laugh now.

"Nah, just some blond guy called Ross Lynch. I don't really know him."

That made Camila lose it even more, and they couldn't stop laughing the entire drive to the freeway.

24

Travis missed the exit.

He almost swore, too, but before he could get the word out, Camila put a hand on his knee. "It's okay, just take the next one and we'll flip around."

The gray-white sky thundered overhead. Wind was picking up again, whipping the palms and swamp grass on the side of the freeway into a frenzy of white-capped drops of rainwater.

They passed a Winn-Dixie grocery store before turning around and zooming back onto the wet asphalt again.

Camila flipped her maps around, following the route with her finger. Travis glanced at the topographic folds, the penciled-in star that marked where Dr. Tabby lived.

Far out in the middle of nowhere, he checked the gas gauge. They'd need to fill up soon. That is, if they were going anywhere after this. Where would this take them? Travis couldn't possibly know.

In the silence of the next few minutes, he replayed the deep growl of Drone Handler J talking to him in his mind. They had the dormant drones with them in the back seat, wrapped in one of Camila's emergency blankets and stuffed under a seat.

What did they need with them?

And what had been inside their abdomens? The doc's blood? Or maybe something else?

"It's here!" Camila said.

Travis swerved into the exit lane just in time, his heart thudding at the suddenness of the transition.

"Ground control to Major Tom!" she shouted. "Come in, Major Tom!"

"Sorry! I—"

"Take a left."

Travis turned just in time, barely making it before the traffic light at the freeway exit turned red.

"Okay . . . now we just drive straight on till morning. Should make Neverland before breakfast," Camila said.

"Any idea what we should ask her?"

"We don't really know much. This article—I mean, it mentions the Malaria Project? I get how that's related, mosquitoes and everything . . . but that can't be what Titus Pharma specialized in, can it?"

"Also need to know what the doc did for them. And Swain and Tabby."

"And clearly there was controversy, especially after the president nearly died in that accident. There had to have been public pushback, or at least opposition from their backers, or they wouldn't have shut down whole divisions like they did."

"We should ask her why someone wants her dead?" Travis said.

The question hung in the air like a weight.

"Right," Camila said. "That, too."

* * *

Ivy crawled across the sprawling estate. It hung from the copper gutters and curled into the cracks between stones on the side of the cottage-style house. It clung to the shutters and drooped over the front entryway—an enormous natural door with bracketed iron over its small window.

Travis pulled in, gravel crunching under the old station wagon's tires. "Do you think she's even home?"

He looked to the left of the cottage, where a circular atrium with intricate wrought-iron brackets and crystal-cut glass was connected to the main house by a mossy path.

Camila shrugged, folding the map back up and double-checking the address over the mailbox with the photo on the burner phone. "She could be parked in the garage."

With the engine off, after so many hours of it constantly rumbling and the world rolling by underneath them, the silence itself made a sound Travis wanted to swat away, like a buzzing cloud pressing against his ears.

He made sure his wig was still secure atop his head and they approached the front door.

Camila took off her sunglasses, held them under one arm, and knocked; it was barely a sound, most of it absorbed by the grandiosity of the door itself.

In the humidity, the wig had become stifling. The sun was starting to disappear. Rainbow rays of sunlight bounced toward him from the atrium as he turned to look around.

Camila rang the bell, a large gonging sound.

"Should've called ahead," Travis joked.

"You're funny."

Knock, ring. Knock again.

Travis was beginning to have déjà vu of finding Alec this morning. He didn't like where this was going . . .

No, he wasn't going to let it happen like this, not again.

He leapt off the porch and peered into one of the windows on the side of the house. The light was on in the cozy kitchen. There was a pot on the stove.

"Dang it," he said.

"Let's do a lap," Camila said, "before we jump to any other conclusions. Okay?"

Travis led the way, pushing them through hedgerows and over jutting sprinkler heads as they popped out of the ground like meerkats for their evening spritz.

After a full circle, nothing.

"Only two places left she could be," he said. "Either the garage, or—"

"The atrium," Camila finished.

They decided the atrium would be the most likely place for her to be. Still, the quiet—the bubble they had over them from being out in the country, the buzzing of cicadas and crickets, the stars beginning to shimmer above their heads—all pointed to something being out of place.

Her two colleagues had ended up dead within less than twenty-four hours of each other. What were the odds that she'd escaped that fate before they arrived?

Nothing on the news, though; they'd listened carefully most of the way here for anything like that.

"Dr. Tabby?" Camila said, rapping her knuckles on the glass door. This knock reverberated through the cuts and slits and iron.

Travis thought he could see a shape inside. "Dr. Tabby, are you in there?"

"We'd like to talk with you, if you . . ." The latch was unlocked. Camila pushed open the door.

The overwhelming scent of the atrium hit them— soils, sweet and fertilizer, and . . . iron. More iron than in the bulwarks of the glass.

"They got her," Travis said.

They got Dr. Tabby.

25

An hour earlier, Dr. Samantha Tabby pulled her long graying hair into a ponytail and tied it scalp-ripping tight. Then she worked on getting the knots of the apron that were just as unyielding. The Muck boots were a tight fit, too, almost too much—but enough to keep her on her toes while she worked in the atrium.

Little amounts of discomfort here and there—that was Samantha's philosophy. How could she ever expect to conquer herself if she allowed every luxury as it came by?

She occupied her time as she waited for her driver— she'd given up driving years ago. In light of the theories swirling around the Titus Pharma scientists, she decided to go visit her sister and lie low for a while.

But first things first.

The Muck boots pinched at her ankles as she pulled open the atrium door. The humidity increased tenfold, creating a nice sheen of sweat on her wrinkled forehead. She wiped it away with a smile and set to work.

She pulled a bunch of roots dangling from multiple wicker-and-iron planter boxes and set them into the wheelbarrow next to her. Then she pushed it around, the wheel furrowing the ground as though she were getting it ready for planting. She continued to clear out little weeds and overgrowth and dead branches here and there—couldn't leave it as it was even if they weren't why she was here. Constant diligence. What would her life be without it? She shuddered to think it.

A moss-and-stone path dissected the circular atrium into four triangular quadrants, each with their own varieties of flora—green, multicolored, some of them kaleidoscopes of diversity. Samantha crossed all the way to the other end of the path she was walking, wheelbarrow by her side, now full of unnecessary and dead things.

Just one more spot to clear.

Samantha bent down, her knees popping. She pulled out the shears from her apron and snipped away at the overgrown echinacea that hid the rusted, half-buried box.

Once she'd thrown the herbs into the wheelbarrow, she dusted off the lid of the box and put in the four-digit combination to unbolt the lock. She took a single breath. Did she really want to do this, now? Yes, of course she did. They were dead, weren't they, and she was next, so if she didn't keep up her diligence, well then . . . Samantha opened the box.

The hinges protested. Decades of oxidization, neglect, soil buildup. She almost had to yank it forward.

But then she'd done it.

She reached inside and brought out the three-ring binder. The pages had browned, some of them wrinkled and stained with water damage.

Samantha stood, cradling the binder like a mother would her child. After wiping dirt onto her blue jeans and relieving some of her sweat on her sleeve so it wouldn't get in her eyes, she opened it. The pages were damp under her fingers, but all those notes—scribbled, typewritten, ink, pencil, all of it together. Like opening a favorite novel she didn't remember was on the shelf, every memory of those years at Titus Pharma came back in a single rush. It'd been so long since she'd allowed herself to think about that time.

The research they'd done, though . . . what they'd been able to accomplish? That had been truly remarkable. Some of the proudest achievements of her life—which was why she'd kept it here all this time. Kept it *here*, of course, hidden in an atrium and not tucked in some archival file cabinet or shelf. Despite the risk of damage, she couldn't let anyone else get their hands on this.

"Ooh." She didn't notice the prick on her skin until the sound had escaped her mouth, a hint from her brain that something had gone wrong under her notice.

A mosquito flew away from her. Already the welt it left on her hand had begun to swell.

A bite she could deal with, but it was a nuisance. And the last thing she needed was a whole scourge of them growing in this atrium while she was gone. What hell that would turn out to be.

Notes still in hand, she checked the atrium door— how had she left it open? That wasn't like her. She really must have been distracted retrieving the notes and throwing away any roots that needed to go.

Well, she'd just fix that now. Wouldn't she? Constant diligence, then back to her work.

Samantha marched down the stone path, moss squishing beneath her almost-too-tight Muck boots.

The plants attacked her. Just a devil's vine at first, from the right of the path, creeping around her ankle. She felt the pressure initially, and her first instinct was to continue moving forward. That's when she landed on her face, nose smacking against the stones with a *crunch*.

Heartbeat slapping against the stones as she lay there,

Samantha waited for her breath to catch up with her ambition. She must have tripped. She'd forgotten to trim the devil's vine, just as she'd forgotten to close the door.

Your diligence is slipping, she thought.

She raised her head, preparing to get herself off the path, only to find that every plant in the atrium was floating. The greens had become emeralds, the yellows bursts of sunshine, the reds oozing drips of blood—and all swirling in an actual cyclone before her eyes, a kaleidoscope of shifting, dizzying shapes in and out, and—

Samantha thought she was going to vomit.

The devil's vine had grown. It wasn't just her imagination now, wasn't her "diligence" slipping and causing problems for herself. It was the actual *reality* of the situation, she understood—the devil's vine snaked along her body.

It was at her throat.

The vine tightened and leaves sprouted against her skin, the new growth like blades trying to slice through her.

She screamed, clawing at it.

That only seemed to egg it on further. No sooner had she succeeded in ripping through it than it climbed into her throat, leaves blooming fast enough to fill her mouth as it forced its way down her esophagus, her windpipe.

The muscles under her lungs contracted, heaving. Bile came up, but didn't have anywhere to go.

Scramble. Lunge for the shears in her apron pocket, bring them up. *That's it, Samantha.*

She opened them up, like metal jaws, and slashed them through a chunk of vine. Blood spurted from the devil's vine, fountains of it red and slick and hot. *My blood?* she thought, but dismissed the idea.

She was free.

She pulled the vines out of her throat. She could feel them sliding and cutting inside her, but she got it all out, threw it down on the path as she stood.

They were out of her.

So why couldn't she breathe?

Samantha reached up to her throat, feeling the slit, the oozing, sticking, congealing . . . *Oh, Samantha . . .*

Samantha fell.

She heard her body hit the stones, then nothing at all.

26

"Not again! We're too late!" Travis said.

Dr. Tabby lay just feet inside the atrium, her body twisted so that her bottom half was flush against the stones, but her face looked up at them, her hand outstretched.

A laceration cut across her neck, deep enough to expose her swollen esophagus. The blood had stopped flowing some time ago, and now it grew in crusted crystalline rivers of scarlet.

The path behind Dr. Tabby was a mess of it. A few feet behind her lay a pair of bloodied shears—Travis had to hold back the vomit that came up at the thought of her slitting her own throat with them—and a three-ring binder, musty, dirty, and half-open by a patch of devil's ivy.

Camila rushed toward her, putting two gloved fingers gingerly at her jugular, while Travis stepped over her body, clenching his fists, telling himself to focus, to keep moving despite the dead woman now behind him. Dead. Four of them now. Three previous doctors for Titus Pharma, one friend. Who was next—and *why?*

"She's dead." Camila swore.

Travis picked up the binder, flipping through it. There

was a lot here, tabbed, handwritten, most of it printed on
an old dot-matrix.

"Travis," Camila said as he flipped through some of
the pages, eyes narrowed, "she has bites on her arm, her
neck. Mosquito bites. Just like what the doc had—and
probably Swain, too . . . I wish we'd gotten close enough
to look."

"Do you hear that?" Travis said. He looked up.

A mechanical buzzing had filled the room, like an old
computer modem—cogs and dials that could almost be
organic. But Travis knew better by now. "We need to get
out of here."

He closed the binder and walked back to Camila,
stepping around Dr. Tabby's body.

"What do we . . ." Camila trailed off.

It was horrible, Travis thought, but it needed to be
said anyway. "Someone will find her. We have to keep
moving."

* * *

Camila took a turn at the wheel, driving them back
toward the city while Travis flipped through the binder.

"I think we need to lay it out," she said. "Everything we know—about Titus Pharma, the killings, the
drones . . ."

Swampland and sheets of hanging algae whooshed
past them. And behind those sheets, in the dusky light, a
flock of birds took off. The sky silhouetted them, turning
them into dark shapes.

"For starters," Travis said, "all of the doctors from
Titus Pharma seem to have been killed with drones present. But how? We both saw the marks on the doc's skin

and now on Dr. Tabby's. So the drones are linked somehow."

"Which means the drones aren't there for surveillance. We need to be more careful. Those little buggers can somehow kill us."

"Maybe this can tell us," Travis said, leafing through the binder from Dr. Tabby's atrium. It smelled like dank soil.

"TITUS PHARMA," the first page read, and below it was what could only have been the company's mission statement.

"*Beneficium maior scientia est.*"

Travis read out the Latin as best he could. Camila gave him a confused look, so he translated it on the burner phone.

"Service is greater than knowledge."

"Huh," Camila said. "A for-profit company based on science, and that's what they choose as their reason for being?"

"It makes sense." Travis was scanning the pages upon pages of notes. "For years after it started, it looks like their main concern was inventing a nanotag for disease control. 'Mass delivery of vaccinations to developing countries using nanotags.' Holy mother . . ."

"What is it?"

"I assume the nanotag is like a marker or delivery method, nano size of course."

"That's crazy," Camila said. "So if you examine someone's blood with the vaccine, then you would see these delivery tags, these nanotags?"

"Yeah, I suppose. So Titus *invented* the drones to deliver the vaccinations. These mosquitoes must be able to extract and inject!"

"I don't . . ."

"Think about it—malaria spreads as fast as it does because of poor water management and low-level health care. So . . ."

"So if you could load up a bunch of mosquitoes with the vaccination, you just inoculated an entire population against it. And they'd barely even know it happened . . . just a little bite."

"Exactly."

Travis continued to scan through the binder, though now he had to shine the burner phone's screen over the wrinkled, browning pages. The sun had entirely set.

Was it really just this morning that they'd found—

Focus.

"Nanotags can be put into the bloodstream, in this case with vaccines attached to them. Let's see—then the nanotags attach to red blood cells . . . that's how they travel around the body."

"The samples," Camila said.

"You don't think there're nanotags in the doc's blood?"

"Yeah, Travis, I one hundred percent believe that. Makes sense. If he was bitten by a Titus Pharma drone, then his blood should have these nanotags in it."

"If we could get into the blood sacks in our drones, do you think we could take a look at the nanotags?"

"Totally."

Travis took off his glasses and cleaned them again with Alec's sweatshirt. And this wig? Geesh—he needed it off *yesterday.*

"Hold on . . ." He narrowed his eyes.

He'd just flipped to the next major section in the second half of the binder. There were full-color printouts with water damage creeping through them, leaving unnatural splatters and rings, and concentrations of color. But Travis made out the images just the same.

The "CLASSIFIED" stamps and streaks of slick permanent marker where information had been redacted sent chills up his spine.

"Travis?" Camila was trying to get a look at the binder but couldn't, not if she wanted to keep them on the freeway. "Is that a bacterium?"

"No," he said, "a virus. It's a copy of the official declaration, but I bet the company has the original somewhere. It's CDC-stamped, too. Titus-1A."

What use would a company like Titus have for a virus? Travis thought. *Wasn't their mission service before knowledge?*

Didn't that mean service before—well, anything else, too?

He continued through the notes.

"Holy . . ." he said. "The virus was *government* contracted. They had Titus make it. Then after, they even subpoenaed Titus Pharma, said they had to make . . . 'the location of the remaining vials of the virus public.'"

"That doesn't make any sense," Camila said.

Nervous all of a sudden, Travis flipped through the rest of the binder, but there was no mention of a lab, or the locations of the virus anywhere. "It's definitely confusing," he finally mumbled.

"So—did they create viruses or vaccines?"

"Both?"

"If that's true, no wonder someone's out to get them. Sounds like the whole operation was hypocritical."

"Why force them to tell the public? Wouldn't the government want to keep something like that hushed up? I mean, especially if they *paid* Titus Pharma to create it? You'd think that'd upset some people."

Camila didn't respond.

Asphalt sped past under Alec's car wheels. A fog had rolled over them from the coast, and Travis could only see several feet in front of them, illuminated by the station wagon's small headlight beams.

"Nanotags . . ." Camila whispered.

He heard it in her voice, a slow-building excitement.

"What'd you figure out?"

"Nanotags on red blood cells," she said. "And they had to make the location of the virus public . . ."

Travis met her eye, confusion washing over him. "We need to see what's in those drones," she said. "That's the next piece of the puzzle."

27

Travis was a blond again, and Camila wore her lipstick and sunglasses. Which meant that when they walked into the ultra-modern hexagonal space that was the Aust Biotech sector of Nive University, they just needed to act like PhD students.

"Evening, Bert," Camila said.

"Evening," Bert replied. He gave her a soft smile and waved her past.

Travis trotted to keep up with her, finding her hand so they could walk through the lobby together. He hoped their disguises would be enough that they were actually unrecognizable on CCTV. And they were just lucky they had the same security guard as last time.

They made their way to the lab Alec worked in with barely a hitch. At seven o'clock in the evening, they were the only ones here. And Alec's ID worked perfectly.

Travis's stomach somersaulted when he saw Alec's smiling face on the plastic as Camila held it up to open the lab doors. He looked at his shoes.

"How are we going to look at those sacks of liquid?" he whispered, taking out the vial and setting it on the counter. They kept as many lights off as possible, and the inky shadows behind shelves and around corners were beginning to spook him.

"Right," Camila said, "the explosive."

"SEM?"

She nodded slowly. She looked as tired of this as Travis felt. But at least they were on the same page. Some more information, and then they could catch some Zs.

"You do it, though," Camila said. "You've actually used an SEM before. I'm afraid I'd break it."

Travis prepared the equipment while she slid the drones out of the vial and onto Alec's ID card for holding.

An SEM, or scanning electron microscope, would scan the surface with a focused beam of electrons. With luck, those electrons would interact with atoms of the blood, producing various signals that contained information about the surface typography and composition of the sample.

In this case, whatever was in the drone's abdomen.

Here we go, Travis thought. He wished he would have thought of using the SEM with Alec instead of the digital 3D rendering.

The entire microscope consisted of a large black box, not unlike a microwave, with a large cylinder directly atop it, and a thicker short cylinder to the left. Computer monitors to the right of it powered up along with the microscope itself, ready to render any images the electrons might find.

When it was ready and humming—the only sound in the big, empty lab was too much like a drone and put Travis on edge—he took the specimens from Camila and gingerly placed them inside the microwave-like door.

Knowing what they might be capable of, he found that being this close to them now made him sick.

Travis started the sequence.

The SEM stirred to life.

He stood back and crossed his arms, pushing the unruly blond hair out of his eyes.

After a few tense moments, the image, which could focus up to one nanometer, came up on the computer screen. Despite the advanced nature of the tech, it still could only be rendered in black-and-white.

The three-dimensional image showed several concave disk shapes, definitely red blood cells. And floating with them, similar disks, but these were clearly synthetic.

"Are those nanotags?" Camila asked.

"Must be," Travis said, confirming their suspicion. He zoomed in and saw that there were a minimal amount of nanotags on the red blood cells, with a number and a word etched on them.

"What's that say?" he asked.

Camila tipped her head to the side. "Thirty-one longitude."

Travis sat back.

"Nanotags in the blood . . . what does that all mean?" Camila asked.

"The drones are attacking the members of Titus Pharma one by one, but it's got to be more than that, though." Travis rubbed his head.

"So this drone has the doc's blood in it."

"Exactly."

"A collection sample. From the victims?" Camila's eyebrows raised.

"Most likely."

"What would they need that for?"

"To find out what nanotags are in them?"

Camila let out a deep breath. "I suppose. But what's the yellow stuff in the other sac?"

"So to sum up, the drones aren't just killing people,"

Travis said. "They're collecting information. A location, by the looks of it."

He shifted the focus of the microscope to the pouch inside carrying the yellow liquid. The machine ran the spectral scan for him.

"It's some sort of chemical." Travis shifted his gaze to another monitor with columns of numbers and scales of wavelengths. "Definitely not biological. Seems to be man-made."

"Wow, interesting." Camila leaned in next to him.

Travis pointed to a bookshelf full of books with similar navy-blue spines with gold-leaf lettering. "Hey, hand me that reference book over there on that shelf."

Camila got up. "Which one?"

"Grab the one with point zero-one-nine to point zero-three-seven."

She touched each spine, reading the numbers before tipping the heavy reference book down and lugging it over to where Travis sat. She heaved the book onto the desk and set it down with a thud. He opened the front cover of the thick book and the spine cracked as he flipped through chunks of pages.

On each page were columns of numbers and names of chemicals. Every so often there was a diagram of a molecule. Shaded globes hooked together with thin bars, representing a 3D drawing of the organic substance.

"I see," Camila said. "Use the number from the scan"—she pointed to the screen—"and cross reference it to the chemical in this book."

"You got it, sista," Travis said, then grimaced.

"Sista?"

"Sorry. I'm just happy we're getting somewhere with this whole thing. Can you find point zero-three-five?"

Camila scanned down the pages with her index finger, flipping them as she went. "Yes, here it is."

"Great," Travis said. "What does it say?"

"Tyrosine," she answered.

He scratched his forehead. "Okay, I thought I could guess from here. Go grab another reference book, please. Ranges point zero-five-nine to point zero-eight-seven."

This time, Camila had to lug back two reference books. "Here you go, master chemist."

Travis smiled as he shifted one of the heavy books to his lap. "Zero-six-five, zero-six-five . . . here it is! Phenylalanine!"

He sat back and rubbed his eyes. "I have no idea what that is."

"It's Google time." Camila opened up a browser in the computer with a secure window. Within thirty seconds, she said, "No, that can't be . . . really . . . what the . . ."

"Peyote," Travis whispered.

"Like peyote, peyote?"

He took control of the keyboard and soon found out that peyote came from cacti, but synthetic peyote was 3,4,5-Trimethoxyphenethylamine.

"And guess what? Tyrosine and phenylalanine serve as precursors to mescaline—peyote," he said.

"So you're telling me that the yellow stuff in these mosquito drones is just peyote? I can't believe it."

"Let me look up number 3,4,5-Trimethoxyphenethylamine here." Travis flipped to the back of one of the thick reference books, found the page, and located the number. He cross referenced the number with mescaline, then looked at the data on the screen from the SEM scan. "This is the issue. The number doesn't match. So I don't know. Maybe some synthetic mescaline on steroids."

"Holy suck! Don't you see?" Camila said. "This is just like the MK-ULTRA Project or Operation Artichoke."

Travis vaguely recalled something about declassified CIA projects and operations. "I kinda remember something about that."

Camila stood up and paced around the room. "The CIA used to use peyote, er, mescaline, on people to run mind-control experiments. They would inject people with different concentrations and chemical variations of mescaline to see what happened. In a nutshell, of course. There was a lot more to it, but this has got to be one of those chemicals. That means that the drone injected the doctors from Titus Pharma with this whatever chemical and caused them to have suicidal hallucinations."

Travis nodded. "I totally buy it. Whoever is running the drones is taking the blood to get the nanotag numbers, then injecting them with a variation of synthetic mescaline so they'll kill themselves."

Satisfied with their work, Travis took a snapshot of the nanotags mixed in with the red blood cells and printed it out. Then he carefully took both drones out of the microwave-like SEM, scooping them up with Alec's ID card like Camila had done and depositing them back in the bottle. He left the ID on the bench.

Camila caught his eye as he set it down, and she nodded her approval. Better that the university take repossession of it than they keep carrying it around. Other than making them look suspicious, Travis felt it would be disrespectful.

* * *

A bubble of joy filled Travis's chest for the first time

in what felt like weeks. Elation, that was what it was. Because—

"We're on the right track," Camila said.

We're doing it, we're getting somewhere.

"Each of the doctors from Titus must have a nanotag hidden in their bloodstream," Travis said. "Whoever's controlling the drones is trying to collect them all—and if they're like the doc's, then there are longitudes and latitudes written on them."

"Locations . . . It's a treasure hunt."

"But for what?" he asked.

"I think we both know," Camila said. "You saw that subpoena from the CDC. They must be looking for Titus-1A."

28

They sat in quiet for a moment. A night drizzle began making whispering, percussive music on the station wagon's roof.

"We should probably get some sleep," Travis said.

"Any ideas?" Camila asked.

We should just sleep in the car, he thought.

But they were already on their way. Camila was driving them to the seedy part of town, someplace she knew where an ID and credit card weren't required for check-in. Travis didn't ask *how* she knew this, only went along with it.

He could practically feel the bed, any bed, beneath him. Could feel every tense strain slowly seeping from him as oblivion began to take . . . over . . .

"I think we're being followed," Camila whispered.

Travis's eyes flew open as he was knocked out of his meditation on how much he wanted to sleep. A sour feeling like acid dropped into his belly.

They passed under an orange streetlamp, and he saw Camila's fingers were curled around the steering wheel, gripping it as though her life depended on it. And she was deliberately keeping her eyes forward.

He turned to see what caused the sudden tension.

"Don't, Travis," Camila said. "Did you *want* to put a sign on our foreheads that says, 'Hey, pick me! I'm an easy target!' Use me, I'm your little—'"

"Thanks for that," he said. "I get it."

Travis glanced out the window as discreetly as he could and saw a pair of headlights on what *appeared* to be an SUV following closer than any vehicle had the right to.

He tried to swallow, but his throat had gone dry.

"I . . ." Camila swallowed. It looked like it took difficulty, too. "I'm going to see if I can lose them."

She turned them to the left, putting real effort into making it look like she hadn't slammed on the brakes.

For a moment, it appeared that they'd put them off their trail. Travis physically turned, looking out the curvature of the back windshield. The street yawned dark and rain-splattered behind them.

They passed under another orange streetlamp.

And not two seconds later, like watching a cheetah move after a limping gazelle on Animal Planet, the SUV swerved, corrected, and was behind them again.

"Nope," Travis said. "We're definitely being followed."

They passed a dead-end sign, and he hoped that wasn't how this road ended, too.

"We should probably ditch the vial," Camila said, keeping them at a steady clip down the ever-narrowing side road.

"What—are you crazy?"

"That's what they're after! That's what Drone Handler Jeremy, or whatever his name was, told you after he *killed* Alec!"

Travis took the bottle out of his hand. Flecks of basil

remained at the bottom with the drones, from when it'd been a mere addition to Alec's spice rack.

"Travis, think about it." Camila's speech was speeding up, and it looked like the SUV behind them was slowly gaining inches. "If they catch us without it, then chasing us down is pointless. And we can go back for them later."

He was still studying the drones, remembering the nanotags stored in them, one of the pieces to a much larger puzzle he was just beginning to grasp.

"No," he said, "I don't think it works like that. That's not who these people are. They *know* we have them."

"And?"

"And what if they catch us *without* them?"

That left her quiet.

"Might just be me, but I think we'd be in a whole lot more trouble without them than with them."

If Camila had a reply, it got lost in the small crash that happened as she hit a metal drum of some kind. Travis could see a homeless man peeking out from behind it, unkempt face scrunched against the harsh headlights.

The street hadn't dead-ended officially, but it might as well have. On either end, project housing soared into the deep navy sky, narrower and narrower until it was basically an alley.

"We're not gonna make it any farther," Travis said.

"Really?" Camila said, voice shaking. "Thanks, Edison."

The hobo scuttled away from the glare, and Travis looked to Camila, gripping the basil-cum-drone jar tight.

"What do we do?" he asked.

But she didn't have to say it.

They were going to have to get out.

Brakes squealed as the SUV behind them came to a

stop. Now it was Travis and Camila the headlights were blinding, bouncing off the rearview mirrors and glass.

"On the count of three?" she said.

But neither of them waited for three.

In a split second, Camila had taken the keys out of the ignition and unlocked the doors, then they sprinted out on either side. He shoved the drones back into his pocket for safekeeping, along with the photo of the coordinates.

He and Camila jumped around more metal drums like obstacle courses and swiveled around a fire-escape staircase that had come unbolted from the brick side and lay against the apartment building, taking up half the alley.

From behind, large doors swung, clacked, and banged shut. Finally, he heard a mechanical click, like a gun being cocked.

Don't look behind—

"You won't get far!"

He recognized the voice.

Drone Handler J.

Travis stopped.

Camila skidded to a halt next to him, grabbing his hand. Both their backs were turned on the men from the SUV.

And all around, the street only began to narrow further.

Looking forward, Travis saw that his fear had been right.

It was a dead end—not even a fence to climb, but a crumbling, solid, brick-and-mortar wall separating them from freedom. He looked down, to a collection of bottles and other debris that had taken seasons of grime and sun exposure. Travis crouched, took out the spice jar, and set it down amongst the others. It looked perfectly at home, especially in the dark.

"We already have the coordinates," he whispered to her in a shaky breath, and stood up.

"You two stop talking now," J said. "Turn around. Put the drones on the ground—I know you have 'em. I want to see your hands in the air."

I bet you would, Travis thought.

A humming modem-buzz filled his ears—louder and more intense than he'd ever heard it, even in the atrium.

Slowly, Camila by his side, he turned his head around. His jaw dropped. Fear crinkled down his spine like jingle bells rolling downstairs.

A thick-set man with a crew cut stood only a few feet from them, holding a remote in his hand that glowed a sickly acid-green.

He smiled at them as, from behind, an entire scourge of drones rose up like a roiling cloud, ready to attack.

29

J must have seen the switch in Travis's expression—the involuntary widening of his eyes, the gape of his mouth—because he smiled and lifted the glowing acid-green remote up. The man was closer to seven feet than six, and his muscles bulged under his jacket. Hair was slicked back like a true villain; it was almost comical if it weren't so frightening.

"See this?" J said. "One flick . . . one *tiny* push, and this army here attacks."

Camila fumbled for Travis's hand, and he took it, intertwining his fingers with hers. He squinted, trying to keep his focus on J, on the swarm behind him. Could they run through it? Probably not. Could they climb up one of the fire escapes and get out from one of the buildings?

Who would that put in danger? Complete strangers, people who wouldn't have wanted to get mixed up in this . . . Travis bit his lip, noticing J was talking again.

"Give us the drones," he said, "and you won't end up like your friend."

"What are the coordinates for?" Camila blurted.

J's eyes widened—the look, on anyone else, might have appeared surprised. Under his crew-cut brow, it was cruel.

"Oh good, you just confirmed the information we needed," J said. "Our other drones failed to get the tags we need. Hand them over. You've got bigger problems. Don't forget you're just a couple of interns, on the run for *murder* . . ."

"Murder?" Travis repeated back.

J pushed a button on his acid-green remote; it blinked. The scourge undulated and pulsed, drawing closer. "If you want to know what happened to McCallister . . . to Swain, to Tabby . . . I can show you. Firsthand."

Travis's heart skipped a beat as the swarm drew closer.

"Travis," Camila breathed, only loud enough for him to hear. "We have the coordinates . . ."

He glanced at her.

"We *have* the coordinates," she hissed again.

Travis turned back to J. The men flanking him in black fatigues had drone controllers hooked to their shoulder straps. The bright glare of headlights illuminated the swarm of buzzing metal insects.

"If we give them up, will you let us go?" Travis said.

"Yes," J said, in what was almost a mocking tone. "We'll let you go."

The beginnings of a plan were floating in his mind, and piece by piece it laid itself in front of him—just enough bridge across to the next action that he could take the first step.

"We have them," he said, "but not with us."

J only looked them over; his expression remained the same.

"What—you think we're stupid enough to *have them* on us?" He got further into the bluff, hoping against hope they'd buy in to it. "We know what they mean to you. Wanted to make sure you wouldn't be able to get your hands on them."

J spread his muscled, callused hands out in front of him. "And *where are they?*"

Travis could barely hear himself speak over the buzz of the drones and the pumping of blood so close to his ears—it was like he was drowning in his own heartbeat. "I can get them for you," he said.

J looked them over, narrowing his eyes. He ran his tongue along the inside of his bottom lip, a predatory action that made Travis shiver. But he clenched his fists against it and made himself stare this man down.

Buy it. Please buy it, please . . .

"You, Travis Grant," J said, "have been a thorn in my side for too long already, you know that? I could call your bluff right now." His thumb hovered over the controller. The men around him in fatigues shuffled back and forth on their feet. "Should I? Should I call your bluff? Have my men search you up and down. Or better yet, have this little army do it?"

Travis tensed, all of his anxiety knotting up between his shoulder blades.

J gestured to a slim guy next to him, with a line of tattoos running up his neck to his right ear. He nodded at the command, then stepped forward.

"Hands out in front of you," he barked to Travis.

He complied, letting the man pat him up and down. When he was satisfied, he did the same to Camila.

"They're both clean," Tattoos said.

"Search the *area*, then!" J said, more than frustrated.

Two other men, who could have been twins with their spiky black hair, came forward and joined Tattoos in searching the area behind them. Their flashlights swept, created wide arcs. Travis noticed a few people watching the scene from their fire escapes, windows thrown wide.

"It'd be a lab vial," J said, "rubber lid, like a test tube.

Easy to spot—wouldn't you think?" He swore, eyes narrowing into slits when the men returned empty-handed. "You would think, wouldn't you? Oh boy, Travis, you just keep it coming, don't you? You just . . ."

Travis shrugged, elated inwardly at his luck, and letting the relief make his lie even more convincing. It relaxed his shoulders. "I told you. We have them. But not with us."

Suddenly Camila's hand pulled out of his, and he turned to see Tattoos, who yanked her hand behind her back and started to drag her away from Travis.

Travis reached out again, trying to pull on her hand, but she was too slippery, Tattoos too strong. Her face twisted in resistance as she elbowed him, making crunching contact with his nose. A dribble of blood ran down his face, covering the tattoos on his neck.

From the corner of his eye, Travis saw the scourge move. In another instant, the cloud surrounded him, blocking out his vision. Several of them landed on his skin but didn't bite. Not yet, at least.

He held very still.

"Travis," Camila said, sounding hoarse as the thug turned her around to leave. He had a firm grasp on her.

Travis flipped his head around, trying desperately to make eye contact with her. "Camila!" he shouted. "CAMILA!"

"It's okay, Travis," she said pointedly. "Just get the drones!"

They dragged her to the front of the alley.

"No," Travis breathed.

Then he heard J's voice through the swarm, as though each drone was speaking it at once, a cacophony chorus of the same voice over and over and over.

"Blood for blood, Travis," J's voice echoed. "How

about that? Blood for *blood* . . . you have twelve hours to get those drones to me, or we kill Camila. Could I be any clearer?"

"Twelve hours," Travis said.

Even his tongue felt numb, and he kept hearing Camila's words pulse through his mind.

He heard the SUV doors closing, heard them peel away, heard a deafening silence descend as the drones flew into the navy sky. But he didn't hear Camila's voice again.

Oh . . . The realization hit him all at once. *What have I done?*

Part 3

ANATOMY OF THE THORAX

> "Legs and wings sprout from the mosquito's thorax. Just as the body, as a whole, separates into three main *corpi*, so does the thorax—becoming three sets itself, each containing exactly one pair of legs. The middle segment carries the wings, balancing out its anatomy almost perfectly to achieve flight."
>
> —*Dr. Zane McCallister, PhD*

30

After finding the basil jar amongst the other trash, Travis called Camila's name and took off toward the opening of the alley—even though he knew it was useless, even though they were almost too far away to hear him now. One elderly woman with curlers in her hair shook her head at him as she went back into her apartment and closed the window.

Camila . . . they have Camila . . .

He could still hear the SUVs navigating the labyrinth that was the inner part of the city. Then he heard something else: a chainsaw-type engine cranking to life.

Just as he reached the mouth of the alley, the broad street opening out in either direction, fog began lapping at his feet.

A squeal, like slamming brakes, was followed by a dull, metal-filled *crunch*.

Travis looked both directions, the fog rising up to eye-level now. There was nothing in either direction, but . . . the sound. It had come from the right, hadn't it?

Or it could have been left, he thought, remembering how tricky sound directions could get when surrounded by multiple walls of concrete and brick.

But he decided on right, where the fog was thickest,

and set off. More sounds ahead of him, like fighting—between who? And why?

He'd never be able to forgive himself if something had really happened to her. She'd told him not to come, and there'd been that entire scourge around him—but if he'd *really* been the saving type, wouldn't he have done something to save her? Fight for her?

His mind said he'd done the best he could.

His heart swelled with guilt as he realized that, if facing a judge and jury on the matter, no, he *hadn't* done all he could.

Travis had stood there and done nothing.

He rounded the corner and put his hands in front of his face, waving away as much fog as he could. His hand waving didn't seem to do much, but something else was lifting it.

The scuffle, only a couple yards ahead of him.

Fog stirred in stretching, limb-like patches, curling away from the scene.

Four of the men, in black fatigues with drone controllers on their shoulders, lay unconscious on the cracked and tarred asphalt. But there was a fifth body. Knocked out like the rest.

That wasn't what made Travis's breath catch, though.

A giant of a man wearing a scientist's white lab coat and breathing through a gas mask stood in the center of that ring of fog and knocked-out men. The coat billowed as another wave of fog came out of the horn of his mosquito-smoking backpack, the white clouds covering his combat boots and cargo shorts. And next to him—Travis saw it just before the fog obscured it again—a soft bag meant for a cello? *Like the instrument?* But instead of the stringed instrument, it was full of things sticking out of it. Bats, golf clubs, lacrosse sticks.

Odd combination, Travis thought, before another cloud of fog blasted against him and he smelled the artificiality of the mixture—the byproducts of a small-cc engine.

"Put your hands up," a gruff voice said through the fog.

"It's okay," he said, not seeing the point of raising his hands if no one could see him. "I'm—I'm not with them. My name's Travis."

The fog swirled around a black silhouette as the man came closer. He was inches away before Travis could see him clearly. Behind, the fog began to disperse, going from a high concentration to a low concentration as physics dictated.

"Travis . . ." the madman growled, gray beard bristling.

It was then that Travis's eyes flickered to the ground by the cello bag, and saw something he hadn't seen before, nestled next to one of the fallen men in fatigues.

The man was Tattoos.

The girl on the ground was Camila.

She stirred, and Travis pushed past the madman with the beard to get to her. He stepped gingerly over Tattoos and reached out a hand. Camila looked up at him, confused at first, then understanding lit her features and she scrambled up, using his hand as leverage.

She's okay, Travis thought. *She's okay, she's here.*

He tried to pull her back from the mad scientist, but Camila put out an arm, catching her breath, and narrowing her eyes as though she were trying to remember something.

"No," she said. "Travis, it's okay. I think . . . I think he's the one who saved me."

"The name's Briggs," the man said, looking around

conspiratorially. "And unless I'm very much mistaken, we need to get you lot out of here. Yes?"

Travis cocked his head. The man looked familiar, now that he had a moment to process it. And where had he heard the name before?

"You're one of the scientists from Titus," Camila said, coming to the conclusion first.

Then it clicked. In his mind, Travis saw the photograph of the eight Titus Pharma scientists. He'd been the gruff, stocky one they'd decided might have been unapproachable.

Well, we were right about that, weren't we?

Mostly, Briggs looked the same, though obviously his beard had changed shades. And there was a way about him that reminded Travis a lot of the doc—if McCallister had been in any way fit before his bouts of coffee and Jack five times a day.

Thinking about the doc in that way, with a man in front of them who could have been his brother, opened up the way for grief to sneak in the back door. Travis suddenly found his heart hurt.

"Hey!" Briggs said. "You two listening? We don't got much time, and I'm not just saying that."

Next to their feet, the men in fatigues were beginning to stir. Briggs brought his fog wand up to the ready just in case, as Travis and Camila scampered away.

"Listen," Briggs said, more quietly, "I've been following you two since I saw you on the news. I knew you were being set up. If you know who I am, then you know that *I* knew McCallister and Samantha and Victoria. And there's been one more, Dr. Cornelius."

Travis's brain did the math.

Four dead; four alive.

"You really think I want any piece of this crap?" Briggs gestured around him.

Travis looked into his eyes, saw behind the rough exterior. "No," he said. "No. I trust you."

31

Briggs led Travis and Camila a block over, into an alley much like the one where J had confronted them earlier with his scourge of drones. Every starting engine, every pump of a brake, sent Travis's eyes skittering behind them. And all the way, Camila held his hand, and he held hers. *In this together*, it seemed to say. After the experience of losing her, Travis knew exactly how he felt about this: It was together, or not at all.

They clambered into the back of a white van, Travis wrinkling his nose up at the smell of stale cigarette smoke, coffee, and general neglect for cleanliness. It was the sort of van used in delivery services like catering, but with back seats jerry-rigged into place with amateur welding. A series of bulky tech hung from the ceiling and lay scattered along the floor, and it all began to sway precariously on threads of copper wire as Briggs peeled out of the alley. Travis could only assume, based on the tech Briggs had been wearing—and which now sat in the passenger seat—that he'd invented it all himself.

Briggs swerved, and didn't bother to slow down over speed bumps, and even hit a couple curbs on their way out of the district. "Sorry," he mumbled, "little nervous."

Travis raised an eyebrow, which he knew Briggs caught from the rearview mirror.

"Yo!" Camila said over the loudness of the driving, the complaining of the engine. "Where are the seat belts?"

Travis looked down around them, realizing they'd neglected to put them on.

"They're attached to the floor," Briggs said.

They pawed at the floor amongst all the junk and found the rudimentary seat belts, locking them around their waists.

Briggs shrugged, the action enough to cause the steering wheel to turn dramatically to the right. Travis and Camila held on to each other to compensate for the g-force.

Travis wiped the fog from inside his glasses, put them on, and blinked until his vision was clear. Then he ripped the wig from his head and let his mushed, sweaty brown hair free. The air inside the van was stuffy, but still he shuddered in relief.

"No point now, is there?" he said. "If we get caught, we get caught. And clearly, the police aren't the real threat."

"You've got that down pat," Briggs said. He caught sight of both of them from the rearview mirror. "How much do you kids know?"

Travis and Camila took turns explaining the last two days, both of them interrupting each other at different points, their stories overlapping as they told him both their experiences and the knowledge they gained. There was a pause after they talked about the doc, and another when Travis told him about Alec.

"It's a shame he got caught in the crossfire," Briggs said, shaking his head. "Should never have happened."

When they'd finished, Briggs was quiet for several moments. *Finally focusing on the driving,* Travis thought.

But then he said, "You've got about half the puzzle put together. There *are* nanotags in each of our blood. They were put there after the CDC got onto us for not making public knowledge of what we'd created. Titus Pharma had a loophole, to keep their reputation clean for the few stockholders they had.

"All eight of us have them. And when you put them together, you get the coordinates to the location of the virus Titus Pharma ended up hiding. Titus-1A."

"Why'd they hide it?" Camila asked.

"Yeah," Travis said, "doesn't it make more sense to destroy it if it's that big of a deal?"

Bump, swerve. He almost hit his head on the ceiling, but gripped the grimy handhold over the door.

"That's just it," Briggs said, "they couldn't destroy it. Don't think they didn't try—that was their first course of action. Best they could do was hide its location. Which is how the CDC ended up getting involved . . .

"You kids have to understand. We're *scientists.* Biologists. Under the same ethics as doctors—'do no harm.' We never intended to make a virus. Under the guidance of our company's . . . *president* . . . we were working on a life-changing project. It was a delivery system, via drones, that could blend in with the environment. Small, non-invasive mass population of a drug. Could be anything, really. A drug to administer to the currently ill, a vaccine to inoculate against future spread. Our president, and the rest of us, we were really concerned with the vaccine side. The first delivery was going to be to combat malaria in Africa. We needed a drug and a vaccine to do it right."

Travis and Camila shared a look. So that prediction had been right as well.

"So of course," Briggs continued, slowing down as they arrived in a more residential area, "in order to do that, we had to run tests. Hundreds of them. With all eight of us working, all hours of the day for years, the test numbers grew into the thousands. The hours would have broken a regular person, but we loved it! It was our passion! Not just on the drones, but on the disease itself. On vaccines for it, on treatments for it. Because it wouldn't do to just *deliver* cures—no, they had to do better than any other cure on the market, be most efficient. Had to beat out the competition, differentiate ourselves. Working that long with a disease like that, constantly putting it up against conditions. It's..." He held a knuckle to his mouth, and Travis saw how difficult it was for him to finish his thought. "It's like we forced evolution onto it. It changed, almost overnight."

"Titus-1A?" Travis asked.

Briggs nodded, pulling into a long drive and turning to them once the van was in park. "It's been one big mess for all of us ever since."

32

Now that the lights of the van were off, Travis got a full view of what he assumed to be Briggs's house.

He let them out of the van, and they watched their step as they got out. From the state of the utility van with all the amateur-welded tech, Travis wouldn't have expected the view of the house that greeted him.

It was old, at least a hundred years, and elaborate enough to belong in a gothic horror film. If it weren't for the sweet scent of tropical plants around him, he would have thought them somewhere closer to New England.

Briggs let them in through a side door next to the garage, and into the main hallway. Travis gawked at the dark wood finishes, the forest-green drapes, the carved leaves on every corner of the crown molding.

They stopped in the kitchen for snacks and water, then Briggs led them to the back of the house and into what must be his study.

The ceiling doubled in height here, and there were two floors to it, half the room turned into a loft where Travis could only see the balcony. The same emerald velvet drapes covered latticed-iron windows that stretched nearly twenty feet high and over the entire back wall.

In front of the glass was a desk covered in messy tech

pieces, dog-eared books, half-filled legal pads, schematics, medical journals, and a brand-new computer that looked at odds with its desk neighbors.

Travis noticed Camila walking toward one of the walls, hand outstretched to a frame that held the same image they had seen in the newspaper clipping on the blog.

"Ah," Briggs said, the wrinkles on his face deepening with his smile, "*that* is the last time we were all together. Before it all went down. There's more, too. Hang on."

As the gruff man searched through the drawers in his desk, Travis saw that his expression had darkened. He'd changed his scientist's coat for a plain T-shirt atop his cargo shorts while they'd been getting snacks. Without all the bulky equipment, Travis saw his build for what it was: muscled shoulders, bulging arms, and a gut that protruded over the button of his shorts. A man gone to seed.

"You think," Briggs said, "that those men that we left back there are dangerous? They're just the front line of it."

He laid out another photo, this one more professional, less journalistic, and unframed. It looked like it had been torn off the wall of the reception desk when the company had been in its prime.

Travis knew immediately who it was, especially in the immaculate suit. Maybe he was younger, his eyes softer, but it was still him.

"That's Cowan," Camila said.

Travis read the title along the white border under his photograph—"TITUS PHARMA, President & CEO."

"He was our leader for a while," Briggs said, lips curling under the graying beard. "We were already working hard on the drones, on the possibility of mass distribution. But he brought focus to it all—I think that's why they chose him. He really wanted us in Africa as soon as possible."

"What happened?" Travis asked, sensing a turn in the story. "Was it the virus?"

"Yes," Briggs said. "And . . . no. Cowan didn't end up being CEO for long. A lot of bad blood. But that didn't matter. The board wanted him out, so we were obliged to show him the door.

"It was because of the virus. One of the interns got sick with it, after it mutated into what we now call Titus-1A. It was the worst-case scenario for a company like ours, the sort of thing that could bring us to our knees in bankruptcy, or worse—worldwide pandemics—and all because of us. The decision was almost automatic for them. Cowan had been CEO when the small out-break occurred. He had to assume extreme responsibility. Like it was war, or some other bull-crap nonsense. Didn't matter about his vision, or all our hard work to change the world. He was just out. I think he took it pretty hard."

Briggs dropped the photograph on the desk amongst the rest of the clutter and switched a lamp on next to the computer. It gave him a sharp under lighting as he sat down in the leather-upholstered chair—like he was hold-ing a flashlight underneath his chin to tell a scary story.

Without Briggs having to say so, Travis and Camila took seats opposite him, scooting in closer, not want-ing to miss a word. This was, Travis thought, the sort of information they'd been after for two days, and he wasn't about to waste the opportunity to get it straight from the horse's mouth.

Briggs snapped his fingers; Travis and Camila jumped.

"In one day," he said, "they dismantled our entire operation. Set up a base camp in our lab with sealed tents, ventilators, full-body hazmat suits. The entire purpose for the company became about the containment of the new virus—as it should have. I don't blame them, but to have thrown everything else out along with it? To discount the years of research and hard work that we'd done? So much good could've . . . anyway, I'm rambling.

"After it was contained, there were so many constrictions with the government, so many phone calls with the CDC, so many subpoenas and trials and testimonies and audits of *every little thing* we had tested, discovered, used. They wanted to know *how* we had created the virus—and always they questioned if it was intentional, if we'd meant to cause harm, which, of course, none of us had. It was grueling business.

"And the company couldn't hold water. The entire purpose for its existence was no longer being executed. Funding dried up, which meant profits did, too, as well as any promise of future profits from the product we'd created. One by one, we each left. The company folded, eventually dismantled. Then disappeared altogether.

"But not before we were each injected with nanotags. And in the cruelest way possible."

"What do you mean?" Camila asked.

"No terrorist can torture a single coordinate out of us," Briggs said, "because we were never told the location. I don't know the coordinates that I or any of my colleagues have. That way we could really keep it secret—but if we ever had to come together, we'd be able to snap the puzzle pieces in place."

Four are dead, Travis thought. *Four remain.*

Almost half the coordinates were already in the enemy's hands.

The enemy . . . who exactly *was* the enemy? It couldn't be Drone Handler J—no, he was just a pawn.

The dawn of a realization was seeping over Travis, looking at the photograph on the desk.

He swallowed, looking into Briggs's eyes to let him know he was ready for the rest of the story.

33

Briggs typed something into a keyboard, then swiveled the computer monitor around so Travis and Camila could see it. The bright screen showed an image much like the spectral one they'd taken at Nive University earlier that night. But the imprinted numbers were different.

"Thing is," Briggs said, "I've contacted all the others. Victoria sent me the results of her nanotags before she died. Same as Samantha and Cornelius. And it's a good thing I did. Overnight there were two more deaths, Dr. Armstrong and Dr. Ulrich. That's six, six of my colleagues just gone. Armstrong drowned in his pool, tame compared to how the rest died. And Ulrich..." He held the bridge of his nose and shook his head. "It's too gruesome to repeat."

"I'm so sorry," Travis said.

"As of yesterday, I had everyone's nanotags except Norcroff's and McCallister's. Until now," Briggs ignored Travis's condolences. "See this? These are Norcroff's coordinates, he was the last one I was waiting on. Just got the email this morning."

"Where is he?" Travis asked. "Is he safe?"

Briggs shrugged. "As safe as he can be, though I wouldn't put it past who we're working against to be able to reach him. He's in Antarctica right now, far enough away I was worried I wouldn't hear back. But who knows?

"Obviously"—he swung the monitor back around to himself—"I didn't get to McCallister in time. If only I'd known."

"What did you tell Dr. Norcroff?" Travis asked.

"I told him to take his blood and send me the nano-tag number, then I told him to contact Cowan and just give him the blood sample. Let Cowan look with his own SEM. It would buy us some time. I warned him that it's not worth dying over, so I told him to just give up his blood willingly. I hope it worked."

Travis's mouth felt dry. He didn't say anything, and neither did Camila.

Briggs let out a dark chuckle. "I've been trying to get everyone's coordinates—you know, before they get attacked by those drones."

"Why?" Camila asked.

Yeah, Travis was suspicious, but she was going full-on interrogation mode.

Briggs continued in the same, almost condescending tone, "After I heard about McCallister, I realized that once they—once *we*—were gone, we'd lose all the coordinates. For good. But obviously I couldn't get a blood sample from McCallister even afterward. The explosion took care of that."

Camila and Travis were still looking at him.

"I understand why you'd be suspicious. The last two days haven't exactly endeared you to strangers. I just want to get as many of the coordinates as possible and try to figure out where the virus is—to *protect* it from the guys who're after it."

"And who's that?" Travis said. "Who's after it?"

"Cowan," Briggs said. "It's got to be Cowan."

I was right.

"Problem is," Briggs continued, "I just can't understand why. After Titus fell apart—really, after they kicked him out of his position—none of us ever saw him again. He just . . . *left.*"

"Makes sense, though," Travis said.

"I'm sure you've been watching the news," Camila said. "Cowan's been all over it. Blaming Travis and me, getting everyone on his side and using us as the scapegoats. Of *course* he'd want to shine the spotlight on himself to make him look more innocent."

Briggs sighed. "True. We need to keep you two safe. But I didn't even realize you had captured drones. Then it clicked why the drones you'd collected must've been so important to them. You have the remaining coordinates. McCallister's blood is in those drones."

Camila raised an eyebrow at him, accusatory. "You were there? Sure took your time to help out, didn't you?"

Briggs shook his head. "It wasn't like that. I'd been following them for the last twenty-four hours, trying to track their movements. I stayed a bit behind to hear what they wanted."

When they still didn't seem to buy it, he said, "Look, I came after you, didn't I? I *saved* you—and Travis." He was getting angry now, the deep growl coming from the depths of his throat. "So don't sit there and tell me I'm not on your side. Believe me, if I was with Cowan, you'd know it."

Silence.

Briggs leaned in closer, the lamplight shining more evenly now across his features. "If you *do* have McCallister's coordinates," he said, "that means we're in business. Means we have all of them—and we can get to that virus before Cowan does. Turn it over to the right people and never have to deal with Titus-1A again."

After looking deep into his eyes, thinking it over, Travis pulled the basil jar out of the hoodie pocket. "You mean these?"

"I thought you told them it was somewhere else." Briggs chuckled. "Huh . . . lucky bluff."

He looked between the two of them, and Travis thought he knew what he was seeing.

Travis could feel the exhaustion trickling through him, slowly congealing his movements. It fought with his mind, which was so alert it was almost painful.

Briggs cleared his throat, reminding him of the doc. "We'll take a look at these buggers in the morning, okay? It's getting too late for this old geezer."

Travis smiled appreciatively. "Now that we have proof of what they're doing, that we're being framed, shouldn't we go to the cops?"

"No way!" Camila said. "You can't trust them!"

"It's an idea," Briggs said, "and I've thought about it. But you know, there's a reason I came in with a fog machine and a cello bag full of weapons instead of calling nine-one-one. By the time they got there, you would've been long gone. The government works slowly. Lives are at stake! I can't let some bureaucratic red tape take weeks to process this information. If I had, Travis would've been left wandering down an empty street if he was lucky. More likely than not, he'd be . . . like the scientists."

The scientists are dying fast, Travis thought. Briggs was right. There wasn't enough time to go through the proper channels. They had enough evidence for themselves right in front of them. As long as they could do something *now*, that was all that mattered. Assuming it was the right thing.

"Why do you think Cowan is doing all of this?" he asked.

"I suppose revenge," Briggs answered. "He left the company hated by us and by all the board members."

"That makes sense," Travis said.

"If that's it," Camila said, "then why not just send all the drones at once and get all of the blood in one night?"

"Location," Briggs responded. "That kind of happened, though, if you think about it. McCallister's, Swain's, and Cornelius's deaths all happened within thirty-two hours of each other. I'm the next closest, so I suppose I'll be next. I'm sure it's locating the doctors. Making sure someone takes the drones to a close vicinity. I can't imagine these little buggers having enough energy to fly across the country, or the world for that matter, to take another doctor's blood."

"So you're just a sitting duck?"

"You'd think so, but I've taken precautions. I've developed an app that alerts me if the frequency is within the range of sound for a mosquito and what I deemed would be a mosquito drone. At a minimum, it gives me a fighting chance. I'm still here, aren't I?"

"I see that," Camila said.

"The thing is"—Briggs shrugged—"Cowan and his little followers will have to be officially implicated eventually. I just don't know if that day is today."

"Right," Camila said.

"You two get some rest. I've got someone I need to talk to before lights out, so you can show yourselves to the guest rooms. The third door on the left—and Travis, there's one for you across the hall, to the right."

34

Camila found her room easily. The door was already propped open, as though it had been waiting for her—an enormous dark wood slab that didn't make so much as a squeak as she pushed it.

"This is me, I guess," she said.

Travis nodded to her, his gut suddenly dropping at the idea of having to leave her. But he said, "Yeah. Guess it is." And then he smiled.

She disappeared into the room and closed the door behind her. Travis stared at the door, biting his bottom lip and feeling like a complete idiot.

What did he tell her? *I don't want to spend the night alone. And I don't think you should, either.*

He couldn't say that. Could he?

A creak from his left made Travis look down the carpeted hall. With the study doors to Briggs's office still open, he had a perfect view of the desk and the curtained windows beyond.

Briggs was on the phone with someone, talking quietly enough that he couldn't hear the conversation. He locked eyes with Travis. *Get some sleep already*, he seemed to say, before swiveling his gaze back to the computer monitor.

Right. Sleep. Of course. How had he been so stupid?

Letting out a defeated sigh, and not quite sure *what* he was feeling, Travis turned around and entered the guest bedroom opposite Camila's.

The bedside lamps had already been lit. Dark green curtains drawn about a four-poster revealed an enormous king-sized mattress and the most luxurious white duvet Travis had ever seen. He almost groaned, thinking about sliding under it.

He let himself into the bathroom attached to the side, not wanting to turn on too many lights. His eyes couldn't take that right about now.

Instead, he stood in front of the mirror, only half of him illuminated by the soft glow filtering in from the open door to the bedroom.

He'd never seen deeper, more bruised-looking bags under his eyes. There were still flakes of dried white wig glue on his forehead that he picked off one by one and washed down the sink. He ran long fingers through his hair, then took off his glasses.

The veins in the marble sink blurred. His reflection fuzzed out of focus. The lamplight grew, if possible, warmer and softer still, until he thought it just might envelop him.

It was the first moment of peace in a never-ending forty-eight hours. There was no adrenaline-induced heartbeat banging on the back of his throat. No blood rush pounded behind his ears. The silence, the quiet, the calm, threatened to give him a headache.

Eyes nearly rolling into the back of his head with exhaustion, Travis turned away from the mirror, stood under the showerhead, and turned it up as hot as it would go without scorching his skin.

The water ran down him in beads and swirls. The

steam cleared away the air in his lungs from the past two days, opened up his sinuses, and brought relief to his pounding head.

He put his arms around himself. The shower was turning cold, which meant he'd been in for a long time. He quickly scrubbed himself off, then toweled dry and saw that, while he'd been in the shower, someone—Briggs, probably—had dropped off a new pair of clothes for him on his bed. They were a little too big, but they would do. And they didn't smell like fire, blood, exhaust, or the acidic fertilizer of an atrium.

Travis climbed into bed.

And stared into the darkness.

His bones and muscles ached.

But the moment he found himself under the most ideal conditions for sleep, it eluded him. It became slippery, gel-like, like a fish he was trying to catch with bare hands.

And the house around him seemed to stare back, empty and alone. And . . .

Is Camila all right?

Of course, she's fine.

But is *she? Maybe I should check on her. Maybe something's happened since she went in her room.*

What if—and this was the worst thought of all—what if Briggs wasn't what he said he was? What if he was working with Cowan all this time? He'd said "the scientists" like he wasn't one of them.

Travis had barely thought it before action followed. He got out of bed, his bare feet warm on the decorative carpet, and began tiptoeing to the door across the hall.

Just to check.

Just to *see* if she was okay. Then maybe he'd be able to go to sleep.

The wooden floor took his footfalls outside as though he wasn't even there.

He knocked softly on Camila's door.

No answer.

Again, a little louder this time.

He heard a shuffling of sheets, a rustle, maybe of a duvet, but no answer. Slowly, Travis turned the handle and peeked.

Light from the hall shot a sliver of yellow onto the four-poster bed that was identical to his. A comfortable but restless-looking Camila was tucked under the white duvet. She was practically drowning in eiderdown pillows.

"Travis?" she whispered, sitting up.

"Yeah," he said.

"You, okay?"

"Are *you* okay?"

He opened the door wider and stepped inside, just a foot, enough that they were facing each other fully.

"No," she said finally.

"Me either. I don't know how I'm going to get to sleep."

"I know what you mean."

"Well look, I just . . . I just came to make sure you were okay is all. So I'll . . ." Travis gestured behind him.

Maybe he imagined it, but he thought he saw disappointment flash across her face.

"Of course," she said. "Thank you."

Travis turned away, moving to close the door behind him.

"Travis?"

He paused.

Not looking back at her, he said, "Yeah?"

"If it's not too weird . . . I mean, we've been through

a lot the last couple days. I'm finding being by myself a little . . ."

"We've definitely been through a lot," Travis agreed. He faced her.

"Would you maybe *not* wanna go back to your room?"

His heart skipped a beat, in an excited, bubbly sort of way. "You mean stay here?"

"Would that be weird?"

Travis shook his head. "That's—no, that wouldn't . . . I think that would be a good idea."

He took a deep breath, swallowed, and closed the door on them so it was just darkness, then climbed into the opposite side of the bed. The duvet and sheets were cold on this side.

"Thanks," he heard her whisper.

She scooted closer, turning her back to him. Tentatively, Travis moved forward, until their bodies met. She was warm, soft, practically vibrating—and for a moment he wondered how he would *ever* get to sleep now, like *this*.

But soon her breathing slowed, and so did his. He wrapped his arms around her, glad beyond belief that she was somehow still here, with him, that Cowan hadn't taken her.

Together, he thought. *Or not at all.*

She was asleep now, and Travis almost was, too.

Before he fully dozed off, though, he planted the softest of kisses on her shoulder. He thought maybe he heard her move after that, but then she was still.

And Travis finally fell into a dream full of clean air and white clouds and Camila holding his hand as they walked toward a dying star.

35

The man the drone handlers *thought* was Dr. Norcroff walked into the lab and sighed at the enveloping warmth. In reality, this stranger looked quite a bit like Norcroff, so it was easy to understand the mistaken identity.

It was because of the beard.

Usually, mistaken identity would not amount to more than excessive credit card bills or the reissuing of a passport. In this case, the mistake would end up costing him his life.

The mistake wouldn't have happened, if it hadn't been for Delia. The man—Dr. Johnson, or Jon Doc to his colleagues—had only come to Antarctica because staying back at home, where every street corner bakery reminded him of his ex-wife, had been too painful. So Jon Doc, a man who preferred the comforts of home, had gone on expedition.

That was his first mistake.

The second, and perhaps most tragic, was the beard.

Just as Jon Doc never thought he'd leave the labs and university classrooms of the United States behind, he'd never *ever* had any inclination toward facial hair. It wasn't just because Delia abhorred it, either. But the fierce winds had proven too much for his baby-smooth skin to handle. Six months in, he'd relented. Another six months later, he was unrecognizable as Jon Doc. So it was an honest mistake, really; it could've happened to anyone.

Jon Doc walked past row upon parallel row of plants growing under tarps that exposed them to the conditions of the world outside the greenhouse. Every time he walked through here, he couldn't help thinking how much it resembled a *reverse* greenhouse—a way to keep them, the scientists, warm while the plants tried to survive the cold.

He checked several thermometers, jotting down the temperature with numb fingers. No, not numb fingers. "Numb" wasn't a concept in Antarctica—mostly because that was the default state.

They were trying to get plants to adapt to colder conditions. And if that proved an impossible task, they were at least going to know how the plants *tried* to adapt. That would give them so much insight into the world of evolution.

The mosquitoes surprised him, though he didn't know what they were for the first several moments after they flew through the airlock.

First, it was a hum that accompanied the hollow flap of the greenhouse's plastic-and-canvas walls. By the time he recognized what it was making the odd sound, one of them had already landed on the back of his wrist—the only piece of skin exposed between his sleeves and gloves.

It didn't feel like a mosquito. There was a weight to it, and it was freezing cold, like pressing a penny to his skin. That was one of the most dangerous things one could do under these conditions. If he weren't in the greenhouse, the metal-on-skin contact would have taken a layer of dermis with it.

Rather than swiping it away, Jon Doc raised it to his

eye, inspecting it further. It *was* a mosquito, as still as death, covered in flecks of ice and snow.

A mosquito? No, that was impossible. Or it should have been.

Of the thirty-five hundred species of the insect, Jon Doc knew, they bred and wreaked havoc on every continent except the one he'd chosen to run away to.

This shouldn't have been here. It was impossible.

A stinging pressure grazed his skin, and Jon Doc shook his hand out in front of him, until the little bugger detached itself and buzzed off.

Not in any real pain, but annoyed, he looked around the greenhouse to see just how many of them had flown in.

But he only saw the insulated sections portioned off and flapping, flapping, flapping in wind that churned, boiling like nitrogen down here at the bottom of the world.

That was when Jon Doc felt them all at once, and from all angles—three on the back of his neck, two on his other wrist, one near his eye, which he tried to slap at but missed, causing him to flush with blood.

He furiously swatted them away, but when they didn't stop, he simply ran, nearly crashing into the flaps of the greenhouse, tangling himself in their plastic sails.

His eyes found one of the monitors above his head, an enormous flat-screen with multiple shots from the CCTV footage live outside of the house's airlock.

Were those . . . KGB?

Yes, he thought, shaking his head. Had to be.

Except Jon Doc was fairly certain the KGB never had animal heads atop their human necks.

36

The KGB men all looked identical to Jon Doc, except those heads, those growling, snarling expressions. And they were making their way inside.

He tried to make sense of it, tried to . . . *The KGB disbanded in 1991*, he reminded himself. There was no reason for them to be here, no reason for them to *exist* at all.

But that wasn't what the monitor was telling him, and he knew he wasn't making up the noise from behind him—the pounding, near shattering of glass as they tried to break in.

Slowly, Jon Doc turned around, needing confirmation that the CCTV footage wasn't just feeding him bull crap.

He'd been hopeful. But in his gut, he knew he hadn't really expected anything less. There were KGB men in red snowsuits—one with the head of a polar bear, one with the head of a lynx, one with the head of a wolf. Another with the head of a hawk let out a screech that eventually did it—shattered the glass of the air locks. The Russian animals stepped inside.

Blinking rapidly, a blurred vignette coating his vision, Jon Doc faced forward. Dizzy. He almost fell over, but righted himself again. Blinked again. Again. *Again.*

If the KGB were here, then he needed to save some of their work for America, right? Keep the red scythe out of it, those bloody traitors to humanity.

In a rare window of clarity, Jon Doc urged his feet to *move*, taking him to a cryo-closet at the back of the greenhouse. He entered his PIN with shaking fingers as the system searched for authorization.

"Incorrect PIN," a voice chimed.

Jon Doc swore—*bull crap* arctic computer speeds—looking over his shoulder at the animal-headed KGB marching forward, marching like they had all day because they knew he was cornered, done for, dead.

He wondered if the heads were a result of some sick commie experiment, just as he entered the correct PIN and the cryo-closet swung open. Jon Doc grabbed several of the seed samples and a jump drive, stuffing them into the pockets of his parka, before running out the other end of the greenhouse.

The air lock whooshed shut behind him, sealing him away from the KGB for now—at least until that hawk opened its mouth. And then he knew all hell would break loose.

One of them—the bear, he thought—roared. Jon Doc heard the ripping of several of the plastic sheets, his heart plummeting at the idea of them destroying the last several months of work.

He could barely see because of the foggy breath in his face. His nose, warm seconds ago, seemed to freeze, the snot in his nostrils congealing at once into small crystals.

Jon Doc pulled the muffler up over his face and stumbled forward. The snow hadn't been cleared from the backside of the greenhouse, and it was almost up to his chest.

Still, adrenaline pushed him forward, and he waded

through as best as he could, spreading his arms wide to clear a path for himself.

He heard something trip from behind, something tumble. *Incorrect*, a voice chimed, muffled by glass and plastic and canvas. Just as he'd suspected . . . they wanted the seed samples for themselves, the rotten commies. They wanted the data on the drive he'd secreted away.

Despite the difficulty of his escape, Jon Doc had to smile at himself for a job well done. The snow didn't seem so terrible to move through anymore.

Silence.

From all around.

Even the wind seemed to have died down.

In his haze, Jon Doc checked over his shoulder, saw an empty greenhouse and an open airlock. *He* hadn't left it open, had he? He wouldn't have.

His heart sped up as he looked all around for where the KGB might be. But there was no sign of their red snowsuits anywhere, no odd animal heads bobbing on human necks.

What?

Whatever snowbank he was working his way through finally came to an end. Jon Doc practically burst through the other side, his momentum carrying him too far and crashing him into the ground.

His beard was wetted with snow, even under the muffler, and after he got his breath back, he checked that the seeds and drive were okay. They were fine, and snowmobiles were lined up here, this close to the lab.

If the KGB were still after him, this would be the best way to escape. Those commies were probably behind enough in tech that they wouldn't even be able to start the things.

Laughing out loud, Jon Doc approached one, putting his master key in the ignition.

It wouldn't start.

Neither would the next one.

Bull-crap things were probably out of gas, he thought.

And there, on the other side of the snowbank, the four KGB men—a hawk, a polar bear, a lynx, a wolf—bobbed along the top, their heads just visible, slits of red just underneath their necks like a slice of blood, dripping as they came for him.

There was no time to try to start the snowmobiles now.

Jon Doc took off running again. Careful not to slip, he cleared patches that he knew were ice crevasses hidden in the sea of snow.

The wind was picking up, and fast, a storm-level wind that brought with it clouds and swirling clumps of cotton that stuck to his beard and wanted to drip into his eyes, to get rid of the rest of his vision completely.

And the KGB were still following him.

A small boulder of ice grew out of the ground, seemingly out of nowhere, and he ran into it, falling face-first again into the snow. It was enough to knock his boot loose, twisting his ankle in an unnatural way.

Grimacing, holding back a scream so the KGB wouldn't hear, Jon Doc sat up, clutching his wounded foot even as ice water seeped into it, and the wind churned the ice on his wool socks until his toes grew numb.

Still, they were following, a steady march.

Need to get out of here, he thought. He needed to get away, needed to make sure the seed samples were safe and in *American* hands. Otherwise, there was no point in leaving the States to begin with, was there? All of this for nothing, and all because he couldn't stand to see that stupid corner bakery anymore on his way into lecture.

Jon Doc stood up, not caring about his semi-injured foot. He could deal with that later in the safety of the lodge. *After* he'd told everyone what had happened, and they'd called in reinforcements or . . . whatever they were supposed to do in this situation.

He limped forward, trying to get a full grip on the seed samples and the drive in his coat. They were falling from the pocket he'd put them in, and he was using his numb hands to try to switch them out, squinting through the torrent, teeth chattering.

But they fell out of his cold fingers, all dexterity lost on him. The envelopes tumbled to the ground, and Jon Doc wondered then why on God's good Earth they'd chosen envelopes to keep them in. Hadn't they thought of a situation like this? How stupid they had been all this time.

The seeds landed in the snow, making little craters where they disappeared.

Jon Doc blinked.

And when he opened his eyes, there they were. Everything he'd worked toward and hoped for, *right in front of him.*

Green things of all varieties in full extension, flush and ready for the sun to feed them. Strawberries, corn, peas, tomatoes, straight out of that bull-crap Antarctica snow, from infancy to maturity just like that.

For a moment, jaw hanging open, he didn't feel the pulse in his ankle. Didn't care about the men with animal heads coming for him from behind.

He only wanted to take these miracles back to the lab.

Letting out an awed breath that smoked and swirled

around him, Jon Doc walked toward those green blush-
ing miracles.

The snow melted; the plants disappeared with it.

And he realized only nanoseconds before the fall that
it was a gorging crevasse he stood before, and not a miracle at all.

The vertigo filled him like a hot soup.

Jon Doc, mistaken for Norcroff because of the bull-
crap beard he'd never wanted to begin with, fell with
bone-crunching finality onto the ice.

37

"Good morning," Camila said.

Travis slowly opened his eyes, this new reality taking a while to defrost in his brain.

"Morning," he said, as though it were the most natural thing in the world, as though they'd said this to each other every time the sun came up for the entire time they'd known each other.

Light filtered through the curtains, through the almost tapestry-like evergreen curtains. A blurriness suffused it, softening it with the touch—or promise—of rain.

Camila was facing him now, both of them simply staring into each other's eyes. Travis found himself getting lost in hers, in those green pools.

"How'd you sleep?" he asked, voice croaky.

"Fine," she said.

"Same."

He couldn't help cracking a smile at that.

They lay there next to each other, wrapped in the warmth of the duvet until the sun got brighter, until the heat of it wasn't comfortable anymore.

"Time to get up," Camila muttered.

"Yeah," Travis said. "Time."

* * *

Briggs was just leaving his office when Travis stepped out of Camila's room. The old scientist raised an eyebrow at him, before cracking a smile.

"Well, you two lovebirds just hurry up, then," he said. His voice was like a rock tumbler. "I let you sleep in, but there's a lot of ground to cover, so—"

"Of course," Travis said. "Ready in a sec."

Briggs nodded. "Breakfast in the dining room. Or lunch at this point, depending on how early you do that sort of thing."

Travis got ready quickly, then met Camila in the hall. An awkwardness had sprung up between them that hadn't been there before, a wall he didn't know how to scale, not this time—and that made him angry.

Freshened up, they met Briggs in the dining hall— what Travis supposed was most people's entire ground floor—and started piling their plates with scrambled eggs and rye toast while Briggs filled them in.

"You were probably wondering who I was on the phone with," he said, looking between them.

Camila shrugged.

"Well, it was a guy who used to work for me. He has access to a lab, and I happened to get my hands on some of Cowan's drones. Had him do a full evaluation."

Travis's ears perked up.

"Good luck with that," Camila said. "We've already tried to get a look inside those things, twice."

Briggs grinned at her, almost a smirk. "What'd you two find?"

She told him everything they knew—from the small mechanics of it, to the blood sack, the yellow liquid they'd identified, and the fact that most of it was made of copper.

"Not bad," Briggs said, chuckling. "Not bad at all—you two actually made it pretty far. I can give you one better."

Travis stuffed his face with a mouthful of wet scrambled eggs, savoring the butter in it and the salty creaminess.

"That yellow fluid," Briggs continued, "is actually a hallucinogen."

Travis scooped more warm scrambled eggs with cheese into his mouth and smiled at Camila. He knew where this was going.

"That's the last bit of the puzzle," Camila said. "I mean, Travis and I both *thought* that might be it, too."

But before she could say more, Briggs said, "You were right, both of you. I see why McCallister hired you on as interns. Did you know it's a compound called mescaline?"

Camila nodded. "The stuff used in MK-ULTRA."

"We realized that's what it was, too!" Travis said.

"Why didn't you tell me that yesterday?"

"I don't know," he said, shrugging and spooning more eggs into his mouth. "It just never came up, I guess."

"Good point," Briggs said. "Yesterday was hectic. Let's make sure today stays the same or crazier." He lifted a glass of OJ and saluted the statement.

Travis raised an eyebrow and looked to Camila, who lifted hers and said, "Hear, hear."

He joined in. "To a more chaotic and hectic day than yesterday."

"I hope our wishes come true." She smiled and took a sip of her juice.

Briggs and Travis started laughing.

"So all the scientists"—he swallowed his toast, meeting Briggs's eyes—"they all got a dose of it and started seeing things. Crap that scared them enough for them to do crazy things to themselves."

"Like swallow gallons of acid," Camila whispered.

Or jump off a building, Travis thought. *Slit their own throat . . .*

"And at the same time," Briggs said, "it collects their blood sample. The perfect combination—the sort of thing Titus Pharma was developing those drones for in the first place."

"That's all fine," Camila said. She hadn't touched a bite of her food. "But that doesn't help us fix this problem."

Briggs nodded.

"Cowan and those guys almost have all the coordinates," Travis said. "They're after the Titus virus."

"Right," Briggs said, "and we're going to fix that, especially with what you've given me. You two, though, you're going to have to stay with me. Cowan knows exactly who you are. Keep your guard up and stay safe while we figure out what to do next. Yeah?"

Travis locked eyes with Camila; it seemed that they had an entire conversation right then, passing between them like radio waves. Muscles tugged at the corners of her mouth—a sign he now knew meant she wasn't sure.

But finally she nodded.

So did Travis.

"You wanna let me in on what that was about?" Briggs asked.

"We're good to stay here," Camila said. "Thank you."

Briggs clapped his hands together. "Right, then. We

need to get to it. Wanna bring breakfast down with you, or just leave it here for later?"

"Down where?" Travis asked.

Briggs got a twinkle in his eye that made him look like the mad scientist version of Santa Claus.

"The lab," he said. "Where else on Earth, kid?"

38

They walked to a wing that Travis remembered seeing from the outside but had entirely forgotten about. It branched to the right of the main house, connected by a hallway done in such a different architectural style, he wondered if they'd stepped into another house altogether.

The transition brought them to a wing that couldn't have been attached to the main house more than ten years ago or so. It brought Travis immediately into spaces he wished he could forget: The Aust Biotech Lab at Nive University, the destroyed lab at the GMMC.

He almost wanted to look under the stainless-steel counters, dig through the glass cabinets glinting with industrial lighting, to find some sort of bomb, or a fleet of dormant drones ready to swoop in on them. *Isn't Briggs one of the scientists?* Travis thought, realizing that Cowan should be after him, too.

Unless . . .

No.

Travis took Camila's hand and squeezed it.

They'd decided to trust Briggs, hadn't they? There was nothing to be nervous about.

"Have a seat, kids," he said, gesturing to the round

industrial benches placed before the stainless-steel counter.

Briggs went about turning on lights, pushing a button on a remote to bring up the vinyl window coverings. They rolled up all around them, revealing walls that were really just glass. They could have almost been outside if it weren't for the half reflections of the lab.

"What are we doing?" Camila asked.

"Photodynamic dye," Briggs explained as he removed a vial from under a cabinet Travis couldn't see.

He thought about emergency buttons, flashing lights.

He shook his head—something that didn't go unnoticed by Briggs, who kept his eye on him carefully as he continued.

"When Cowan's drones finally get to me, I want to make sure I'm injected with a boatload of this stuff. That way they'll end up sucking out dyed blood. If we're lucky, it'll make Cowan's drones more visible even in daylight. And if we're *really* lucky, it might just interfere with the nanotags, make them more difficult to read. Though don't quote me on it, kids, obviously I haven't had the time to test that bit. But"—he shrugged—"any opportunity to slow Cowan and his guys down, right?"

Travis sat, nerves beginning to churn in him again at the idea of Cowan's drones finding them, of Briggs preparing for it because it was *inevitable*.

Briggs lifted up the dye, which was a deep cerulean, like someone had taken a sample of the ocean, but instead of becoming clear water, it maintained its shimmer, depth, and hue. He almost looked funny, the burly, bearded man squinting to make sure there were no bubbles left in the vial.

Then he moved to a cabinet and took out a sterile needle, the point of which he promptly broke by using his teeth to open the packet, spitting the tear of paper and plastic onto the floor. He used one hand to get the needle out, uncap it, and insert it into the rubber cap of the dye.

Both of them sat quietly while he loaded the needle, flicked the air bubbles out, squirted a sample of it into the air so it was fully loaded, then promptly inserted it into the crook of his left elbow. Briggs barely grimaced as the cerulean dye disappeared into his veins.

After a moment, he sighed, throwing out the needle into a biohazards bucket and flexing the considerable muscles in his arms. He then proceeded to do a series of exercises, alternating sets of push-ups with sit-ups. "Gotta get the blood pumping through me."

When Briggs was done, he sat on the floor, legs up against his chest, arms crossed. He was catching his breath, beads of sweat catching in his gray beard.

"Now what?" Camila whispered.

It was clearly meant only for Travis, but Briggs answered. "Now," he said, "I wait to get bit. Cowan's drone's will bite me, suck my fluorescent blood, and inject me with mescaline. The belly of those drones will be full of my glowing blood, and we can track them to where Cowan and his goons are hiding out. You kids get in a spot where you won't be seen. Let's get this done once and for all."

A feeling of uselessness was beginning to settle over Travis. Now more than ever, he itched to act, to *do something*, anything. "What should we do in the meantime?"

Briggs must have heard the earnestness in Travis's tone, because he smiled. "When I'm bitten, I'll signal you both to come tie me up."

He got up, walked toward a glass cabinet, shuffled through several labels, and finally pulled one out. He got out another needle and did the same thing to these contents as he had with the dye. It was thick and white in a way that reminded Travis of soured milk.

"This," Briggs explained, "should counteract the hallucinogen. After you've tied me up, give me this. So I don't . . ."

"So you don't . . ." Camila said.

"Right," Travis said.

Briggs got out bright yellow neon rope from another cupboard and put it where any of them could grab it.

* * *

The lab had grown almost entirely dark.

Only the shape of Briggs's head as he looked left, right, behind, forward again—as he'd done a hundred times over the last several hours—let Travis know that he and Camila weren't alone.

They had cuddled up in one corner of the lab, the hallway-facing side without windows. Camila had fallen asleep nearly two hours ago, head resting against Travis's chest.

He wished his breathing could be as even as hers, almost baby-like in its consistent *in, out, in* rhythm. The arm he had around her had fallen asleep forever ago, but he wasn't about to move out of this position. Geesh—he wasn't that insane.

"Briggs," Travis hissed.

He saw the scientist's head swivel his direction.

"Do you think they're still coming?" Travis asked.

Briggs let out a breath, a heavy, surrendered sound— still strung up on a trapeze line, about to fall.

"It's hard to—" he was saying, but he stopped.

Travis held his breath; he'd heard it, too. A low hum like a nineties modem turning over and over and over.

Camila held up a hand in her sleep and swiped at something, and Travis nearly went cross-eyed trying to see the little shape in the near full darkness of the lab.

There—just enough of a glint to . . .

"Get ready," Briggs said.

Travis jumped; he hadn't known the other man was so close to him.

Briggs was reaching out a hand. Travis could just make out its broad shape. "Any . . . second now . . ."

39

Camila stirred.

Travis put his numb hand on her shoulder, squeezing it, trying with everything in him to convey the importance of staying quiet.

She gasped, but seemed to know to stay silent.

"Come on . . ." Briggs was whispering. "What are you afraid of, huh? You little bugger—come *on* . . ."

The drone buzzed forward, flashing.

Travis held his breath. He felt Camila hold hers, felt her heart beating against his own rib cage, almost in sync.

Briggs hissed, cursing. "That's it," he said, breathing through whatever it was doing to him. "Now, kids. *Now.*"

Travis and Camila scrambled to their feet. He grabbed the light switch closest to his head, enough so they could see.

Briggs was clutching his wrist. Travis saw the bruising, blood-filled sore bubbling up, just like it'd done all over the doc. Thinking of the doc was enough to break his momentary stupor.

He and Camila moved as though they'd rehearsed it, each of them grabbing one end of the rope, keeping an eye on the drone as it bit Briggs again near the neck, then took off for the ceiling, circling around the single bar of light.

Briggs's eyes were growing large, pupils contracting, mostly whites now. He wheeled his head around, as though seeing the world for the first time. Whatever he saw drew the gruff man's features into squints and wrinkles and tear-filled frowns.

And more mosquitoes were joining him, a veritable scourge that made Travis want to cringe back. But they didn't seem to have any interest in him or Camila—just Briggs.

"No," Briggs whispered. "No . . . no . . . please, that's not what I . . . You don't... *understand.*"

He growled the last word. Travis and Camila took that as their cue. They pushed him down into a metal chair. He landed with a thud, the chair driving back several inches.

Before he could get up, they'd gone on either side of him, putting the rope against his chest. Travis and Camila twisted around Briggs like it was a maypole dance, quickly getting several layers of rope on before moving to his feet and wrapping those as well, and finally securing it all with five knots.

No, ten.

"All right." Camila waved her hands. "He's good, he's good, you don't—"

Briggs growled. It was an animal sound, bearish, brutal, like it was ripping up the bottom of his throat.

"Travis!" Camila yelled. "The drone! No, don't worry about him, I got it. I'll inject him with the counteragent!"

She was holding Briggs down, making certain the ropes did their job, while Travis got their TracFone from his pocket and shone the flashlight toward the mosquitoes that hummed erratically through the air before them.

The dye had done something to the drones. They now glowed the same cerulean color, getting even brighter and more obvious in the beam from the light.

He looked around for something to trap them in, but there was nothing in his immediate vicinity.

And it didn't matter—because the moment he turned his head back toward the drones, they'd already fled down the hall toward the main house, a small, twisting cloud of metal and electricity.

With Briggs recovering and gasping behind him, Travis bounded forward, still clutching the glowing phone. The pounding of his sneakers echoed off the glass walls of the connecting hall, muffling again as he made it into the main house.

He kept the phone held up to the level of his eyes. *Keep it in your sights. They're gonna go friggin' rogue if you don't.*

Travis rounded a corner and found the cloud that was the scourge, floating like iridescent fish lures in a dark, swampy lake. Silently as he could, he followed them, all the way into the library. The air felt cooler here. He just made out the slit of dusky night outside the cracked-open window.

And just like that, the drones were gone.

"No, no, no," Travis muttered, flipping around and shoving his way out the front door, toward the side of the house with the open window.

He flashed his phone light around.

Nothing glowed back at him.

No bright blue fish lures buzzing.

A squeak of hinges, and then Travis heard footsteps joining him in the front yard.

"Where'd they go?"

Travis turned to see Camila, out of breath, coming to stand next to him.

Briggs followed behind, grizzled face looking as though it were about to melt off him. Where before his beard had only made him rugged, now it seemed to add decades onto his age.

"I—" Travis threw up his hands. "I don't know. I don't know where they went. I *had* them."

"Kid," Briggs was saying, "it's okay. Just calm down." He wheezed, coughing up phlegm. "We got one thing right. We got that dye into those three. Tracking them just got a whole lot easier. They're somewhere in these trees. We just gotta track 'em down."

40

Travis rushed inside as Briggs gestured them in. They half jogged into his study, where Briggs took several gulps of straight vodka before digging through a cabinet and bringing out three heavy metal flashlights.

"Time to follow these suckers," he muttered, though Travis couldn't quite tell if he was talking to him and Camila, or merely to himself. Maybe all three.

They shone their spotlights outside, concentrated, steady yellow beams.

All Travis could make out were the trees—a forest line so solid, so thick, it might as well have been a wall.

Briggs stumbled forward, getting his bearings. He took a moment to stand straighter, and Travis found himself admiring the old scientist's courage, the tenacity it must take to still be moving forward after what he'd just undergone, after what he had seen, whatever it was.

Flashlight beams waved back and forth, creating a glimmer, like fairies in Peter Pan. A small cloud of blue-colored fireflies wove in and out of the trees, away from the house.

Briggs flashed them a wide grin. "Found 'em," he whispered.

Wet, dewy grass swished beneath his feet as Travis

walked forward with the others. He kept his gaze on the slow-moving cloud, now creating a very non-mosquito sort of line that snaked through the trees.

They entered the trees. Travis was careful to be as quiet as possible, but it was difficult when all he wanted to do was run after them. He steeled his patience.

"Travis." Briggs's gruff whisper was closer than he thought it was. "You keep a razor eye on them, you hear? Camila and I, we're gonna go back to get the van."

Travis nodded his agreement, keeping his eyes forward.

He heard them retreating behind him, and his heart constricted.

* * *

By the time Briggs and Camila showed up with the van, the iridescent scourge of mosquitoes had led Travis through to the other side of the palm trees and onto the main road.

And they'd picked up speed.

A few cars passed him, but they didn't pay him any mind.

Travis wiped the sweat from his forehead, but even then it wasn't enough to get the dribble that fell into his right eye. It coated the back of his hand as he tried to swipe it away, and that only made it worse.

He squinted his way forward, the roots, mangroves, and wildflowers snagging at his toes and heels. He stumbled, but tried to keep pace.

More salt burned his eyes, and that was enough.

Instead of looking forward, instead of monitoring his feet, Travis could only close his eyes and yell out as vertigo shot through him. The metal flashlight clattered forward, rolling unevenly across the asphalt.

Travis got on all fours, shaking his head, yet his vision was still blurry. And he looked frantically for the scourge he was supposed to be following—still there, still flying.

Get up.

Headlights flashed across him. Travis's own shadow elongated the line between road and swampy, snaking wilderness.

"Geesh, dude, what happened?" Camila was by his side, pulling him up. Briggs grabbed the flashlight, handing it back to him.

"Doesn't matter," Travis said.

"Good," Briggs said. "'Cause we gotta get a move on if we're not going to lose them."

* * *

"Why are they sticking to the road?" Camila asked.

She and Travis were again in the back seat of Briggs's van, speeding down the highway connecting the larger metropolitan areas. But so far, it was still only swampland on either side.

To their left, a thick line of shimmering cerulean chunks of metal flew forward as easily as though they were made of paper-mâché.

"I mean," Camila continued, "if they're drones, wouldn't they have some sort of GPS system? Like, I don't know, a way to navigate without needing a road?"

"Path of least resistance," Briggs said, his voice low again, in that way of his that made it seem like he was talking out loud to himself. "Why make your own road when there's one right here? Cowan probably doesn't suspect—*couldn't* suspect—that we'd be following all this time."

Travis met Camila's eye and shrugged. *It's a theory.*

And just like that, semi-jungle became urbania, then city.

Following them through the city became the most difficult part. Traffic kept them from moving too quickly in Briggs's white catering van, so Travis and Camila took shifts following them down concrete paths, ignoring the stares and honks in their direction, until eventually Travis saw them disappear in the propped-open top window of a skyscraper with a glimmering sign over the front entrance that read "Coro Innovations."

He dropped his flashlight beam, certain of what he'd seen, that glimmering swarm being eaten, sucked in by that top-floor window. He called Camila with the Trac-Fone.

"Coro Innovations?" she said, asking him to repeat.

"Yeah."

It sounded like she was turning to Briggs. "You ever heard of that?"

Travis could hear him grunting but couldn't make out the words. He got a whiff of a hot-dog stand somewhere down the road, another of a Cuban restaurant across from him. Everything was sweet and thick. Traffic buzzed about him, replacing the incessant hum they'd been following for well over two hours.

"Hold on," Camila said, "I think we're . . ."

But she didn't need to finish. She and Briggs pulled up, parallel parking in the recently vacated spot, and receiving a loud *honk* from an annoyed driver for their abrupt leaving of the street.

"Briggs says to get in," Camila told him, still on the phone. She didn't roll down the windows, didn't open the doors. "If this is where Cowan is, the last thing we need is for him to spot one of us outside the front lobby."

Travis's blood ran cold. What if he had been spotted? He'd been so reckless. With a gulp, he hung up and clambered back in, slamming the van door behind him.

Briggs was staring through the front windshield at the skyscraper that seemed to go up forever.

"Well now," he said. "That is interesting. Isn't it."

41

"Coro Innovations," Camila said as Briggs pulled away from the curb and the skyscraper jutting from it. "Didn't you say you've heard of it?"

He nodded. "Heard of it—didn't make the connection until now."

"Do we go back to your place?" she asked. "Lay low and do some research?"

"Won't work," Briggs said. "I'm supposed to be dead, remember? If that's really Cowan's idea of putting this baby to sleep, my house is the first target. And now that we've found out where their HQ might be? Not a . . . hold on . . ."

Instinctively, Travis looked back. A line of pulsing headlights were behind them, row upon row.

He thought he recognized the black SUV two cars away.

Even as he watched, the traffic slowed—but not the SUV. It barreled left, barely missing a silver Prius, before cutting off the car just behind their van.

"Just like I thought," Briggs said. "Even getting as close as we did was too much."

"When are they ever gonna stop?" Travis asked.

"They won't," Camila said. "Not until they have the

vial with the drones with McCallister's blood. Which is at your house, isn't it, Briggs?"

He didn't say anything.

"Briggs?" Travis asked.

"It's not at the house," he said. The man was . . . *sheepish.*

Travis took off his glasses, which were fogging up in the humid van, and wiped them clean. "What do you mean?" he asked.

Briggs reached over with his right hand—his neglect of the steering wheel bringing them dangerously close to the adjacent lane—and popped open the glove compartment.

A basil jar rolled around inside, the doc's drones clanking against one another as Briggs pressed the brake too hard again. "Couldn't leave them at the house," he said.

"So you brought them here for them to find?" Travis said, incredulous now of this entire setup.

"Travis," Camila said, "calm down. Think about it. It's better they're with us. They probably would've already gotten them by now."

They're still going to get them, Travis thought, looking behind him as the SUV gained speed. "We sure that's them?"

"Who else would it be, kid?"

Briggs put both hands on the wheel, which was comforting. But not enough. "Only one way to find out," he said. He jerked the van to the left. Travis and Camila held on to each other to keep from tumbling around.

"It's gonna be okay," he found himself whispering to her, surprising himself with the words. "I got you."

And I'm not going to let them take you this time.

Camila caught Travis's eyes, the green of hers twinkling with headlights from every window as they refracted, stretched, and left again.

Her lips twitched up into a smile. "That so, Casanova?"

The engine revved as the wheels spun faster beneath them, the axels practically grinding together.

"I'm serious," Travis said. "I—"

But he didn't need to finish.

Camila's head came forward, lips locking on his.

A flock of *Rhopalocera* took flight in him, rising in his chest, and he kissed her back. She was soft but fierce, and he returned every bit of it, hoping she could sense just how much he meant with it.

"Okay, kids," Briggs was saying, "maybe later, huh? We're officially in a bit of a situation."

They broke apart, Travis awkwardly rubbing the heat of his flushed neck and unable to stop smiling—at least, not until he saw that the SUV had followed them down the side street and was—

Bam!

The SUV smashed into the back of the catering van, forcing Briggs to step on the gas even harder. Still, the jolt was enough to put a little whiplash in Travis's neck. He blinked his eyes, most of his body still absorbing the shock, seat belt tightening against his chest and beginning to constrict his airflow.

"Hang tight, you two," Briggs said.

They sped by cafés. A couple stared at them openmouthed as they passed. Travis saw another pull out a phone and was just about to dial—maybe three certain digits—before they'd sped past.

They zoomed past a hotel, a restaurant, and a used bookstore with paperbacks wilting out in the Florida

humidity—what a stupid idea, what an absolutely ridiculous thing.

And the SUV was only feet away from them again.
Travis saw the crack in the back windshield, a battle scar
from their last run-in. He took Camila's hand, the grinding, smoking engine the only sound. He wrinkled his nose
at the smell of burned rubber, of bubbling, burning oil.

The city they'd been in the thick of not minutes before
was dissolving. Skyscrapers seemed to melt down and
buildings became flatter, more spread out. Blocks became
visible again, the palm trees the highest things around,
with crumbling alleyways on all sides.

"Briggs," Camila said urgently. "We've got to lose
them, right? Any ideas?"

"Go until they run out of gas," he said. If it was a
joke, it fell flatter than their back passenger tire.

Travis glanced at the gas gauge, noticed how low it
was dropping. What did they have left? Maybe twenty
miles?

The road widened out, and Travis saw the SUV swerve
to the left, half of it going into the adjacent lane. If there'd
been anyone there, they would've crashed. *And they still
might*, he thought hopefully.

But then the SUV pushed on the gas.

Headlights landed on Travis, but he looked anyway,
blinking through it. "Briggs . . ." he said warningly.

"Yeah, I see it, kid."

The SUV sped up one last time, and then the driver
jerked the wheel to the right.

The front of the SUV collided with the side of the
van, and in a flash, Travis saw the world outside spin—
saw the van's wheel turning of its own accord and Briggs
letting go.

They were spinning out of control.

And then equilibrium ceased.

Like a carnival ride, Travis's stomach floated into his throat, and then the seat belt jerked him against the seat.

Not just spinning now—*crashing*.

Rolling forward. Shattering metal, scrapes on his skin, squinting his eyes—holding on to Camila, and trying to protect his head.

He heard someone scream.

Then everything stopped.

42

"Camila!" Travis croaked, coughing on fumes. Spilled gasoline stung his eyes as he heard some liquid gushing and gurgling close to his head. "Camila, are you—"

"I'm okay." Deep breaths, close to his ear. He was surprised he could even hear that, as everything else seemed to have become the equivalent of an unfocused microscope lens. "I'm okay, I just . . ."

But then she groaned.

"Kids," Briggs said from somewhere close by. "Try not to move, just in case something's broken."

"Yeah, screw that," Camila said. She let out a gasp as she moved. Travis heard fluttering glass shards and knew that she was going to get out of the van—and he was going to join her.

Whoever had wrecked them couldn't be far behind.

They were probably just waiting for them to crawl out of this shell of a van.

Travis did a quick inventory of his body—trying to breathe evenly, touching sore spots. Bruised and cut up, he concluded. But as far as he knew, nothing was broken.

He was upside down in the van and had to struggle with shaking fingers to press the release button on his seat belt several times before it finally let him go with a snap, rolling back into its placeholder.

Travis fell forward onto the ceiling, now the floor, knee bruising against the overhead light button. It was like stepping on abandoned Legos on a hardwood floor.

Camila was already crawling out of the window closest to her. Briggs had kicked out what remained of the windshield and exited the van. With a gasping breath, Travis followed and slowly stood up next to them, taking in the sight of the wreckage.

He didn't have long to see it.

The black SUV, unscathed except for a vicious dent in the corner of the hood where it had hit them, revved its engine and flashed its lights.

And men in black fatigues—drone controllers perched on their shoulders—were getting out from all sides, the SUV's doors flapping open and closed like wings on a mosquito's thorax.

Travis froze.

What do we do now?

He glanced to Camila's leg, slowly oozing blood. She glared at the men, a furious fire lit behind her green irises, dreadlocks spread around her face in a chaotic array. Travis remembered what she'd said about being a fighter.

A glass cylinder was being pressed into his hand. He looked up to see Briggs giving him the drones with the doc's blood. The last piece to the puzzle of Titus-1A's location.

"I got this," Briggs said, winking.

Before he could even begin to doubt again, Travis put one arm under Camila's shoulder and pulled her along with him. He took off running, Camila limping but keeping up.

He heard some metal clang behind him, as though

Briggs were picking something out of the van's wreckage. "It's all right, fellas. Surprised to see me? You know—"

The rest became a blur, replaced by the sting of breath in his lungs. Never had Travis thought that something as simple as respiration would become difficult. Camila winced through the pain, and he tried not to pay too much attention to the trail of blood they were leaving on the pavement.

A dense fog crept around their feet as they ran, and Travis couldn't help smiling, knowing what Briggs must have done. *I hope he got away,* he thought.

The reflections in an alley-shop window caught his eye. Travis and Camila, almost fused together, limped along. And something else rippled behind them. Someone else.

They'd left Briggs alone, he realized.

"Travis," Camila whispered.

"I know. I saw," he said through gritted teeth and pinched lungs.

The men in black fatigues walked with a steady step, approximately three yards behind them.

Like predators toying with their meal.

Without needing to say a word, Travis and Camila picked up their pace, their footsteps uneven over the concrete. More reflections rippled, more men in black joined the first few . . . and then Travis heard the hum.

His lungs screamed at him now—and Camila's limp was becoming more pronounced.

Travis's heart contracted as he realized the inevitability of what was coming next. Unless Briggs jumped in to save the day with a magical van to replace his first, they were going to be taken.

You have twelve hours, Drone Handler J had told

them. And well, it had been well past twelve hours, hadn't it? These men weren't about to let them go.

"Travis," Camila whispered, her grip growing vice-like.

"Yeah?" he said back.

"Travis . . . I . . . I'm so sorry—"

Camila tried to go a few more steps, seemed to be reaching even for the next street, the end of their slab of sidewalk. But she didn't even make it that far.

Her bloody, twisted leg collapsed underneath her, and Travis lost his footing as she fell.

Concrete scraped his forehead, taking off the skin from his palms.

And within seconds, the men in fatigues had caught up to them, hundreds of little drones hovering about their heads, some of them still glowing with the cerulean dye from Briggs's bloodstream.

"That's it," one of them was saying, before touching a button on a headset Travis couldn't see. "Cowan? This is Drone Handler Q. Those interns from the control center? We got them."

The drone scourge attacked, and they blacked out. It was like dying by a thousand cuts, but this time it was dying by a thousand drone bites.

Part 4

ANATOMY OF THE ABDOMEN

> "Contained in the mosquito's abdomen, secreted away in ten body segments, the digestive, reproductive, and respiratory systems work around the clock to make sure the insect has enough oxygen to mate and continue to find fresh blood."
>
> —*Dr. Zane McCallister, PhD*

43

Travis didn't remember losing consciousness.

But now that he was awake, sitting on a folding chair, with a head that drooped and lolled like a bowling ball in a sack, the gap in his memory cracked open wide.

Those interns from the control center? We got them . . .

Travis . . . I'm so sorry . . .

This is Drone Handler Q . . .

Travis yanked the black hood off himself in a whoosh, and light pierced his eyes, a thousand needles stitching into his pupils. He squinted his eyes shut and tried to get ahold of himself, of his surroundings.

The muffled sound of feet walked away from him—like he was in the middle of a sealed room.

He forced his eyes open again. Frantically, Travis looked around, the bright light only worsening his headache.

He tried to piece a timeline together, a loose one full of assumptions. They'd gotten to them. He and Camila had ended up falling. Maybe they had given them a drug or some sort of sedative, hooded them in case they gained consciousness, then taken them . . . here . . . wherever on Earth that was.

Travis was in a box. A clear twelve-foot by twelve-foot plexiglass box. And that box was housed in a large warehouse.

No, that can't be right.

But it was.

And he wasn't alone.

Camila groaned awake beside him, head turning from side to side, and eyes shut tight against the light after she removed her hood. They weren't tied up in any way, likely, he thought, because that would have been redundant.

An enormous tube led out the top of the box, like a bare-bones HVAC system.

"It's going to be okay. We're going to be okay," Travis said over and over, his voice shaking.

He thought he caught Camila smiling, could almost hear her muttering, "Drama queen," under her breath.

They were trapped at the epicenter of what he could only think of as a warehouse—enormous, with enough room for a 747 to fly through one end and out through the other. All of it was lit with industrial lighting. A circle of these lights stood on stands, illuminating him and Camila inside the plexiglass as though they were on display in some macabre museum.

He pictured their bodies, his and Camila's, pinned to the plexiglass like the stag beetle was on the canvas, nothing more than a specimen for observation now. Worth more dead than alive.

His gut dropped.

His head pulsed . . . what had they given him and Camila? Just a sedative, or something more? Was it possible he was hallucinating this entire scenario? Maybe they'd been bitten all over by the drones, and he was only lying on the concrete outside some alley shop, with Camila next to him, just waiting to die?

No. He shook his head. *No.* This felt real. It had to be real. And until he had evidence to the contrary, he wouldn't allow himself to go down that rabbit hole. Those sorts of thoughts wouldn't keep him alive. And if this *was* real, he needed all of him present. He couldn't go forward second-guessing himself at every turn.

"How are we going to get out of this?" he whispered. "Any ideas?"

"They're probably listening in," Camila said.

"And you'd be right," a commanding voice boomeranged through the space.

While Travis had been taking in the enormous warehouse, a tall man had walked in, flanked and followed by dozens of men and women in black jumpsuits, black ball caps, walkie-talkies strapped to belts, and drone controllers on one shoulder. They each carried the furtive, serious look one might have in a naval academy.

Or, Travis thought, *a funeral. Our funeral.*

He immediately recognized the man leading them, in his navy-blue suit with white pinstripes and the diamond cuff links that only worsened Travis's headache with their star-point shimmer. The dimpled Windsor around his neck, and the thick sun-faded hair. Even under normal circumstances, Travis would have had a hard time ignoring the implied superiority—the power, if not arrogance it all exuded.

And he wondered if Cowan had always been like this, or if it had only happened after the whole "service before knowledge" stint at Titus Pharma. Had that been a lie?

"Of course we're listening," Cowan said, his voice smooth with a practiced control. "How do you squish a bug, Travis?"

He could only stare the tall man down from his muffled place in the plexiglass cube. Humiliation rose as a pink blush in his cheeks.

"You listen for the bug," Cowan said. "You listen really closely . . . *bzzz* . . . do you hear that? *Bzzz* . . . and then, when you have it in your sights—" He snapped his fingers, bending forward to look at them like they were swamp mosquitoes in a Mason jar.

The snap sound traveled with such cracking force against his headache that Travis winced, hating immediately how much power that seemed to give Cowan over them.

"You two viruses, you little bug interns, are interfering with our code—our conduct, our mission. We've listened for you. We've sighted you. We've got you. You're under my boot now, and all I have to do . . ." Cowan leaned forward again, and his toes came down on the concrete in a very deliberate squash motion. "Do you two understand?"

Travis bit his lip. Maybe if he played innocent—ignorant, even—that could buy them both some time. *Time before what? Torture? Incarceration? Framed and turned over to the cops? Killed—like Alec, like the doc?*

Calm down, man, geesh, Travis told himself.

He took a breath. Camila's eyes on him from the side gave him strength even though he felt exactly as Cowan was describing him—like that bug caught in a jar.

"What are you planning on doing?" he asked.

Cowan raised an eyebrow. "You mean Briggs didn't tell you?"

Travis shared a look with Camila, so deliberate and innocently played, it might as well have been planned beforehand.

He inwardly smiled at how in sync they were.

"No," Camila said. She shook her head. "He didn't tell us much of . . . well, anything, really. Did he, Travis?"

He shook his head.

Cowan smiled, then reached into his breast pocket, where he took out a vial no larger than a blood-sample tube. Inside, two dead copper drones clinked around against one another. Travis knew by the sinking feeling in his gut that these were the ones that contained the doc's blood.

"It's all about finding the location of Titus-1A," Cowan said. "It's going to be my avenging angel."

44

This time, the look Travis and Camila shared was genuine, thoroughly organic, and only fed the fire of Cowan's apparent enjoyment.

Travis squirmed in his seat; every muscle complained, asked to be stretched. The air thickened, putting pressure on his lungs. Almost unconsciously, he looked around the plexiglass cube, perhaps for some way out, some other access or airflow.

He only saw the HVAC vent above them.

What is that for? It doesn't seem to be pumping in fresh air.

No time to contemplate, not now. Camila was talking, taking up the conversation since Travis had been too momentarily distracted by the claustrophobia.

"'Avenging angel'?" she said. "Is that what this is all about?" Travis recognized the real incredulity dripping into her voice. "All of *this* because you're sore about losing your job?"

That did it. It was brief, but the built muscles around Cowan's jaw twitched.

You're on to something—keep going.

"I didn't lose anything," Cowan said. He chuckled, spreading his arms wide. "You're looking at the founder and CEO of Coro Innovations. These drones would never have seen the light of day if it weren't for me. I lost *nothing*."

Again, though, that twitch.

Travis didn't know yet, but it was worth prodding. So long as that didn't end with his waking up the hornet's nest.

"Then why all this fuss with the scientists?" he said. "Why go after all eight of them individually—why look for the virus at all?"

If not for your job, then . . . Travis waited for him to fill in the blank.

"Oh," Cowan said, "don't misunderstand. This *is* about avenging. But not over some silly *job* or title. It's so much more than that."

Camila paused, then said, "*Beneficium maior scientia est.*"

Cowan whipped his head toward her, apparently surprised that the words had come out of her mouth.

"Exactly." He chuckled, a smile widening all the way to his eyes. "*Spot on*! Thought those words actually meant something to people."

"They did," Camila said.

"They still do," Travis added, thinking of Briggs.

"No," Cowan said, "those words died a long time ago. Right when my scientists stumbled on something they shouldn't have. Titus-1A. Made the company scramble, panic. First thing they did was shove me off the boat—'cause I kept talking, you know, about how we were going to change the world." He bit his bottom lip. "We spent years developing the tech to *eradicate* disease in developing countries, where the traditional system was too broken to work. *Eradicate* it. The things we were going to do with that tech . . . But no, one little mistake and all trust was lost—think of all the lives we could have saved!"

"What mistake?" Travis asked carefully.

"The virus. Then the subsequent fear that we couldn't escape. The *fear*, you know, that was the real bug. Except, no one was around with the balls enough to squash it—before it ate its way into the board members' ears and ran around in their brains until they were mush, until all they cared about, all they could see, were dollar signs and bottom lines and not enough time.

"You wanna talk about viruses? They're the viruses. Titus Pharma. They're still kicking, did you know that? Working underground, no longer public. Don't want people to know about them. They're still out there, doing business, taking up space while the rest of us scramble. I've poured *everything* into what I got here with Coro—and Titus got it just because they were there first. Because they were afraid, they were cowards. Because they made one little oopsie and forgot the entire reason they existed. Tell me how that's possible? How you can forget it all just like that, just for the payout? They might be cowards. But I sure am not. You know that, both of you do."

"So that's it," Travis said, careful with his words—trailing that line between provoking and angering. "You spent, what, a fortune? Developing these drones? All so you could get the nanotags out of a handful of scientists and release, probably, a worldwide pandemic?"

He stopped, taking a breath—thinking that maybe he'd finally gone too far.

Briggs was right. This is about revenge and hatred.

He did have to give one thing to him, though. Avenging angel was the right phrase for that, melodrama and all.

"Don't worry," Cowan said, "we have the drone tech,

remember? It won't be long before the CDC gets wind of the virus they thought Titus had put to bed years ago. They'll shut everything down, take names, guns blazing, the whole bit. And when the world is sick and dying, and Titus has taken the blame for it, they'll finally see."

"See . . . what?" Camila said, practically whispering it.

"Finally see that tech like ours is necessary. These are real problems, and just because some of them have been going on longer than others doesn't mean they don't deserve to be fixed. This could finally make the world see. Knowledge isn't everything. Money shouldn't go to knowledge only—there are other pursuits just as worthy. These drones, what I've worked on, they'll finally do what they were meant to do."

The reality of Cowan's words was finally sinking in, beginning to make its home under Travis's skin, standing up the hairs on his forearms, breaking a sweat out on his forehead.

Cowan was going to release Titus-1A, then wait until the investigation proved it was Titus Pharma's fault. And after his framing of Travis and Camila, Travis didn't doubt he had the power to do just that, then come to the world's rescue with a new tech—one that could administer the vaccine to mass populations.

Then people would finally see the value in the invention he'd built his life on.

And he'd make a pile of cash while he's doing it.

The irony of that nearly tripped Travis. It almost made him gape with his mouth open at what he was hearing. But he figured pushing Cowan to the limit with insults would only do them harm at this point. He kept his mouth closed.

"And now, thanks to you two little bugs," Cowan

said like he was speaking to puppy dogs he wanted off his lawn, "I finally have the last piece."

He shook the blood-sample vial with the copper drones before tucking it back into his navy-blue pinstriped suit jacket. Travis thought he saw "Prada" stitched on the inside in shining red silk.

"But why us?" he asked. "You had the drones with McCallister's blood all along. I only caught a few of your precious little drones. Why kill us for those?" He pointed to the vial.

"That's the rub," Cowan said. "We recalled the five remaining drones to base just to find out you had captured the only ones that had extracted Zane's blood. I would say you lucked out."

Travis thought back. The way the drones flew. More sluggish than the others, heavier or something. That's why he was able to capture them. They *had* lucked out.

But now their good fortune had run out.

"Go ahead and open it up," Cowan said to the man closest to him, turning away from Travis and Camila. "And don't close it for anything."

The man, face riddled with acne-scar craters, stepped toward a small panel next to the plexiglass cube that Travis hadn't noticed before—just out of his line of sight behind a corner where two sheets of the glass met.

He entered a code, and the vent above Travis and Camila whirred to life like he'd just turned on the AC. Except . . .

Bzzz . . .

It wasn't cold air coming down that vent at all.

With an almost sympathetic look in their direction, Acne Scars turned and marched, with the rest of his comrades, out of the warehouse.

Camila was the first to scream.

45

So it was to be torture, then. Torture or death by—

Mosquitoes poured from the wide-open tube above their heads.

Travis couldn't believe how many. But something was off. He took a deep breath and realized what had pinged at the back of his mind—the thing that felt so odd about the swirling, darkening cloud around them.

These weren't drones. They weren't cold metal with hallucinogens, but a *true* scourge.

He'd been in situations with more insects than a lot of people. There'd been that one trip to Kenya his senior year of high school, and he remembered wading through an entire swamp full of mosquitoes as large as his thumb.

The over-the-counter bug spray didn't cut it. The only way to protect yourself was to go straight to the source—covering your arms, legs, neck, and face in a slick layer of DEET. You had to be careful, though, *because it could ruin your tech if you weren't careful. Camera lenses, plastic on phone cases . . .*

This information ran through his head quick as a beam of light, and yet it was entirely useless. Travis was certain not even DEET would be able to deter *this*.

Camila was screaming, swearing, reaching out for

his hand. He took it. They would do this together. They would find a way out of this *together*—even if he had no idea what that would look like.

They were, after all, in a sealed plexiglass box, trapped inside a larger box, with a scourge and a spotlight like an exhibit.

They weren't meant to get out of this.

All of this happened in a split second, and then the biting started.

First at the softest parts of his skin, close to pulsing, swollen arteries. Then his neck, his wrists, so many stinging proboscises at once that instead it felt like someone had dragged swaths of stinging nettle across his skin . . . slowly, torturously . . . leaving red blotches behind that burned so badly, all Travis could think about was how to peel his skin away with his own fingernails.

But someone was holding his wrists before he could reach for any of these places.

Travis squinted through the swarm to see Camila shaking her head. "Only makes it worse, remember?" she shouted.

He shook his head. What did that matter now? He almost wanted to laugh, but realized that the moment his mouth opened, several mosquitoes broke from the swarm and tried to wriggle between his lips. One stayed and bit his lip, which swelled and itched.

Just when Travis thought it might be bearable, that maybe if he breathed through his panic and slowed his heart rate, he could sit through this, bear the bites, he heard a *whoomp* pass through the vent, echoing through the tube.

A moment later, the scourge—already thousands of mosquitoes thick, enough that they all but covered the plexiglass, the floor, chairs, and their arms, legs, and necks—multiplied by what could only have been a factor of ten.

Camila swore as a fresh wave of thirsty, buzzing vampire insects dropped on them.

The panic in Travis swelled along with his bites, as though it had been his heart someone had dragged nettle over. It burned and beat, and he couldn't open his mouth, could barely breathe through his nose. Keeping the mosquitoes from his mouth was turning into an exercise of endurance.

And besides that, he couldn't *see* anything anymore.

Everything was an undulating, dynamic cloud of insects, of buzzing wings and heads and bulging abdomens pregnant with blood.

Where was Camila? Which way to a wall?

If it weren't for gravity, he wouldn't have even known where the floor was, because it was identical to the ceiling, thick with inches of mosquitoes.

Travis waded through them and found a solid sheet of plexiglass that he pounded on. Dozens of mosquitoes burst under his touch, covering his front and hands with pus and hot blood. It smeared the glass, the putrid stench of it strong enough that Travis gagged, and he was forced to cover his mouth with both hands to keep the mosquitoes from entering.

Somewhere behind him, over the buzzing he knew would haunt his dreams for years to come, Camila pounded on an opposite wall.

Their efforts were dull, and of course no one listened.

Need to find Camila.

If they were going to continue to endure this, or maybe even go down this way, Travis wanted to do it together, not on the other side, trying something they both knew wouldn't work in the end.

The mosquitoes squished under his shoes, their bodies a resistance like wading into the breakers of an ocean. And more continued to pour down the shoot.

Somehow, he found Camila's hand in all the chaos.

The sight of her through squinted eyes, covered from head to toe in the crawling things, like some Old Testament curse, sent a tremor through his body—and just as he realized the full gravity of what they were caught in, they started to crawl up his nose.

Their wings flapped in his nostrils, and they were biting, crawling, wriggling.

In a panic, Travis tried to blow them out, but that meant he had to take a breath with his mouth wide open.

And that was enough to let what felt like the entire scourge in.

They surged between his lips, nestling next to his gums, forcing their flapping way into the back of his throat.

Travis gagged and heaved. But even after he'd vomited into the sea of mosquitoes, still they came. They came like never before.

As the last dribble of bile fell from his lips, Travis reached up with a hand and scooped a handful of the twitching legs and bloody abdomens out of his mouth, spitting and heaving on the legs stuck between his teeth— the way they clung to his tonsils like a mistaken hair in food.

He looked around, eyes wide. *Camila. Camila, where are you?*

How had he lost her? Hadn't she just been here by him? Two seconds ago?

The fight-or-flight adrenaline took off at full speed in his body, and he was ready to break down the plexiglass cube with his bare hands if that's what he needed to do.

Travis heard her, coughing and gagging.

There, only a couple feet away. She was on the ground, her body twitching as she swallowed the scourge.

He could see her swollen eyes swiveling around—just the whites of them—looking for him.

Travis scooped one last bunch of mosquitoes from his own mouth, clamping it shut as though he'd wired it with irons, and swatted away as many as he could so he could breathe through his nose again, then kept one hand over both nose and mouth, like a mask, working hard to keep it sealed.

That pocket of air was enough.

He tried not to puke again as he swallowed down the remaining pieces of mosquito in his mouth.

He bent down, scooping a hand into Camila's mouth and swiping out a handful of mosquitoes, enough that air rushed into her chest.

But that didn't matter.

The mosquitoes only surged and covered her body entirely, barreling down her mouth again.

With his free hand, he tried to pull Camila up from the floor. But she'd become dead weight, unconscious, and he wouldn't be able to do anything at all if he took his hand off his own face.

Camila wasn't moving. He couldn't even see her anymore.

Travis looked around.

He did the only thing he could do—the *only thing* other than lying down next to her. Travis ran to the nearest plexiglass wall and pounded with everything he had.

His fists splattered blood.

46

The shadow appeared like a miracle. Or an omen. Travis had a hard time telling the difference now.

Seeing the outline of anyone at all was a relief after thinking they'd been left entirely alone to their torture. Whether this shadow had come to end it, even if momentarily, or save them from it, seeing it was, he concluded, miraculous.

Travis coughed on the pieces of insect still in his mouth, breathing the same bubble of air that had been trapped between his fingers for several minutes now.

His vision was beginning to blur, blue stars appearing in his periphery, closing in on him as the shadow grew closer.

He pounded on the plexiglass, until he couldn't tell anymore which blood was the mosquitoes' and which was his own bruised, cut-up fists.

His knuckles boiled, sore and stinging. Still he continued to pound. He opened his fists, smashing what felt like a hundred mosquitoes at once. He tried to wipe the guts away, the twitching wings, the eyes like fish eggs.

They smeared all over the glass, but Travis got enough cleared to see out, to try to make sense of the blur approaching the box in the harsh industrial lighting—the *only* thing keeping the scourge from blocking out all the light.

Travis's heart leapt when he saw who it was, too good to be true.

And maybe it was . . . he and Camila had chosen to trust him, but that didn't mean anything. What if he'd been working with Cowan this entire time?

He stayed behind, Travis thought, the split second of relief coin-flipping, landing on an electric dread and spreading through his whole body. *Stayed behind— maybe just* pretended *to fight for us.* But what if he'd led them toward Cowan on purpose?

The scourge swarmed.

Camila was suffocating.

So what did it matter? *What else are you going to do, Travis?*

"Briggs!" he yelled.

Tiny black blood-sucking insects latched on to the soft and hard palate of his mouth, clogging his trachea. He didn't even recognize his own voice. It came out in deep rattles.

Pounding on the glass. *"Briggs!"*

Briggs saw Travis. He *saw* him, Travis could see it in the shock on his grizzled face. He strode toward the glass in his Sorel boots, cargo shorts swinging with materials he must have salvaged from the van. He had on a white lab coat that said "Coro Innovations"—so stolen, or . . .

Please, Travis thought. *Please be on our side.*

He didn't know what he would do if Briggs just stood there in the Coro Innovations coat, if that graying beard turned up in a smile—or worse, indifference.

"Briggs . . ." Travis croaked.

He noticed the fog banking up against the plexiglass

from the outside, diffusing the light so it was one bright canvas—a Renaissance painter's idea of heaven.

Briggs knelt at the pole with the keypad, pulling a small screwdriver out of one of the cargo shorts pockets.

The biting had grown to a numb thrumming on every inch of Travis's exposed skin, the stinging-nettle sensation in harmony with the grinding, humming machine rising up as one all around him.

Briggs was fiddling some more, but Travis couldn't see what happened next, because mosquitoes covered the smudged section he'd exposed.

No.

He smudged more of the bugs away, only to see two guards approaching Briggs.

But the older scientist didn't waste any time on them. He stood in an instant and threw a fist to the first one, smashing his jaw. Blood spurted, and the first guard took a moment to recover while the other one grabbed Briggs from behind.

But Briggs shook him off, landing a blow to his stomach—once, twice, three times. He slumped to the floor, and then Briggs knocked the first one out completely.

The oxygen in his hand wasn't enough, not anymore.

"Briggs . . ." Travis breathed into his hand. Now he thought about it, he wondered if he could even hear him this muffled by insects and fingers and glass. "Please, Briggs . . ."

Mosquitoes covered his window again. He didn't have the strength to stop them.

His lungs burned for him to breathe in more, but he couldn't, wouldn't give up fighting just yet.

"Camila," he said. "What do I do? What do I do?"

A hiss ran through the box, like pressure released

on compressed air. And then white-hot smoke filled the entire space.

Travis squeezed his eyes against the burn, holding his breath. The smoke—not fog—inundated the mosquitoes like hot water. Immediately the scourge began dispersing, the density distributing through the warehouse.

Travis looked through watery eyes toward Briggs, who was standing up from his kneel at the key box, pocketing the screwdriver. Briggs's eyes widened, and Travis wondered exactly what he looked like that would give someone that expression.

He stumbled away.

Briggs pulled him into an embrace, a quick slap on his back a couple times, a bracing grasp on his shoulders.

"Where's Camila?" Briggs said when he pulled away.

Travis turned to the plexiglass cube that until ten seconds ago he thought he might die in. Thousands of mosquitoes billowed from the now-missing fourth wall, which had fallen to the floor. They ribboned up and away, following the law that most things do: High concentration to a low concentration . . . and at the epicenter of that concentration . . . Camila.

She lay motionless while a few stragglers still poked at her skin.

"Oh . . ." Briggs said. He swore under his breath.

Travis rushed back into the box, nearly slipping on the sludge his walking had caused inside.

He knelt down next to Camila, pulling her head up under his arm. "Talk to me," he said. "C'mon, Camila . . . talk to me."

Travis glanced at Briggs, who stood only a couple feet off, looking as though he did not know what to do.

"What do I—" Travis started.

But then Camila shifted. Her mouth opened, and she

vomited over her side. Mosquitoes and bile rushed over the plexiglass floor, almost indistinguishable from the bloody mess already covering the surface.

Travis sighed, the relieved, shaking sound grating his throat.

Camila coughed, closing her eyes and wincing against pain and stinging bites all over her. "Drama queen," she whispered.

47

It's okay. I can trust him. I can trust this man.

The proof of it was all around Travis. The smoke curling toward the ceiling was so thick and potent, it was as though they were in some sort of glade, noon sun shining through a fog and trying to burn it off. The humming of the mosquitoes flying in all directions only added to the illusion.

Alarms blared.

Two shapes by the plexiglass cube were stirring—the guards Briggs had knocked unconscious, though not for long, it seemed.

"Can you walk?" Travis asked Camila.

"I think so—just help me up?" Her voice sounded just as grated as his.

Travis gave her two arms, then let her lean on him as she had in the alley right before they'd been captured. He tried not to think about that too hard, instead focusing all his attention and energy on getting them *out*.

Flashing blue lights shot through the smoke.

"There's an exit just behind us," Briggs whispered. "An emergency one—doesn't matter 'cause the alarm's already going off. Go—go, go, go!"

Travis helped Camila out of the box, and both followed Briggs's lead to the other side of the enormous warehouse floor. The smoke, combined with the thousands of mosquitoes still swarming around them, seemed to work to their advantage.

But Travis knew it wouldn't last long.

Shapes swirled past them, but no one came to them directly. No one except . . . one face came out of the gloom, recognizable. It was Acne Scars, the one who'd sealed Travis and Camila into the plexiglass tank and released the scourge on them.

They froze, all three of them. Briggs brought his hands up, balling them into fists like he was ready to fight. Camila held on tighter to Travis.

The guard looked them over. Then he heard—or pretended to hear—something in the distance and charged off through the smoke.

Travis let out a breath, the sentiment shared by Camila and Briggs. And then they were running out the exit door, and *real* afternoon sunlight was blinding him. It was hot; the asphalt boiled off water into the air that clung to Travis, the reeking blood and insect guts and vomit surrounding him.

"All right," Briggs said, "this is all I got, so we're dealing with it, all right? Don't want to hear any complaints."

And with that, he manually unlocked the Geo Metro that had replaced the catering van.

Travis couldn't help grinning.

* * *

The car was stolen, that much was obvious from the hula-hooping, solar-powered bobblehead glued to the dash with what could only have been super glue. It didn't slide an inch, even with Briggs's erratic driving.

It was all Travis and Camila could do to keep their eyes open as the speeding turned to a consistent rumble, and it became clear they'd gotten away, at least for now.

Camila nestled her head against Travis's chest, and there he remained with her, their breathing syncing up as adrenaline burned away, and he was left only with the sting of his bites and an ache in his muscles that stretched through every limb. Swollen mosquito bites covered his exposed skin, including his forearms and the back of hands. His face felt swollen. Thousands of mosquito bites were sending signals to his brain, overwhelming him to the edges of insanity.

Need to scratch! But where? Everywhere?

Travis thought he saw Briggs shooting a look in their direction every few minutes, but if he noticed anything at all, he made no comment on the situation, save for a small smile.

When at last they pulled back into Briggs's mansion, it was with bleary eyes and legs like straw that Travis got out of the too-small car.

"Won't they be watching?" he asked, a little confused—because hadn't they decided only *hours* ago that this wasn't a good idea?

"Of course," Briggs said. Then he shrugged. "But they have all the coordinates now, so their priorities have shifted. Make no mistake, they'll come for us, but they're looking for the virus first."

Briggs shoved his key into the front door and opened it.

Travis agreed, but there was also a certain surrender to the futility of their situation, which he understood. Cowan and Coro Innovations had *drones*. They knew he and Camila had escaped, and they'd always been able to find them no matter where they were.

So, he thought, *might as well go to the place we know we can maybe find answers*—i.e., Briggs's lab.

He and Camila held engorged, stinging hands as they walked back into Briggs's house, following the sound of footfalls down the dark-paneled halls and into the ultra-modern hallway leading to the lab where they'd waited for the drones—which felt like a lifetime ago. It looked much the same to Travis.

Again, he had to tell himself that he could trust this old scientist. But there was an itch he couldn't shake that had nothing to do with the thousands of bites puffing up his swollen, aching skin. It was the thought that there was something Briggs still hadn't told him and Camila. What was it?

Travis took himself to the first-aid closet next to the entrance, took out two bottles of an antihistamine ointment, and began attending to Camila's swollen, raw, inflamed leg, as well as the cuts and bruises on his own skin. They took turns wiping the anti-inflammatory ointment on their exposed skin, wincing at the satisfying pain it caused as it sunk into the bites.

While they recovered, Travis saw Briggs logging into one of the sleek computers.

What now? he thought.

Before he could ask the question out loud, though, Briggs said, "Do you two remember when I said I have all the coordinates?"

"Yeah . . ." Travis said slowly.

He and Camila sat on one of the stools, both of them still working ointment onto spots.

She narrowed her eyes.

This is it. This was the turning point, Travis was sure

of it—where his intuitive itch that something was wrong turned into a mountainous problem that screwed them over.

He cleared his throat, waiting for what Briggs would say. He racked his mind. What had been special about last night—other than their giving Briggs the doc's nano-tags with the drones, nothing stood out . . . except . . .

"The phone call," Travis said.

Briggs nodded. "I didn't want to tell you earlier, didn't want to freak you out. And if it didn't pan out like I thought it would, I didn't want to unnecessarily get your hopes up either. I was . . . *worried* that they might have gotten to him, but . . ." He paused. "Looks like there was a mix-up."

"What do you mean?" Camila asked.

"Norcroff," Briggs said. "He was supposed to be in Antarctica, but he hopped on a plane the second he got my email a couple days ago. He's back home, here in Flor-ida. The other man on his team, it seems, was mistaken for him. Sadly, they found his body in an ice crevasse late last night."

Camila let out a sickened groan.

"I think Norcroff realized he wouldn't be able to waste any time," Briggs said. "He told me all that on the call."

He angled the monitor so they could see. The screen swirled. The image in the program focused and zoomed until only one thing remained on the screen aside from the two strings of numbers in the upper left-hand corner. The longitude and latitude made up of the eight scientists' blood, finally come together at . . .

A farmhouse.

48

The farmhouse looked to Travis to have been built in the early 1900s, painted daisy yellow on the outside, with white shingles and decorative gables—straight out of the sepia portion of *Wizard of Oz*. The view showed the farmhouse from above, like a satellite—or a drone—had taken the shot. The grass and cracked drive around it seemed almost blown out in the direct sunlight.

"Of all the secure places in the world," Camila started, "they chose—"

"Those secure places would be where exactly?" Travis asked, only half teasing.

"I don't know . . . the Pentagon? Area 51? MIT?"

"MIT?"

"They chose a *farmhouse*?"

"Hide it in plain sight," Briggs said. "No one would think to look there. And I'm sure Titus—or the government—owns it anyway, so who's snooping?"

"But I mean, it could easily be a top-secret bunker," Travis said. "You see that all the time, don't you? The farmhouse is just a cover. Bet it goes for miles underground."

"Easy there," Briggs said. "Let's not get too carried away. This isn't some crap comic."

"Isn't it?" Travis threw his glistening arms up.

Camila was smiling at him.

"What?" he asked.

She bit her lip, shaking her head. "*Conspiracy, man . . .*"

"Well," Briggs said, "hope you two are up for more disappointment, 'cause—"

"Oh shut up," Camila said, some of the hoarseness in her voice coming back in a croak. "If we're gonna do this, we might as well dream, right?"

Briggs and Travis both laughed.

"Where is Auntie Em's place, anyway?" she asked.

Briggs did some typing. The image zoomed out at an almost dizzying speed, and then a blue digital river snaked from the farmhouse to what Travis assumed was Briggs's home.

"Nine hundred miles away," Briggs said. "It's just inside the Georgia border."

Travis raised an eyebrow. "In that Geo?"

"No, not in that Geo," Briggs said, with a smirk that made the old guy seem so much younger. "The van wasn't the only vehicle I own, I'll have you know."

"*So*"—Camila picked up the bottle of ointment and squirted more into her palm—"what's the plan, guys?"

"The logistics are going to be the most difficult part to tackle." Briggs ran a hand through his gray beard. "Do we know if Cowan has the same information as us? Will he be prepared for us to come in? Is he watching right now and doesn't even need the rest of the coordinates? And *how* do we go in? Guns blazing, or smoke guns out? Or do we need to be covert?"

"And the virus," Camila said. "We don't know how it's being stored."

A terrible thought occurred to Travis. "What if we release it just by moving it?"

We haven't even really had to think of fail-safes before. He sat back, letting out a breath.

The enormity of what they were going to do—what they *had* to do, if they were going to stop this virus from being released, and more people from dying like Alec, Doc, and the other scientists—was settling over him. The clean air of the lab suddenly felt too thick and dirty to breathe.

"I think no matter what," Briggs said, "we can safely assume that Cowan and his people aren't going to be far behind us. We need to be prepared for some type of fight."

"What's his deal, anyway?" Camila said.

"Cowan's?"

"Yeah," Travis said, "I didn't exactly buy what he told us."

"What did he tell you?" Briggs asked.

Travis summarized as best he could everything Cowan had told him, including his reasons for releasing the virus—to blame it on Titus Pharma and bring them down, and then for his Coro Innovations drones to come to the rescue.

When he'd finished, Briggs huffed. "Well, that's because he left out probably the most significant part. It's not exactly something you tell when you're trying to be the big bad guy about to squash some bugs."

"What happened?" Camila asked.

"After the board voted him out of the company," Briggs said, "Cowan went a little crazy. He lost it . . . I mean, can you blame the guy? Everything he'd ever worked for, his entire life purpose, just ripped out from under him. The slogan was his idea, you know—and we scientists, we all voted on it. Thought it was such a clever idea. The board, not so much.

"The last I heard, he had become obsessed with something. His wife—she and I were good friends for a while—didn't know what it was. He was out every night. Was he getting himself drunk? Sleeping around? Was he doing drugs? We just didn't know, and no matter how crazy the explanation, we entertained it. He was erratic, gone all the time . . . and then months would go by without any contact.

"At one point, she finally called the cops on him, only to find out he'd been staying in a hotel just five miles away. His room was full of equipment, laptops, different phones. The police investigated it, and none of it was illegal, of course. But that's when she gave him the ultimatum. Either he quit what he was doing and come home, or she was going to leave him.

"That was the last time I spoke to her, years and years ago. She told me she was leaving him. I guess he was working on what would become Coro Innovations. Which . . ." He typed something and peered at the monitor. "Looks like it's about to go bankrupt."

"He really needs to be the cure to something," Camila said, "and fast, or his entire business collapses."

"I bet he's poured whatever fortune he made from Titus into this," Briggs said. "Which means the man is effectively broke."

"And he lost his entire family," Travis said. "Because of Titus Pharma."

"Or so he thinks," Briggs said.

"No, but that makes sense," Camila said. "He blames them for his family walking away from him—probably even for losing his money. None of that would have ever happened if Titus had just stuck to *his* plan and kept him as president. Then they could have delivered medicine with drones, saving millions!"

"Now, this seems personal," Travis said.

Briggs nodded. "Which really just means he's nearly unstoppable. People with a why that big aren't going to just stand down."

No, Travis thought. *He's going to fight with everything he has.* He'd told them as much when they were trapped in that plexiglass box in the warehouse.

Cowan fought for everything he had.

Except . . . that he *hadn't.* Had he?

Cowan thought he'd been the courageous one. The action taker, the one who didn't run away from his problems, instead running *to* them. To solve them.

But he'd failed to run toward perhaps his biggest problem of all. And it had led to his losing everything that ultimately mattered.

Titus isn't the only bad actor in this scenario, Travis thought sadly.

Obsession could be its own form of cowardice.

Camila was looking between Travis and Briggs, a big smile on her red face. "Right—so when are we driving down the Yellow Brick Road?"

49

"Holy—" Travis's mouth widened as the garage door finished opening.

He didn't know why he was surprised anymore by what Briggs continually pulled out of his sleeve, but now that he saw the fleet of vehicles, he thought he understood the mischievous, even juvenile, gleam in Briggs's eye when he'd asked about taking the Geo all nine hundred miles into Georgia.

Because *of course* they wouldn't need to.

Lined up just as neatly as the utility vehicles had been in the GMMC, in perfect parallel diagonals, was a fleet of . . . well, *everything.*

There was another of the enormous catering vans. A Rolls Royce Phantom seemed to size Travis up and down, as though asking if he knew exactly what he was in the presence of. There was a black Ferrari, a Porsche SUV, a Mercedes-Maybach, and at the very end, a Bentley.

Travis hid his laugh with a cough, which was realistic, given how sore his throat still was from all the hacking and vomiting he'd done earlier. "So I'm assuming we're taking the van?"

"Are you crazy?" Briggs said. "If we get into another chase like that, we won't stand a chance in that brick."

Briggs approached the wall, where Travis saw a thick glass cabinet with a keypad. He entered the pin and took out a fob from one of the many hooks. The lights to the Porsche flashed.

"It's a hybrid," Briggs said, "so it gets better gas mileage. The Royce would suck my pocket dry."

"And that's the only reason?" Travis asked, incredulous.

Briggs shrugged. "Running out of gas in a chase is a bad idea. There's also the maneuvering thing. She can make some wicked sharp turns, so if we need to, we'll just—" He mimicked flipping the wheel around and made a whistling sound.

Travis shook his head. That would've been an accurate representation of Briggs's driving ability with or without a flock of black SUVs on their tail. "Porsche it is," he said.

*　*　*

Camila met them in the garage a few minutes later. Travis could smell the ointment on her, a gentle mix of mint and aloe. He felt tired from the massive histamine reaction from all the bites, but that was nothing compared to how bad they looked. Red and swollen. Camila whooped with excitement when she heard they would be taking the Porsche Cayenne SUV.

The temperature outside dropped significantly as storm clouds rolled overhead. The humidity still made the work sticky, but it was at least bearable now that they had cloud cover and a low drizzle to keep the heat down. A breeze blew into the garage as Briggs barked orders out to Travis, who in turn would roll his eyes at Camila, and then the cycle would start all over again.

But eventually they had packed the Porsche with all sorts of protective clothing—from poncho nets they could wear against mosquitoes to hats, gloves, smoking backpacks, and a flamethrower. Then Briggs had them change into Kevlar suits, each with holsters for a pistol and two magazines.

"Are you sure?" Travis asked, feeling the weight of the pistol against his left thigh.

"You ever shot one of those before?" Briggs caught Camila's eye, and she nodded.

"I got it," she said.

"Got what?" Travis asked, confused.

Briggs had already gone off to tie down the rest of their equipment, and Camila stood directly in front of Travis. *I've never seen her so serious*, he thought.

She didn't look him in the eye as she asked for the pistol. Travis handed it over. The gust of wind from the open garage door smelled like breaking waves, like seafood and coral. It was a strong enough gust to blow her heavy dreadlocks behind her shoulders. He watched a bead of sweat roll down Camila's temple.

"What?" she asked, playing with one of the mechanisms on the pistol.

"You're beautiful," Travis said.

She scoffed.

"I'm serious," he whispered.

"I know you are," she said, finally looking up. "That's the whole problem. You sound ridiculous."

They locked eyes, and there was nothing ridiculous, Travis thought, about the way she was looking at him. He fought the urge to wipe the smudges from his glasses, the itch to push away his unruly hair. He knew how ridiculous he must look, but she didn't seem to care.

He wanted to do it now, before they were off again.

The car ride would be long, but there wouldn't be any privacy. So if he felt this way *now* . . . if he could say it *now* . . . well, then he had to, didn't he?

Camila spoke before he could push the words out of his mouth. She held out the gun, showing Travis its length.

"So this is the handle, the trigger, the grip. The safety's here." She showed him the switch behind the trigger. The long side would be red if it was ready to shoot. "And that's probably the most important thing you need to know. Keeps you safe, me safe, Briggs safe. But, you know, mostly you."

"Right."

Briggs slammed a door shut somewhere else in the garage. Other than that signal to his presence, however, Travis felt entirely alone with her.

She had caught the way he was looking at her again. But she took a breath and continued where she left off. He watched her hands grip the steel, moving back and forth across it to get the clip undone. She held up the rectangular magazine, showing him how to disconnect it and how to put a new one in.

"Got it?"

"Sure."

"You *sure* you're sure? You don't sound—"

Travis acted on instinct. He stepped forward and wrapped his arms around her back.

And then, with the hard, metal pistol pressed between them, Travis pressed his lips to hers. She was soft, salty, and she didn't hesitate to kiss him back.

He broke away first, because he was beginning to breathe heavy, and he needed to *say it*, before Briggs returned.

"I love you," Travis said.

She searched his eyes, still smiling from their kiss. "You're just saying that because we're about to die," she said, looking away.

Are we? Are we about to die?

Did it matter?

"No," Travis said. "I'm not."

"Kids!" Briggs bellowed.

Camila stood on her tiptoes and gave Travis one last kiss. It lingered and seemed to hover there like a butterfly even after she'd backed away.

"We better go," she said. "It's a matter of cat and mouse and who can get there first."

50

Night fell. Fast food sat like a rock in Travis's stomach. He'd tried to catch Camila's expression once every half hour or so, and sometimes she met his eyes and gave him a smile. Other times she was asleep, on his shoulder or against the opposite window. He'd almost felt bad leaving Briggs up front by himself, but the strange man seemed unbothered.

He was glad he'd said what he did to Camila, glad to understand his feelings at last, and be able to express them. But her reaction . . . *Well, she didn't reject you,* he told himself. She hadn't exactly reciprocated, either. What she *had* said—*you're just saying that because we're about to die*—made it seem like she didn't believe him.

Was that it? Did Travis have to make her believe he was telling the truth? And would he even have the time for that?

He shifted, perpetually uncomfortable now. There was so much he wanted to discuss with Camila, and more than anything, he just needed to get out of this super-duper luxury motor vehicle and find the virus.

* * *

Travis and Camila were taking turns reapplying the mint-and-aloe antihistamine to each other's hard-to-reach patches of skin when the dirt road Briggs had taken them down ended abruptly.

No house stood anywhere near them, as far as they could tell, but there was a chain-link fence with curled barbed wire on the top. Blue flashing lights stretched for miles in either direction. Electric.

Camila let out a whoop. "Conspiracy," she said. "What I've been friggin' saying from the beginning. *Anything* could be in there."

"Okay," Briggs said, an unusual terseness in his voice, "you two just sit tight. I'll be right back."

It took only ten seconds after he'd left for Travis to disobey the order. Camila followed after him, and together they approached the fence with Briggs. This far away from the ocean, the only smell Travis could pick up was damp cottonwood, mixed with the sickly-sweet stench of manure. Crickets chirped under their feet. An owl hooted somewhere off in a darkness that was so complete, Travis felt like he could reach out and bunch the pitch black between his hands.

Briggs marched to the trunk, opened it, and began rummaging through one of his duffels.

"What can we do?" Travis asked. He actually *shivered*. Was it nerves?

"Here." Briggs handed him a set of wire cutters.

"And if there's an alarm and cameras?" he asked.

"Of course there are," Briggs said, voice picking up as though he were losing his patience. "That just means we're on a timer the second we drive through that fence. But we're on a timer anyway, remember? Cowan's had his eyes on us from the beginning, too. We need to do everything we can to stop him."

The stress in his voice wore off onto Travis. Briggs was right. The car ride, and his *personal* thoughts, had made him lethargic and slightly complacent. Now, urgency swept over him all at once.

He set to work cutting the links of the fence, Camila next to him with her own pair. With each cut, sparks jumped out, threatening to land on their hands. The wire resisted, but several bone-cracking snaps later, Travis had made his way up most of the length, and so had Camila. He stood on his tiptoes, getting through the barbed wire, glad for the rubber on the handle to keep him insulated from any residual electricity that might be flowing through it from the electrical portion of the fence.

"That's good enough," Briggs said.

Travis handed him the wire cutters, so did Camila, and then they each got back into the Porsche while Briggs tied a thick metal chain from the cut portion of fence to the grille attachment on the front of his luxury SUV.

Then he got in and revved the engine into reverse.

Tires spewed mud, covering most of Travis's view out the side window, and they started to fishtail.

"C'mon . . ." Briggs was murmuring. "C'mon, you little—"

Travis didn't hear whatever came out of his mouth next, because the wire snapped, flying over their heads and scraping along the windshield. His heart jumped, but he tried to keep his cool as the Porsche came to a stop.

Briggs whooped, then got out to remove the chain.

Once back inside, he put his hands on the wheel in the ten and two o'clock positions, something that seemed awkward with his burly, callused hands. He was far too reckless of a driver to even *appear* this normal.

But Travis thought he understood what was happening in his mind.

This was it. They could turn back still, even drive the full twelve hours back to the house and the lab and home—whatever might be left of it. But the second he put the car into drive, they would cross the point of no return.

Briggs shifted gears, and the Porsche punched forward.

51

The road continued as it had before, seemingly into oblivion, as far forward as the fence had been long. It was hard to make out with the lights of the luxury vehicle off. They used the moon as their only source of light. Cornstalks cast eerie shadows across the road from fields on either side.

A flock of quail fluttered to flight on their left at the approaching car. Grasshoppers smashed into the windshield, smearing over the glass as Briggs wiped them away with fluid and rubber, making Travis feel queasy and out of breath. The plexiglass box wasn't far from his mind.

And then there were the mosquitoes.

They mixed with the gnats and grasshoppers and occasional moths that got stuck between the wipers. They were the hardest to spot because they blended in so well with the weeds, hiding between the ropy fronds of a wild willow, or swarming away from a patch of reed and bluegrass. Every one of them put Travis's teeth on edge.

The farmhouse seemed to sprout from the soil, a quaint yellow building amidst a backdrop of velvety-black canvas. Briggs pulled up next to it slowly, killing the engine the second it was in park.

"What now?" Travis asked.

"We go on foot," Briggs replied.

"Okay, sounds good."

"First things first," Briggs said. "I'm going to get our supplies ready. I'm going to see if I can't find some blueprints for this place."

Behind them, the trunk opened. Hot night air filled the stuffy cab; the leather seats felt sticky.

Briggs tapped on the window.

Travis jumped.

Briggs pointed to some sort of thin tablet. "Come on! We don't have a lot of time left!"

Travis swatted the mosquitoes away from his face, nearly gagging when a moth got too close to his mouth, attracted by the bright white lights shining from the Porsche. "Don't get bitten," he said.

"Seriously, Sherlock?" Briggs replied.

But Travis could hear the smile through the sarcasm. The Kevlar and protective clothing they wore helped to ease his panic about going out into the night, which seemed to belong to mosquitoes.

With the light off, though, the insects calmed somewhat.

He could only see the silhouette of the farmhouse now.

And as the flare of the car lights melted from his vision, the stars came into focus.

So much space, he thought. And yet he couldn't make out most of it. If he thought about it, there could be anything beyond the farmhouse. *Is that a tent?* He squinted, but it didn't make the image any clearer.

Anything at all.

Briggs waved the thin tablet in front of them; it seemed to be a backlit ink display, like an e-reader. Made sense, Travis thought. Long battery life, fairly resilient.

"Blueprints!" Briggs said.

"Where'd you find those?" Travis asked.

"Hacked in," he said, turning the tablet on and pulling up one of the first files.

Camila swore. "I was right," she said. "Oh my—I was *right*."

The blueprints showed that the farmhouse was indeed just a cover. The reality of the space lay underground, a labyrinth of connected tunnels and wings, designated with names that denoted a series of labs.

As nervous as Travis *knew* she must be—because she was just as nervous as he was, right?—Camila seemed at odds with that emotion as she excitedly jumped up and down.

"What'd I tell you?" she hissed.

"So we just need to figure out how to get inside," Travis said. "Maybe there's another fuse box or something."

His mind spun with the idea of secret compartments, codes, and doors that weren't doors at all, but keys to open another passage.

"I was thinking we'd try the front door," Briggs said.

And Travis was about to agree with him, walk up those wooden steps, and jiggle the farmhouse's handle, when an enormous siren filled his ears.

He grimaced, covering his ears with his palms, wondering just how many decibels were required to make the human eardrum bleed. He was certain it was close to *this*. But then a voice came on over the siren, and Travis's gut did a somersault and a half.

"Shift three commencing," the voice said. It was robotic, monotonous, and somehow overtly . . . *kind*? "Drone Handlers K through O, please report to the main loading dock. Energy conservation off. Shift lights commencing in five . . . four . . . three . . . two . . . one."

A flash. White and all at once like a meteor strike.

Travis watched through the fan of his fingers as the farmhouse became the foreground of a much larger scene, enormous industrial lights like the ones at the warehouse humming into existence.

And they weren't the only things in the airspace that were humming.

Coro's drones flitted around the lights and equipment and vehicles in a series of infinity loops, figure eights of buzzing, electrified copper.

An entire operation veritably surrounded the farmhouse, complete with a series of insect-like flying machines parked in a neat row next to the biggest canvas tent Travis had ever seen in the field. A flag flew above it in enormous corporate lettering: "CORO INNOVATIONS."

Part 5

THE PHYSICS OF FLIGHT

"Unlike other insects and fowl, which fly by forcing air downward, mosquitoes must create negative air pressure by rotating their wings at each upstroke and downstroke. This in turn creates 'wake capture'—the unique ability to harness energy from their previous beat and supplement lift."

—*Dr. Zane McCallister, PhD*

52

Travis heard Briggs swear, and the old scientist put out an arm as though he could shield them from being seen. The tablet still glowed with the blueprints. Somehow, Travis thought blueprints didn't matter nearly so much now.

Cowan got here before us. Norcroff must have followed Briggs's advice and sent Cowan a blood sample. The realization rolled through his body, until it reached his toes and zinged back up again. *Our entire plan is moot. Geesh.*

"Inside the house," Briggs whispered. "Now."

For a moment, Travis couldn't move. His eyes tracked every movement behind the farmhouse, every flit of a light, every shuffle of someone in a dark suit with a drone controller on their shoulder. And the *drones*—his eyes couldn't even track them all. They swarmed and circled about, many of them flying into a single white tent, where . . .

An idea was forming in his mind.

"Travis," Camila whispered.

He looked to find that she was practically pleading with him to move. Briggs had already walked up to the dark farmhouse, picking the lock.

How do we even know it's empty? The dark windows

meant nothing if the surprise they'd just gotten was any proof. But where else were they going to try to hide and figure this out?

Shaking from nerves now, Travis took Camila's hand and began to walk forward. His glasses fogged up from the moisture in the air; he'd need to wipe those off later.

In his peripheral, Travis noted a yellow biplane, designed for crop dusting, parked on the side of the farmhouse. And behind that were two helicopters with "Coro Innovations" stenciled onto the side of them.

Just before he passed onto the porch of the farmhouse, its dandelion walls blocking his view, Travis thought he saw small boxes marked "Canisters" being stacked on top of one another and loaded into the back. *What's in—*

But Briggs had already opened the door, and Camila dragged him through it.

* * *

Travis was guided by the odd lights that fanned in through the blinds and curtains. Light switches mocked them from the walls, but he stayed away from them—and it seemed they'd become venomous snakes to both Camila and Briggs, who wouldn't so much as lean against the wall just in case they flipped one on and exposed themselves.

At any rate, if there were drone handlers or other Coro Innovations employees in the farmhouse-that-was-never-a-farmhouse, they didn't show themselves.

Sitting around the square kitchen table, blinds closed next to them and chrysanthemum-patterned curtains drawn, Travis knew that Camila and Briggs were listening for the same thing as he was: the spinning humdrum of a drone. The three of them were watching, and waiting to see what would happen next.

Travis's gut twisted. How were they supposed to beat someone who was so many steps ahead? *What else have they planned that we're just flat ignorant of?*

He nearly jumped out of his skin as a pulse of blue industrial light shot through the chrysanthemum curtains and landed on them, sweeping from side to side.

He held his breath, and so did Briggs and Camila.

"I saw them loading something into that plane," Travis whispered, and he told them about the canisters he'd seen.

Based on what Cowan had told them, it was obvious what these contained.

"They've already gotten to the virus," Camila said.

"And I bet those canisters are full of drones," Travis said. "They're going to dispatch them."

"Which means," Briggs said, "if we're going to do anything to stop this, we need to make sure that plane doesn't get off the ground."

He cocked an eyebrow at Travis, then at Camila, as if to say, "You sure you two are up to the challenge?"

But Travis didn't have the chance to respond.

"I have an idea to start dismantling the operation," Briggs said. "Throw a wrench into this whole thing."

Someone walked toward them. Voices reverberated through the dusty glass windowpane. Travis closed his eyes and breathed in the dust-tinged air. *They're going to find the Porsche, and everything in it.*

"We need to take this to the basement," Briggs said. He gestured to the blueprints still lit up on the e-ink tablet on the table, then picked it up. "There's a way out into the field from there, a false cellar door we should be able to get out of."

More sweeping lights through the front windows.

Travis and Camila didn't need more convincing than

that. They stood and followed Briggs to a pantry door. They stepped inside and closed the door behind them just as they heard steps creaking on the porch and the hinges of the front door.

Briggs pushed on the shelves in front of them, exposing the dark hallway behind. He went first, then Camila, then Travis, who closed the hidden door behind them, silencing the entire world and bringing them into full dark.

Behind them, people flooded the dandelion farmhouse.

53

Briggs kept the tablet lit in front of him, the glow on his face bouncing forward into the concrete tunnel. And it *was* all concrete, miles and miles of it slowly sloping downward like a mine shaft. Wires ran above their heads—red, blue, green, yellow—clumped together with zip ties and going who knew where.

Travis finally took off his glasses and wiped the fog from them. His hair felt greasy, and sweat collected on his upper lip. He'd sprouted scruff that normally he would have shaved off days ago, and it scratched and prickled against his cheeks. For not the first time—but probably the last—Travis thought about what it might be like just to turn around, drive out the way they came. Live to fight another day.

But that wasn't how this worked, and he knew that now. Camila had helped him see that, and that thought made his chest swell with emotion.

There would be no hoping to fight another day. It was never going to be perfect, and nothing was ever going to go exactly according to plan. Which meant the only option for him, for anyone, was to put one foot in front of the other. To walk the path he was on *now* and find a way to make it work. He couldn't control the outcomes, couldn't control everything that happened to him, but he could control how he reacted. He could fight today. Right now.

Travis thought of Dr. Tabby, throat slit from cutting shears, a hand still reaching forward as though he could help her, when there was nothing he could do. He thought of the limp hand falling out from under a white sheet, Dr. Swain, pieces of her splattered across urban concrete. He thought of Alec, his body sprawled over his own couch, a place that should have been his safe haven. And finally, he thought of the doc. His body burned and simmering from the inside out, bite marks all over him—a sign Travis had come to recognize as more ominous than any gunshot wound.

And then he thought of the tens of thousands of people who would end up dying horrible, painful deaths in ICU beds because of Cowan's inability to face his own reality. No, Travis would not be that coward. And these deaths were going to stop. *Now.*

He clenched his fists and put one foot in front of the other.

The long concrete hall opened up, the wires splitting off and *up* toward a ceiling that towered—and he could see that because the fluorescents flickered to life the moment they entered the room.

He gasped.

It was as though he'd stepped onto the set of his favorite science-fiction movie or, more to the point, his dream lab.

Chrome and stainless steel glittered all around, with tech so advanced, he'd never even seen it before. He guessed that one of them was a microscope, another a sort of splicer. All of it stood dusty and unused. As though they had spent several years studying the virus at first, but then had abandoned ship and left the property up to bureaucracy to handle.

And we all know how well that works.

Briggs was consulting the e-ink tablet again, pointing to a small fire-escape-type ladder at the far end of the room that led to a square opening in the ceiling with a twist handle. The opening was on the side of the house by the copters and plane.

He set the tablet down and began rummaging through the dusty lab. "We need to protect what's left here and use it as evidence against Cowan."

It was clear where the virus had been stored, because those areas had been wiped clean as things had been moved. Travis even noticed mud on the rungs leading up to the manhole door in the ceiling. Cowan's cronies had clearly taken the virus from here and brought it to the surface for distribution.

He fondled the gun still strapped to his side, going over what Camila had told him about it—where the safety was, how to change out a magazine . . .

Briggs shuffled back to one of the tables with three bulky metallic things that clanked together, the sound ricocheting off the concrete walls like it was a main play in a game of racquetball. Two midsized tanks were labeled with the periodic table sign for hydrogen. And there was a blowtorch the size of Travis's forearm.

"Oh," Camila said. "This'll be fun."

"Protection," Briggs said. "You never know what we'll need to use these for."

"And what about getting caught?" Travis asked.

Briggs looked at him as though he'd missed the most obvious thing in the world. He tapped his backpack. "Fog 'em out, Travis. Geez. Keep up."

The friendly dig was enough to alleviate some of his nerves. He nodded. "What are we waiting for, then?"

Camila found a canvas bag for the hydrogen canisters and the blowtorch. She strapped them to her back, and then Travis got in line after her and Briggs, who fiddled with some of the dials on his pack and did a test spurt of smoke that floated through the room, almost viscous in the way it wound down to the floor and curled toward the stools and tables.

"Ready?" Briggs asked.

Travis nodded.

"Yup," Camila said.

And then Briggs started up the ladder, Camila next, then Travis. The metal burned cold under his palms, but he worked his way up anyway, slowly, step by step, breathing through the nerves coursing through his veins.

Briggs paused at the trapdoor.

Travis tried not to look down. Vertigo swam in his belly; he thought he was going to be sick any second now.

But then a grinding, metallic *whirr* sped down toward him, and he looked up to see the trapdoor pop open. Blue light spilled in.

And Briggs shot smoke up into the night air.

54

Fog billowed from the opening, draping down toward Travis, even concealing Camila from him for a moment.

He only knew the white fog, smelling gently of rain and fresh things, before the grinding of one of the Coro Innovations copters caught his attention and he remembered to move.

Even the fear of heights disappeared as his heart rate sped up, forcing him to *move* if he wanted any of this to work.

Travis wasn't thinking anymore. He was acting.

Camila grunted as she lifted herself up and out of the ground. He followed suit, looking around in the billowing clouds to get his bearings.

A spike of panic shot through him. He couldn't see *anything*—not Briggs or Camila or any of the thugs or scientists.

Then he made out a shape not too far away from him, as Cowan's people began to shuffle around him, barking orders to one another.

"Get the boss on the phone—something's going down!"

Travis did his best to shut them out. With any luck,

they would mistake his shape for any one of them. That was the point, after all.

The enormous shadow began to solidify the closer he got to it, feet pounding through silt and pebbles and fallen cornstalk leaves, silky and slick. The shadow took on angles and lines.

Fog hadn't yet reached this far, and Travis found himself stepping into clear air, the fog coming from behind like an ethereal cloak. He stood in front of a tent made of clear plastic, flapping slightly in the small breeze the fog's pressure created.

Inside, three people were working on a makeshift assembly line. Three people he recognized. The confirmation that they had been with Cowan—even though Travis *knew* before that they had to have been, though he couldn't have pinpointed it at the time—filled him up with rage.

These people—Biceps, Redhead, and Wristwatch, the non-EMTs—had stood over the doc and knew exactly what had happened. Had known because they were drone handlers.

They were Dr. McCallister's killers.

And they were prepping Cowan's avenging angel from inside their makeshift lab.

Biceps carried a set of white canisters from the more open end of the tent through a double airlock, and into a much more sterile end, where Redhead and Wristwatch waited for the batch.

Travis held his breath. They hadn't seen him, not yet. He kept eyeing those lab coats, those pristine white coats that said someone had made something of themselves. Here they were being used to do harm rather than good.

They don't deserve them, he thought.

He'd wanted one of those coats all his life. And he was

still going to get one, he reminded himself, after this was all over, after they'd done the right thing and gone back to normal life—but maybe that time could come a little early.

It could only help, right? And as long as he was turned around . . .

Travis crept closer. Most everyone except for these three seemed concerned with the fog and distraction occurring behind him, so he stepped toward the tent, locking eyes with the process the three were doing, while also eyeing the lab coats.

The assembly line was a conveyer of drones, each held up on small pegs, like one might use a needle to pin a real insect to canvas. Biceps set the canisters at the end of the line and unscrewed one, while Wristwatch injected a purple substance into a hypodermic needle. He then approached one of the drones and injected it in an access point to one of the liquid sacks in the abdomen.

Evidence! Briggs said to find evidence!

Oh geesh, he'd been right. It appeared they were putting Titus-1A into the drones, so instead of a hallucinogen when someone was bit, they'd get sick. Just like the West Nile virus and malaria-carrying organic mosquitoes.

Even more reason he couldn't let those copters out of here.

The number of drones Travis saw was dizzying. And still, Wristwatch continued to inject them, while Redhead dropped them carefully into canisters, which must have connected with the tech wirelessly, because the moment they dropped in, a light turned on, flashing green.

All they might have to do was set a canister down in a city park and the tech would do its job by itself. Each of the drone handlers had controls at their shoulders; at the touch of a button, a hundred people could be dead.

Travis had seen enough.

He moved forward to get the lab coat, maybe a good disguise, and then he would be on his way back to find Camila and Briggs, hopefully unquestioned.

Biceps, Wristwatch, and Redhead all stayed focused on the conveyer belt.

Travis put his hand between the plastic at the front of the tent, opening it enough to step through. His heart pounded so hard, it hurt his lungs, and he found himself holding his breath—which only made things worse, so then he tried to breathe quietly, in through his nose, out through his mouth.

Every inhale made too much noise, almost stopped him from overhearing their conversation, about what was going on, and about who had and hadn't died.

Need to get evidence.

These three—they weren't like the acne-scarred man who'd pulled the trigger on the mosquito torture on him and Camila in the warehouse. These three didn't care. These three actively believed in everything Cowan was doing and would do anything to make sure that he succeeded.

Travis felt in his pocket. He slipped his phone from his jeans, held it up, swiped to the camera app, and took a picture of the operation.

I've got the evidence.

That filled him enough to take one last courageous step, put his hand on the lapel of the nearest white lab coat, and—

He froze.

Biceps had seen him.

There was no waiting for recognition, to see if the guy even remembered him. It was clear by his frown that he did. Travis watched the muscle in his jaw twitch, saw his arms flexing and unflexing as he put down the canister.

No turning back now.

Travis grabbed the lab coat and rushed out of the plastic tent, Biceps running close on his heels.

55

Travis shrugged into the lab coat, the newness of it on his shoulders spurring him on. He felt like he could do anything in one of these.

The white flaps billowed behind him as he sprinted away from the tent, arms pumping, He filled his lungs with air, though it was splotchy with fog.

He heard Biceps running behind him and felt a degree of satisfaction when the large man grunted in frustration trying to keep up with Travis's lighter frame.

Cornstalks smacked into his face, scratching at the already sore spots on his neck and cheek where he'd been bitten so many times by the scourge in the warehouse. He was thankful the Kevlar suit protected the rest of his itchy body.

The stalks closed in around him, forcing him to slow down and squeeze between the lengths, the sticky leaves becoming razor sharp on his forearms and fingertips. He brushed them away as best as he could.

And the ground—he stepped directly into an irrigation trench, ankle-deep in muck and stagnant water. Mosquitoes buzzed around him, real ones, and Travis had to close his eyes against the memory of that plexiglass box.

You're not trapped this time, Travis. You're not trapped, just move!

But the cornstalks pressed into him from all sides, and he felt almost more trapped here than he had in the warehouse.

It's just a few little bugs. Insects. Entomology.

The tall corn grass rustled behind him. "Come out, little bug," Biceps mocked, voice deep and dripping with arrogance.

Travis fought the panic in his chest as he tried to pull his foot from the irrigation ditch. He got it free and managed to break enough stalks to keep moving forward.

Mosquitoes swarmed about his head, his hands, but he told himself, *as long as you keep moving, they won't be able to get to you as easy.*

The air was sweet in a way that only corn could create. The earthborn sugar swirled through the mud and humid air like cotton candy. In Travis's panic, the scent only served to make him more nauseated.

Stuck again, mud, stalks around him.

He took a deep breath. *You can do this.*

He tugged his lab coat tighter around him and pulled the collar high. *Think about something else. Think about something else and just move.*

Sir Vincent Wigglesworth, Travis thought, shoving a stalk away from his face and hearing it crack back as he turned sharply. *He wrote . . . he wrote* Insect Physiology. *We wouldn't know anything about organ systems of insects without it. Vincent Wigglesworth.*

Carol. Camila wanted me to call the truck Carol, but I insisted. Why?

Because this is what you do, Travis.

Even though he was scared of these mosquitoes now and was paranoid about the bites on his neck, he'd never stop being interested. Because he, Travis Grant, "did" insects—even though he'd promised Camila never to use that term again.

These mosquitoes were *not* going to best him.

He swatted them away with his hands and practically screamed as he moved his way forward through the cornfield, turning his head about him to see where he needed to head.

But an enormous muscled shape was closing in after him; Travis could see the biceps rippling as he pushed away the corn. In the industrial flash of light that shot through the cornfield from the base camp, he made out the sneer.

He faced forward and continued to pump his arms, angling away so he was making a circular path back toward the flashing lights and the fog beginning to creep along the muddy, irrigated field.

He's not going to stop, Travis realized.

If he was going to make it, Biceps needed to stop following him. And there was no way Travis could beat him in a physical altercation.

His face flushed as he remembered the gun at his waist.

Still pushing forward, scraped along by the leaves' edges, Travis flipped his head around to get his bearings. Biceps was just feet away from him, angrily pushing away the stalks as he made his way forward.

Travis weaved in and out, breath turning heavy as he picked up the pace. The cornstalks were thinning now, and the fog moved in and over his head in earnest, concealing everything but what was directly in front of him.

The cornstalks became shadows of ears and hands and limbs reaching up into a sky that had become a blanket of pulsing, flashing white. He heard shuffling and a siren wailing up ahead.

Crush, fall, crack.

Travis whipped around, pulling the gun from the holster. He checked to make sure the safety was off, that the red paint shone at him, fluorescent and bright by the clip. Then he raised the gun with both hands like Camila had shown him and checked the sighting and made sure the little dot was on the shadow's leg.

"This is for Doc," Travis said. Then he took a breath and squeezed the trigger.

The kickback ricocheted up his arms, pulsing in his shoulders. It also meant that his aim hadn't been where he thought it was. Shaking, Travis dropped the gun, which splattered as it hit the mud. There was no time to reach for it.

As Biceps emerged from the fog, Travis noticed the bullet had struck him, not in the thigh as he'd intended, but in the abdomen. The muscled man held the wound with a grimace, shaking in rage. His run slowed, but miraculously hadn't stopped.

What is this guy made of?

Ears ringing from the shot, Travis turned and ran full speed through the remainder of the cornfield. Up ahead, he saw the outline of a biplane and helicopter, with their bays open, and two people shuffling between them.

He ran, clutching the stitch that needled through his side, hoping and praying, that the two silhouettes were—

Arms reached around him from in front. *"Travis!"*

It was Camila, holding on to him for dear life and shaking. "Where *were* you?" she asked, voice higher-pitched than he'd ever heard it.

"Doesn't matter." The second silhouette was Briggs. "Glad you're back, kid. Let's go."

"I got some evidence," Travis mustered the energy to say.

Just then, he heard the sound of breaking cornstalks behind them, and saw the multiple people and drones that were beginning to gather in the dissipating fog around the copters. Among them were Biceps, Redhead, Wristwatch, Acne Scars, and Drone Handlers J and Q.

"Right," Travis said. And the message was clear.

56

Travis ran to cover on the side of the farmhouse near the porch. There was nowhere to go. They had to stop them.

He turned around just long enough to see Briggs screwing something together—the blowtorch, the wand for the smoke. And he knew what was about to happen.

"On my signal!" Briggs shouted to him.

He saw Camila bite her lip as she watched Briggs go.

Briggs nodded to both of them and then clambered forward. The old scientist twisted the handle on both tanks he had been carrying and then lit the end of the hose. The gases mixed and a fireball blasted with the force of Greek gods. He torched the cornfield, and Travis could swear Briggs smiled as the Coro thugs retreated deeper into it. They were safe for now.

"I've got one of the canisters," Briggs said.

"And I've got a photo of the inside of one of those tents," Travis added.

"I think that's enough evidence. Let's get out of here," Camila suggested.

They snuck around the farmhouse. Then stopped.

A tall man stood there. He took off his sports coat and flung it to the ground as he undid the perfect Windsor knot around his neck and flicked away diamond cuff links. He loaded canisters into the spray mechanism of the old crop duster. They must've retrofitted the plane to accept such a canister, because three of them fit into the spray mechanism like shells into a shotgun.

Cowan.

Cowan had already turned toward the cockpit. He sat down comfortably in the pilot's seat, turning the key to On and grabbing the joystick sitting between his legs. He must've pressed the ignition button, because with a loud hiss and thwap, the prop started spinning at a deafening speed.

"I've got to stop him!" Travis yelled over the plane's sound.

"What are you going to do?" Camila asked.

"I don't know. Aren't we making all this up as we go anyways?"

She hugged him. "I know you can stop this. I'm going to help Briggs dismantle the operation. You know, like he said, throw a wrench into this whole thing."

Travis looked into her green eyes. "If I don't make it back . . ." He leaned in and kissed her. This was the most courage he had ever had in his life.

The plane started to pull forward and Cowan readied it for takeoff. He was just going to use the well-manicured backyard as the runway. Travis snuck around to the front of the farmhouse and sprinted to the rear of the plane as it pulled forward.

He continued to run at full speed as his lungs filled painfully with foggy air. Heaving himself onto the rear of the plane, he pulled with all his might until he positioned himself in the rear passenger seat. No time for the seat belt.

They were up above the cornfield now, and all Travis could see out of the windshield was a deep navy sky turning lighter and lighter near the horizon as the sun began to rise.

The plane's propeller buzzed and hummed up Travis's legs as he formulated a plan. Just then, Cowan noticed him. He looked back with his upper lip in a half smile. Travis needed to make a move, but before he could, Cowan spoke to him over the roar of the small biplane's engine.

"You know, I never could figure out," he said over the mechanical whirr, "why *you* kept coming after those scientists. Why you were such a pest!"

Did he really not know?

"You killed my friends!" Travis yelled. "And we were being framed for the murder of all the Titus Pharma scientists."

Cowan shook his head. "Your friends killed themselves!"

"Yeah? Alec did that all to himself?!"

I can still see his blood on the walls.

"That was an unfortunate loss."

Travis shook his head. "No—you would have killed anyone who stood in your way. You told me yourself. You're willing to let tens of thousands of people die from this virus just to get back at Titus Pharma. Why?"

Cowan's profile smiled; it gave Travis chills.

"I'm taking action," he shouted. "Doing what no one else would do."

"But out here? In rural America?"

"The media is all over Coro Innovations right now. I've made quite the name for myself. But there's been a ton of speculation, too. A lot good, but some bad. We couldn't go back. Coro is going dark, Travis. We are staying out of the media's eye. We require a rebirth. Our phase two, here at this farmhouse. After I release these drones,

I'll position myself to be America's hero. The illusive star. Curing all while Coro Innovations dies."

"You can't be serious!" Travis yelled.

He saw Cowan's hands tighten on the joystick.

"I know about your family," Travis said, knowing he was treading in dangerous waters, but out of options. There was nothing to use physically here, nothing he could hold, so this was the only plan he had to go on. "I know how they left you because of what you turned into."

"And what did I turn into?" Cowan asked.

Travis steeled himself, knowing what he was about to say next would definitely anger the man. After all . . . *It's the one thing he despises most in the world.*

"A coward," he said.

Letting out a huffing breath, knowing he only had seconds to make the right move before Cowan was on top of him, Travis centered his attention on the cockpit. But g-force pressed him against his seat, pinning him there for a moment before he realized Cowan was reaching for him, grabbing him by the neck of his T-shirt. Travis had no other option, so he hooked Cowan around the neck and pulled him out of the cockpit seat, causing his knee to hit the plane's joystick—the flight pattern was awkward and labored as they mowed down jolting stalks of crop.

Cowan scrambled to the pilot's seat, righted the plane, and turned back to Travis sitting behind him. "You stay there," he said. "You're going to kill us both."

Travis surprised himself with what he said next. "I don't care! It's better for the two of us to die than for millions to die from this virus."

Cowan pressed his fist into Travis's chest before turning back to piloting the plane.

He grunted but stayed still for just a moment, collecting his thoughts. What to do next? He looked around, trying to find anything in the small passenger seat that he could use to defend himself. Could he knock Cowan unconscious and fly the plane out of the cornfield?

If Cowan was angry, he hid it well. He laughed, switched some knobs on the control panel, and swerved them closer to the ground. "Would a coward do this?" he said in a maniacal tone.

Travis expected to hear a "muahahaha!" He ducked forward, hiding behind the back of the front seat.

Cowan turned the biplane sharply to the right. The canisters clanked below them.

How sturdy are those canisters?

As Cowan dipped the wings back and forth, jostling the canisters, Travis's jaw dropped as he remembered what was inside.

Must be some power move.

Then they sped upward and away.

A few hundred yards in the distance, yellow-orange light flashed toward them, followed by a *BOOM* so loud, it shook the plane.

They must've blown up the two choppers so the rest of Coro Innovations couldn't get away. Briggs and his flamethrower.

Cowan maneuvered sharply again, and Travis realized he was trying to dump him, fling him out of the plane.

He scrambled for the seat belt. Could the plane really fly upside down? Was that good for the canisters? He couldn't remember if he saw some TV show where planes like this could flip. It didn't matter, he still quickly slipped his arms though the shoulder straps he was sitting on and grabbed anything he could find to hold on to just before Cowan looked back and attempted to roll the plane.

57

Sirens blared below. Travis saw, as though he were in a carnival ride, flashing lights of blue and red. Help, maybe? Cops? Had someone called the cops?

But just as he began to register the swirling lights and sounds, Cowan steered the plane in the other direction, away from the authorities. They flew over vast fields of green stalks of corn.

Travis couldn't think. Out of options, he was exhausted. Sweat began forming on his palms, slicking the handle he held and making it impossible to hold on indefinitely.

Come on, Travis. Think.

Would he still be able to do anything about the drones at all? They were in the middle of nowhere, after all.

Yes. There was still hope to keep the virus contained.

You just have to take out Cowan and land this plane.

Right. Not a big deal. He could totally do this.

Travis's glasses fogged up, slipping down the bridge of his nose as the adrenaline pushed sweat onto every surface of his skin.

The plane righted ever so slightly as Cowan changed course.

That gave Travis enough leverage to readjust his grip

on the handle, so he could pull himself up into more of a seated position. The bicep in his right arm tightened, sore already from having to hold on with Cowan's sporadic flying. He fought the urge to scratch one of the thousands of bites.

He looked around the passenger's cockpit for anything.

Then he spotted it, an old tattered Carhartt jacket. A plan came to him. He carefully hooked it with his left foot and slid it toward him.

The *moment* Cowan turned his attention back to the windshield, Travis screamed and rushed forward, putting the jacket over Cowan's head and tying the arms against the seat.

Cowan's hands reached behind him, stronger than Travis's, and clawed at his wrists, grabbing ahold of him. Travis leaned back, pulling the sleeves of the Carhartt with him so he could try to suffocate him. He had long since succumbed to the idea that he would die up here, with this man.

"You should never have been able to do this," Cowan yelled with a muffled voice. "You little bug! Infiltrating everything, *ruining* years—wasting millions of dollars! You've done enough! No more impossible places at impossible times, no more lucky escapes. This ends now."

Cowan squirmed around and faced the back passenger seat, ripping the old jacket off his head and letting it flutter over the side of the plane. Travis's heart sank. The plane became a sort of chaos in equilibrium, where he wondered just which gust of wind would send them crashing back into the cornfield. Or maybe they'd run into some grain silo, or a water tower, and they'd be nothing but ashes and smoke, nothing left for Camila and

Briggs to find. And the strange thing about the whole situation was he was at peace with it.

But Travis had something else to worry about now.

Cowan had stood up from his seat and pulled a punch back. Travis squeezed himself into a ball, bending over his knees. Cowan punched with the fury of a storm. The man was strong, and even though he was only able to punch the back of Travis's head and back, he became nauseated. The last desperate attempt to dodge the barrage of punches was to move. But where?

His chin hit the buckle of his seat belt and split open. He focused on that. Time slowed and a drop of blood landed on the latch of the belt, bringing him back to reality that time was running out. Travis grasped the seat belt latch and lifted. Squirming out of the shoulder straps, he threw himself onto the floor, wedging himself between the seat and the back of the front pilot seat. At least the pain had stopped for now. He contorted into the fetal position as best as he could.

With Travis subdued, Cowan turned his attention back to piloting the plane. Travis watched Cowan's feet from underneath the seat. As he contemplated his next move, he noticed a fire extinguisher. The latch was loose, and the tank tapped against the side of the cockpit, beckoning him to reach out and grab it.

Travis gingerly reached forward, unhooked the latch the rest of the way, and slid the extinguisher back to where he was wedged.

He was quick to get up this time, ignoring the pain in his head and back, eyes widening as he tried to catch the breath that had been knocked out of him. Whistling wind rushed through his hair, sending it in all directions.

He pulled the extinguisher up over his head just as Cowan turned around, and then Travis swung the canister with all the force he could, smashing the blunt end against Cowan's face.

The resulting impact that rang through the whooshing air was enough to make Travis sick, but he couldn't hesitate.

He pulled back his arms and whacked him again. Cowan slumped after the second hit. Travis sat back, looking at what he'd done, breathing hard and feeling both horrified and relieved. Adrenaline surged through Travis's veins just at the thought of Cowan regaining full consciousness. So he reached forward, hooking Cowan under his armpits, and using the leverage of the back seat he pulled Cowan toward him in a bearhug. With the wind rushing by, even with Travis's surge of strength he was surprised at how well it worked. Cowan slid over his head onto the tail of the plane. Travis turned to witness the event, but Cowan, back to full faculties, slid down the side of the plane and out of sight.

58

Travis peered over the fuselage and blinked in surprise—Cowan hadn't plunged to his death. The man had hooked his arms in a panel of MOLLE material made to secure pesticide tanks under the plane. Travis had a flurry of mixed emotions. Just mere moments ago, he'd wanted Cowan dead, but now seeing the man struggling to pull himself to safety made him pause. What should he do? Pilot the plane? Could he leave Cowan to his own survival?

Travis looked over the pilot seat to make sure autopilot was still engaged. With the green button confirming that the small plane was holding course, he reached as far back as he could. Within moments, he was grasping Cowan's hand.

Looking past him to the ground below made Travis dizzy. Cowan's feet dangled past the flapping MOLLE material, making it difficult for him to climb back up even with Travis pulling him.

Screaming from exertion, Travis continued to tug, but they were both being pulled by gravity, the plane rocking violently forward in its erratic, pilot-less trajectory, constantly angled so that they were falling.

The pull of his arm hooked on the headrest of the passenger's seat and the strain of keeping his grip on Cowan was beginning to pull his shoulders apart. The muscles in his back strained, stretching beyond capacity.

Cowan began to slip.

"No!" Travis grunted through clenched teeth. "No, I got you!"

A new thought wormed back into his mind. The original thought. *You could let him go. You could let him go right now, and this could all be over.*

That would be the easy way out, though, just letting him die. He thought of Camila's face, and he knew that he had to keep a hold of this man, this person who had caused so much pain because of his own.

Travis would keep his humanity.

"Don't let go," he yelled to Cowan. He grunted again. "I'm gonna pull you back in, okay? And then we'll get this plane on the ground!"

"Then what?" Cowan yelled, the wind nearly drowning out his voice.

"You turn yourself in!"

Cowan cracked a wide grin.

What? Travis thought, suddenly anxious. Did Cowan know something he didn't?

"You want me to play the coward, huh?" Cowan grunted, chuckling.

Then something shifted in his dark eyes.

And Travis saw, for the first time since that photograph in Briggs's office, Cowan the human being. Not the flashy man on the news, not the cuff-link adjusting, mustache-twirling villain outside a mosquito-filled plexiglass box. But a man who felt lost and confused and couldn't understand the things that had happened to him.

"*Coward*," Cowan whispered. Like he couldn't believe the word was coming out of his mouth.

Cowan let go.

Horrified, Travis watched as he disappeared into the vast sea of cornstalks.

The plane jolted—it was the call he needed to get out of his stupor. Trying not to think about what he'd just seen, he turned around and pulled himself into the pilot's seat.

Autopilot wasn't going to cut it this time.

He put the headset on and pushed a button on the dash labeled "Communications."

"This is Travis Grant in"—he looked around, shrugging—"a yellow crop duster?"

At the same time, he took the joystick between his legs and slowly pushed it forward. Even the subtle movement was enough to jolt the plane.

He tamped down the worst of the nausea as the plane righted itself. Then he took a breath and did as his instincts told him to do, shifting the joystick so the plane banked to the left and was eventually turning around.

Travis sighed, leaning back into his seat. That was when he realized someone was talking to him from the CB, their voice coming in crackled, but clearer the closer he got to base camp.

"Hello?" a man was saying. "What's your status?"

Travis scrambled to push the foam mic closer to his mouth, practically swallowing it in his haste to answer. "This is Travis Grant," he said. "I think I'm coming back to the farmhouse."

"Travis, this is Officer Steadman. I'm going to help you land."

So I didn't imagine it. The carnival-ride flashing lights.

Below him, Travis watched the trees and cornfields catch fire with the sunrise as firefighters battled the blaze. Briggs had saved him with that fire.

"Officer Steadman," Travis said, "I don't know how to fly a plane.

"Just do everything I tell you," the officer said, "and we will land this together."

There was a silence that lasted too long.

"Travis," Officer Steadman said. "We have eyes on you. Can you carefully move the joystick to the left? Just a bit. I'm just lining you up."

Travis did as he was told. He didn't feel like he'd moved much, but Officer Steadman confirmed that he did good.

Then, gulping past the guilt, he told him about Cowan. "I'm not sure where he fell," Travis said.

"Thank you," the officer said, "we'll get a party out to search for him."

Search for the body, you mean, Travis thought. He knew how high up they'd been; there was no way Cowan had survived. But Travis didn't bother correcting him.

"Travis," Steadman said, "we still have eyes on you, twelve o'clock. Straight ahead. There's a dirt road leading to the house that you should be able to land on, no problem. We'll guide you through it, step by step."

"Right," Travis said. He leaned forward, listening carefully as the officer told him just to touch down gently as he could and then cut the engine.

"Gravity should do the rest."

"That's what I'm afraid of," Travis muttered to himself.

He saw the road and Briggs's Porsche by the yellow farmhouse and wondered if both he and Camila were okay.

Just as that thought crossed his mind, he felt the wheels slam into dirt, throwing up plumes of dust as he came in hot.

"Very good," Officer Steadman said. "Now reach down on your left side and slowly pull the brake."

The plane slowed. Relief that his life was spared washed over him.

He let out one last breath, then cut the engine.

59

Two paramedics zipped up the body bag over Cowan's body. Surprisingly, it had only taken them an hour to find him. They'd sent out a drone and looked for indications of a fall, which really left only one option about two miles away.

One by one, the cops began putting away their flashlights. A couple of the German shepherds they'd brought with them still barked and pawed at the ground.

Travis watched all this from where he sat on the farmhouse porch.

Camila sauntered up to him.

"Whatcha got there?" Travis asked.

She held up a hardback-book-sized handheld controller. "Drone controller," she replied. Then she threw it on the ground.

"Oh."

"Yeah, I was doing some flying of my own. While you were up there dealing with Cowan, some of the Coro thugs released a few mosquito drones. Briggs used his flamethrower to threaten them, and I grabbed the controller and brought all those little buggers back. They're contained now."

"Impressive," Travis said.

"Thanks." She sat down by him and put her tired head on his sore shoulder. But he didn't care. They were safe. In the opposite direction, Briggs was having an animated conversation with a stockier version of himself. Norcroff. Thick beard, Einstein hair. He'd gotten their message and had been able to call in the police as backup. Travis wondered what might have happened if it *had* been Norcroff out on the ice. Would they even have stood a chance of winning?

The amount of luck involved made his stomach turn.

What *didn't* make him sick, though, was what he saw straight ahead. The view actually made him smile.

Biceps, Redhead, and Wristwatch were being led into the back of cop cars, along with everyone else who'd worked for Coro Innovations. Even if they weren't immediately guilty as employees, they'd still need to give statements.

But Travis knew those three in particular *were* guilty. They were the drone controllers responsible for the first death, the doc. And now they were going to get what they deserved.

"Listen . . ." Travis was thinking about what he'd said before they came here.

"Yeah?" Camila answered.

Before he could open his mouth again, another voice boomed, "Kids! You two crazy cats. Who woulda thought you had it in you?"

Briggs was striding toward them, the pockets of his cargo shorts swinging too heavily with all the equipment he still had jammed into every square inch.

The older scientist took the initiative to sit next to Camila, so all three of them sat on the porch, staring out at the scene: the cops rushing through tents, the flashing lights, the crunch of dirt and gravel as cars came in and out.

If it hadn't been for the obvious chaos, it might have been a peaceful morning. A breeze stirred up the cool air trapped in the cornfield from the night, and birds sang in far-off trees.

"It's a good morning," Briggs said. Travis was surprised by how much emotion had snuck into his voice. "A good morning . . ."

Camila met Travis's eye, and he could see her trying to apologize for the interruption. But he rolled his eyes and cracked a smile. *No big deal.*

Two cops were walking toward them, a man with a red mustache and a woman with her black hair in a low ponytail.

"You three Travis, Camila, and Briggs?"

"That's us," Camila said.

"Props," the woman with the low ponytail said. "A lot of people would have backed down from what you three did. Even if it was . . . *unconventional* . . . it saved a lot of people's lives."

"But," the man with the red mustache said, "we still need you to come down to the station to give your statements."

"'Course," Briggs said.

Travis and Camila nodded as well.

"You can just follow behind," the one with the mustache said. "I trust you won't get lost. And not many people drive a car like that around here, so you'll be easy to track down if you do." He smiled.

Briggs chuckled. "Will do."

"We'll be leaving in just a few minutes," the woman with the ponytail said.

Then their radios crackled, and the two cops excused themselves.

Travis looked from Camila to Briggs and could barely believe everything that had happened. *Maybe we can go back to normal now.*

Briggs finally seemed to catch on to the fact that he'd interrupted something. He looked to them with a crooked smile that twitched his graying beard. "I'll get the car ready," he said, slapping his knees as he stood.

He disappeared into the driver's side of the Porsche several paces away, leaving Travis with Camila just as he'd been before.

He cleared his throat, wondering if *he* should say something first or . . .

"Hey, so . . ." Camila spoke first.

"Yeah?"

"About what you said . . ."

His heart sunk. Geesh—was he about to get his heart broken?

"I've been thinking about it," she said, nodding. "And when I saw you get into that plane, and I . . ." She looked at him. Tears glistened in the corners of her eyes.

"I honestly didn't know," she said, "if I'd see you again. So I promised myself if I saw you again, I'd tell you the truth. I love you, Travis Grant. I really, *really* love you. And you know I mean it because we're not even about to die."

She laughed, as though it were the craziest thing in the world—but here she was, and Travis loved her for it.

He smiled, everything around them suddenly growing lighter like he'd sucked in helium from a balloon—a rush to the head. "I love you, too," he said.

Then he kissed her. A kiss full of everything he wanted their future to be.

In between kisses, she said, "And I'm going to go to school with you so we can be together."

Travis's heart warmed with excitement.

Camila kissed him again, only breaking away and giggling when Briggs honked loudly, signaling the end—and the beginning—of the craziest part of Travis's life.

EPILOGUE

"Reports confirm that the eight scientists in question were part of an original team in a biotech company previously known as Titus Pharmaceuticals. Six of them are dead, plus the blackballed CEO Cowan—and though police originally thought several of the deaths to be suicides, we now know that they were targets of the late Dr. Cowan, who used nano-drone technology and hallucinogens to induce the scientists' deaths."

The reporter paused, deferring to another anchor, who continued the story. Travis, bending down to finish packing up the last of his books from his bedroom, looked up to the small TV on the corner of his dresser, wondering if they'd mention Alec at all.

"Dr. Cowan was the CEO and founder of Coro Innovations, another biotech company that sought to replace Titus's role in the industry for the past ten years. It seems that Coro focused mostly on the 'innovation' portion of their title, as most of their capital was pulled recently due to lack of profit. Where did all that money go? It seems it went directly to finding a little-known asset created by Titus Pharma well over a decade ago. A virus known as Titus-1A."

Travis put the paperbacks into the box, which he then taped over and labeled with a strong-scented Sharpie.

Then he looked around the empty room, the comforter-less bed, the empty closet.

The pinned stag beetle in a frame sitting on his dresser behind the TV.

"That's right, Stefan. After a debacle with the CDC, Titus settled to have that virus—an accidental mutation, according to sources—hidden by the government. Reports state that the location was hidden across eight nanotags inserted into the original scientists' bloodstream, scattered like puzzle pieces, and that this is what prompted Dr. Cowan's attacks. The virus has since been contained and reburied in an unknown location."

Travis sat on his bed, the springs in the uncovered mattress squeaking in response. He wondered how the one in the dorm would feel. Would it be too soft to fall asleep on? Or so hard he'd prefer the floor?

"Knock-knock," someone said.

He turned his head to see Camila standing in the doorway. She had a drink holder with two coffees and a wax-paper bag.

"Thought you could use a pick-me-up after all that packing," she said.

"That's the understatement of the century," he said, shifting his legs so she could sit next to him on the bed. Camila handed him his coffee and then snuggled up next to him.

Travis rested his head on her dreads, smiling. As it turned out, he wasn't the only one the doc had been impressed with. After getting home, she'd found a letter from the University of Florida, wondering if she would like to apply. According to what she'd told Travis, she didn't have to think about it long. It was too late for the fall semester, but she'd be a full-time student in the spring. Still, she decided to move to the city now—too many bad memories here.

The blond reporter, Erika, said, "As for the two Interns who were originally suspects in the explosion of the Grand Marsh Mosquito Control center, both have been cleared. According to police reports, they were, quote, 'instrumental in the discovery of Dr. Cowan's intentions and the containment of Titus-1A.' In a short statement from Travis Grant, he said they're grateful that it's all over, and that he'll be attending college at the University of Florida in the fall."

Camila sniggered. "You said that?"

"Shut up," he said, feeling his cheeks turn red.

"He also said he'd like to thank his friend, Alec Prescott, saying that he won't be forgotten. Alec, an intern scientist at Nive University, was caught in the crossfires of Coro Innovations. A vigil will be held at the quad in front of the Aust Biotech Lab on Nive University's campus this coming Saturday from eight p.m. until midnight."

Camila and Travis sat there a little while longer, watching as the commercials flickered over the screen. He drank his coffee and nibbled on some of the scone she had brought him.

"We should get going," Camila said, lifting her head from his shoulder.

Travis gave a pretend whine, to which she rolled her eyes and kissed him. "Drama queen," she said. "Come on—it's a bit of a drive."

Travis grinned as she got off the bed, pulling him with her. He grabbed the last box, the one with his paperbacks in it, and was about to turn off the TV and head out when he heard the end of the news story creeping up.

"Why did Dr. Cowan do it?" Bruce asked Erika. "Do we know?"

"There are speculations," she said, "and we have the testimony of over a hundred Coro Innovations employees. But his real motives may never come to light. Dr. Cowan was found dead at the scene of his own crime, apparently having fallen out of a flight vehicle."

"Money?" Bruce asked. "Prestige? Revenge?"

"All we can do is speculate at this point, Bruce, but all leads point to an evil man determined to get revenge. Those heavily involved with Coro and its crimes are being investigated and prosecuted accordingly, but as for the mastermind—that remains a bit of a mystery."

Both anchors smiled at the camera, all of the weight of the conversation suddenly deflating. Travis felt a little sick.

He set the box down and unplugged the TV.

He noticed the framed stag beetle one more time on the dresser. Priceless. A gift that he could no longer give.

Travis's throat grew tight. He picked it up, noticing the sheen on the beetle's wings, its Latin name rolling through his mind like a song: *lucanus cervus*.

And then another Latin phrase—*beneficium maior scientia est*. Something the doc had actually lived by, until the day he died. Camila's surprise letters of recommendation were proof enough of that.

He thought of every belief Cowan had held about Titus. *Not everyone was like that*, Travis thought.

And wasn't that just a choice, anyway?

"You coming?"

Camila was in his doorway again. Her eyes flashed to the stag beetle, and although her expression changed, she didn't say anything.

"Yeah," Travis said. "I'm coming."

He carefully put the beetle in its frame on the closed cardboard box of paperbacks and followed Camila out.

THE END

As a kid, Tyler H. Jolley always had a knack for storytelling. When he grew bored of old fables, he created his own exciting and unique worlds. Many years later, he still had so many new ideas and stories swirling in his head, but with nowhere to share it. That's when he put his pencil to paper and let the creative juices flow.

His debut novel, *Extracted*, came out in 2013 and swiftly became an Amazon Best Seller and Spencer Hill Press Best Seller. *Prodigal and Riven*, the second and third books in The Lost Imperials series were released in May of 2015.

After a brief hiatus he restructured and returned to writing. His Adventurous Ali series has received much praise. To date, he's released four in the series.

When he's not writing, you can find him at his orthodontic practice, mountain biking, or on the hunt for the perfect doughnut.